ALSO BY PHIL GEOFFREY BOND

My Friend, the Cat
All the Sad Young Men
The Disney Diaries
My Queer Youth
Small Town Confessions
The Fall of Mrs. Parsons

The Last Year at Low Tide

Phil Geoffrey Bond

Chess Books
New York

Chess Books
A Division of Above Deck Entertainment
P.O. Box 188
Garrison, NY 10524

First Chess Books paperback edition October, 2018

CHESS BOOKS and design are registered trademarks of Above Deck Entertainment, LLC, used under license by Above Deck Entertainment, LLC, the publisher of this work.

For information about special discounts for bulk purchases, please contact Above Deck Entertainment special sales at 1-845-379-4233 or business@abovedeckentertainment.com.

Cover designs by Kenneth Holcomb
Author photo by Christine Ashburn

Manufactured in the United States of America

ISBN-13: 978-0692628096 (Chess Books)
ISBN-10: 0692041850
ISBN-13: 9780692041857

"History, despite its wrenching pain, cannot be un-lived. But if faced with courage, need not be lived again."

— Maya Angelou,
On the Pulse of Morning

1

Fall, 2026: Malibu, CA

THE WAVES MUST have been angry. They were enormous today, their white caps crashing down upon the shore. The waves had woken Everett from his sleep throughout an already restless night. Now the water, bathed in the slight sun that struggled its way through darkened clouds, slammed itself right up against the coast, sending the water further and further inland, tiptoeing across the smooth, tan sand. Gradually, bit-by-bit, the waves would have their way. The tide would come in, where it would settle for the afternoon.

Another four measures to scribble out. It wasn't flowing this morning, none of it, not as it once had, certainly. The notes stared up at him from stark white staff paper, still mostly blank, as though he had disappointed them, placed them in an absurd pattern that only he alone could ever understand. He second-guessed each rest, each crescendo, every triplet. The time spent placing the notes upon the staff had been wasted; precious time he could never recover. Into the trash with it all, bass clefs, treble clefs, key signatures and all that accompanied them.

He gazed about the little living room, providing a respite for his eyes and mind. His little room at the edge of the world, mostly white and grey, decorated with sea shells and knick knacks acquired over a lifetime: paperweights, books, artwork, candleholders. No photographs, though, no reminders, everything in his life devoid of nostalgia.

He had opened the French doors wide early that morning, at sunrise, to let in the warm sea air but now, a distinct chill filled the room as the breeze ruffled the powder white curtains. The wind off the coast blew through his body, a frigid cleanse. Tides, scribbled notes on staff paper and sunsets: this was his life now, the routine of which he counted on. And each day, it seemed, the waves grew louder and the beach eroded further. One day soon, surely, the water would creep into his little dwelling, wash over him entirely and carry him out upon a vast swell.

The change of season in Malibu is subtle, certainly not as dramatic as back East. Fog, a chill in the air, a sweeping rainstorm rather than the turning of the leaves or an arctic blast of snow that might inspire contentment. At the very least, a more profound change of season was something happening, a pendulum of sorts, a reminder that the Earth continued upon its' rotation. The monotony of monotony can be overwhelming if one is unaccustomed, a notion all too familiar to all Californian transplants.

The phone rang. He ignored it. He knew who it was and it made his stomach churn. *Not today, please. Just allow me this day, please, this one day. This little patch of my own, just allow me to call this my own, free from the confines of expectation. Let this one day, this stretch of hours, belong to me entirely.*

With every ring, his body tensed and his head throbbed. Finally, it stopped. Devoid of any sort of voice mail, there were no messages, which worked well for him. He inhaled the salty air and it seeped all the way down through his bones. One more breath of ocean before shutting the French doors, one final flirt with nature, and then just himself and the innards of his own private universe — this sanctuary by the sea where he would perch till the end of days, the waft of the sea breezing through his now mostly white hair.

The air was still now as his attention returned to the eighty-eight keys, black and white, standing at attention like a meddlesome empty canvas. And so, back to the blank staff paper and his finely sharpened pencils as he sat on the little wooden bench. He would try again to not merely write the music, but to *be* the music.

His last chance. Tide was headed out.

Fall, 1996: West Village, New York City

It was raining. Again. It had rained off and on for four days straight. He looked out from behind the upright piano at the sea of bar patrons, slugging back Cape Cods and watered down shots of God knows what while lighting cigarettes. The plunking of his keys could scarcely be heard over the din of chatter and carelessly loud laughter. It was only a matter of time before someone, surely, would approach his piano and slather their request at him: "Do *Piano Man*. Sing that *Piano Man* song, piano man." He dreaded it.

The room was a perfect, dimly lit triangle. He sat at the out of tune instrument in one corner, slightly elevated on a hollow 3' by 5' "stage," crudely constructed from warped wood slathered with black paint, scarcely large enough to encompass both himself and the instrument. Windows surrounded the room, staring out into the dark Manhattan night. The walls were painted a bland sort of dark green and the floors consisted of little more than chipped linoleum, no doubt installed sometime in the seventies. It was a place one should never have the misfortune to see by daylight. The Pillow Factory had been there for all eternity, or at least since the late sixties when someone had the bright idea to turn a real estate office on the corner of Christopher and Seventh Avenue South into a piano bar. Thirty years later, here it stood with its perfectly preserved grime; fingerprints and shadows from the heyday of Village nightlife which had trudged on and evolved into what it was today: sanitized in a way, yet also more aggressive with new sounds, new faces and new attitudes. And here he sat in the middle of it all, solitary at the keys, an immovable rock amid the great swirl of a parade.

Thunderstorms had enveloped all of Greenwich Village and all of the entire world, for all he knew, pounding down upon the sidewalks as the city's residents darted determinedly between confused tourists whose cheap umbrellas had long since turned inside out in the slight wind. Winter was upon New York. Already, leather jackets were out in full force and a distinct chill filled the air that blew through the pores when venturing out of doors. Picturesque autumn would last only a few short weeks this year. Summer would evolve into winter in what was less than a finite moment. It was all about to change. It was time.

Where all of these people came from, he never knew. They had crawled out of their caves in the pouring rain to seek the comfort of others in this tiny dark room filled with fellow creatures of the night who craved a good show tune as much as their nightly alcohol fix. What did it give them, he wondered, as he gazed out over the sea of crappy haircuts. What did this place supply that kept them coming back night after relentless night, putting dollar bills into his tip bowl and singing along with *Don't Cry for Me Argentina*? A sense of community, he supposed, a habitat, even an artificial one — *home*. Even he had been blinded by it, years ago, during his first few nights at the piano, thinking he had found *his* people — the endless party that would not ever end. But eventually, the lights came back up and everyone was exposed for what they really were before scurrying home like so many roaches fleeing the light of day.

A rotund woman in her forties fought her way through the crowd and approached his piano. He recognized Molly Brown immediately. That was not her real name, of course, not even the gay men who had been her only companions for decades knew her real name. She was dressed in spandex pants that hugged her enormous thighs — like two oblong water balloons right before they pop from overfill. A frilly mini skirt with fringe and some sort of sequins were wrapped around her ample waist which she wore with a lime green pull over. She had her own style, he was always forced to admit. She refused to hide her girth, but rather, she celebrated it, and he always admired this. Truthfully, he was always relieved when Molly approached, because it meant that he could take a break from providing mere background music for a while as Molly was surely about to take the mic and belt out a tune.

Actually, she only knew one song, but it had become tradition over the years for her to sing it, and a Friday night at The Pillow Factory wouldn't be much of a night at all if she didn't. It was a Hollywood classic, and before that a vaudeville classic, but Molly managed to put her own unique stamp on it, much to the delight of the finely quaffed men in the room wearing too tight jeans. She didn't need to hand him any sheet music, it was a plebeian dance the two of them performed every week — like a roller coaster they had ridden hundreds of times together, each of them knowing exactly when to expect each turn, hill and loop. All that was needed was a knowing look between the two of them and his hands played her introduction from memory. She began it as a precious ballad. A hush fell over the room and everyone ceased their conversations to peer through the smoke. She had that ability, the means to silence a room and demand attention.

Oh my men I love them so
They'll never know
All my life is just despair
But I don't care
When they take me in their arms
The world is bright alright.

It was as though a factory's noisy machines had ground to a halt and a pin spot had picked up this lonely factory worker, standing atop her machine, crying out with her brazen voice. He wondered, had she not looked the way that she did, had she been a traditional beauty with slim hips and doe eyes and all of twenty-four, would this crowd even give her the time of day?

No. They would likely rush her off stage with polite applause. But given her singularity, her originality, her uniqueness — she was celebrated and admired amid a room of similarly lost souls.

Some of the guys in her normal circle of acquaintances dabbed a tear or two from their eyes, even though they had heard her sing it a million or more times. Perhaps the tears were shed merely for dramatic purpose, for these gentlemen of the night were always fraught with drama, mind you. But they were kindred spirits, those men and Molly Brown. The single spotlight designated for whomever might decide to sing in front of the piano was only about four inches from the top of her head, and it cast an eerie glow upon her obviously bleached blonde hair, stiff with hairspray. Cigarette smoke wafted through the incandescent beam of light as she inhaled all of the air in the room into her oversized lungs:

What's the difference if I say
I'll go away
When I know I'll come back on my knees

(Spontaneous laughter always occurred at this point. She rolled her eyes in a knowing wink, a rehearsed and time-honored gesture she had perfected for this particular moment in the song, and then pressed on with her confession):

Once more.
For wherever my men are
Especially if they're here in this bar
You'll find me there!

The song really kicked up at this point and he dressed it up with flourishes on the piano, making the tuneless, ancient instrument sound like the force of a thirty-piece orchestra. Molly basked in the spontaneous applause from a room full of admirers mingled with various tourists who felt as though they were getting the real "New York" experience.. He watched her silhouette from behind the dilapidated piano, directly in front of which she stood in all of her diva glory. He knew that in the morning, she would surely have to face reality — tromp back into some unglamorous office somewhere in midtown where everyone addressed her by her real name and she no doubt dressed in tight suits and wore conservative shoes. But for right now, on this makeshift stage and in this hovel of an establishment in the West Village, she was the star she had initially set out to be.

Most of the staff had known Molly for much longer than he. There was a small theatre up a dark and rickety flight from the main piano bar and she had once starred in a number of small revues up there, ten years and perhaps one hundred pounds ago.

He felt a kind of kinship with Molly, a shared reality. We all start out ready to take on the world; grab it by the horns and force it around to our own liking, create new platforms, new vistas, celebrate new ideas, change the norm: perform in the world with *intent*. But as time passes, we huddle in a corner and hope that the world ignores us, for a blessed change. Hope that we can just *pass*, remain upon this Earth without penalty. The ambition of our youth beats us up and never lets us forget it in later years, something he was just coming to learn. Once the world has fucked with you, demanded the bill, one seeks merely solitude and the chance to go predominantly unnoticed more than anything. No matter how she might complain about what she called the "shit show" her life had become, what Molly wanted most of all was for things to remain exactly as they were, and he knew this. Anything more would frighten her or worse test her confidence. She had found her niche, her own personal habitat. Making fun of it all, this dive that had become her palace and the state of her obsolete performing career, was her own definitive brand of artistic expression. It was her own unique home, this tiny stage, and nobody could decorate it like she could. Here came the big notes now, which she held three or four times longer, at least, than indicated in the music. Good old Molly, as reliable as pigeons on statues.

She finished, holding the final note for a good thirty seconds of pure belt. The applause that followed, cheers and wails and "yeeeessss, girl!" were deafening, of course. He smiled but hid behind his piano, his shield, and contemplated what he could play next to bring the crowd back down before another big climactic moment of the evening occurred, which he hoped would happen soon as moments such as these were always followed by a pass of the tip bucket. His quandary was soon answered for him as a young kid with just a wisp of sandy blonde hair, definitely underage and already drunk from two watered down cocktails, approached the piano. He was short and slight, clad in form fitting, unwrinkled blue jeans that still smelled of fabric softener and a bright blue button down, the color of which matched his hopelessly wide eyes.

Here it came, he was certain of it. The young squire was either just off the bus or more likely visiting from Cleveland or Toledo, the star of his hometown productions, a likely Barnaby in *Hello, Dolly* or Rolfe in *The Sound of Music*, mouth open and full of wonder to be in New York City, riding all of the rides and tonight, hanging out with the grown ups whom he emulated and would surely be amongst regularly in just a few short moments in time. He was pretty and talented, and everyone back home had said so. What would happen to him? Would he move to the city and get caught up in the swirl of rent and romance, only too soon to feel the wrinkles upon his skin and calluses upon his feet? Or would he indeed triumph? Look back upon his salad days with a sneer and a giggle? Perhaps New York would be his oyster — why not? Perhaps he would, with fanfare, land his dream job on Broadway and maybe it would all just be the stuff that dreams are made of. It happened, after all. He had seen it. And then sometimes, it didn't.

No matter. For tonight, the young tenor (they're always tenors), strode up to the piano in his impossibly blue shirt, tapped him on the shoulder and peered into his face with a toothy grin that radiated beneath all of that perfectly placed hair of utter blondness. "Do you know *Piano Man*?"

Autumn, 1989: Cambridge, MA

Cambridge, Massachusetts is a perfectly polite place. Shortly after the Fall semester begins, hundreds of trees throughout town begin their slow evolution to crimson and then rust, their leaves littering the narrow streets that permeate the little town that is merely a facade, an excuse of sorts, an empty cell that houses the nucleus that is the dual universities of Harvard and MIT.

His shift began at 6 P.M. More of the same tonight, he knew. He would start on the floor, taking orders for the dinner rush. But once things died down, he would be relegated back to the kitchen to scrape plates and send glasses through the industrial dishwasher. He didn't hate his job, far from it. On the contrary, it provided him a respite from the real world of classes and exams, a place where he could escape into the security of the mundane while still feeling useful. Nothing to overrule nor sustain, no tortes or Habeas corpus; just plates to bus, orders to take and tips to collect. As long as, whatever he did, he did it *well*, this was all the satisfaction he needed. Over the semesters, he had developed a mastery of his duties at the diner, and he prided himself in this. He could handle his tasks, control them, be in charge.

He watched from behind the register, ball point pen behind his ear and apron around his waist. Oh, *they* had just rolled in — the pretty people. A whole gaggle of them had congregated that night, huddled next to the garden windows that overlooked one of many town squares. He was among them — from his Ethical Law in an Evolved Society (whatever that meant) class. Yes, the one who loved to spout his paragraphs long diatribes in front of the professor, a grey-templed man of sixty who dressed in bow ties and always pretended to look interested in his long-winded student but, he knew, was as lost as the rest of the class.

He peered at his classmate from behind the counter. He thought that his theories were interesting, profound, even: brave. He was also certainly something to look at, but he would keep that to himself. It was of little consequence, anyway. Tonight, the tweed and corduroy crowd had graced The Mass Ave Diner, and he would need to take their order. As he approached the table, studying the lot of them, he knew an invisible wall would go up, separating his existence as a student from that as a member of the working class, and this was just fine. They would all pretend not to know him or ever to have seen him before, thankfully. He arrived, pad and pen in hand, ready to begin the familiar foxtrot he always danced with a table full of self-proclaimed elite scholars such as these.

"It's Mr. Crisp, right?" he extended a hand, the one with the eyes. "We're in Ethics together." Here was this smug young scholar, thought Everett, reaching a hand down into the ghetto to slum, to greet the less fortunate, the apron clad servant. He did not reciprocate with his own hand.

He readied his pad and clicked his retractable pen. "What can I get you?" He couldn't stand it when they forced familiarity on him, it embarrassed him and he never knew what to say. He was just a servant, and he would prefer not to blur the lines.

"Mr. Crisp here plays the piano," he informed his fellow diner-goers. "He's good." He peered into Everett's eyes proudly, as though he were the superhero who had just revealed the masked man, proud of his service to humanity. There was an awkward pause as Everett glared at this presumptuous boy with too much goop in his hair, trying surely to emulate his well-bred father whom everyone knew was a Connecticut Senator. People in his inner circle, Everett had overheard, had taken to referring to him as "the gentleman from Connecticut," which they all found oh so amusing.

"I saw you playing at Bridget's last night, right before last call." He was the kind of person who, when speaking to you, led you to believe that you and he were the solitary inhabitants of your own private space of time, as though you had both escaped for a holiday on his private island where even your slightest eye twitch would be examined and applauded. He had endless charm, it was obvious to even the termites that surely inhabited the wooden booth upon which he and his menagerie currently sat. But it was merely a trick, inherited from a political family the same way coal miners pass on iron lung to their children, or Dutch shoemakers once taught their trade to their own offspring.

"So I'll have the burrito, hold the onions, hmm?" The blonde girl with the tight perm, seated too close to his ethical classmate, blurted out, a little two abruptly and with a certain amount of disdain, eager to rain upon whatever phantasmic chalk drawing seemed to be evolving between the gentleman from Connecticut and this aloof wait person. Although, if she were his girlfriend, she must be used to this, his endless interest in everything and everyone who surrounded him, his reckless flirtation, his frequent invitations to complete strangers, to random waiters, to vacation on the private island of him where nothing but you mattered. The young woman's narrow eyes, somewhat obscured by the tight curls of her bad yet undoubtedly expensive perm, met Everett's, and he knew it was time to get the job done, no more and no less. Around the table he went, collecting orders, before he stopped at the ethical Ethics student.

"And for you?"

"Why do you work here when you can play like that?" The rhythm of the evening stopped yet again; all eyes at the table landing first upon the tweed man and his shiny, chemical-laden hair, then upon Everett, his sleeves rolled up and his black hair sticking up in a defiance against gravity. His cheap tie (part of the uniform), was tucked inside his shirt between buttons, half way down his chest, to avoid it falling into a random cup of sauerkraut or grazing someone's maple syrup glazed pancakes. Everett cleared his throat and re-clicked his pen. Too many lines had been crossed, and he resented it.

"I can't help myself. Try as I might, I just love the cheeseburger deluxe." He collected the menus and made a hasty retreat. It always pissed him off when the barrier between student and employee was broken and he was even more frustrated that that had been the best line he could come up with in retaliation. Why couldn't they just maintain the facade, pretend like everyone else? He wished them all back to their eloquent gold coast homes or at least out of the Mass Ave Diner, the one place where he found relief and could swim in thankful same-fullness.

He rang in their orders and was drawing their beers from the tap when there was a hand on his shoulder, squeezing it just a little too hard to be casual. "Sorry. I didn't mean to embarrass you or — be out of line, I guess." It was him, whatever his name was — snooty and arrogant, congregating with the lepers, the help.

"I'm not embarrassed."

"You blushed," his giggle was accompanied by a sly grin, like he had caught an adolescent boy with a dirty magazine. He personified the word suave, the kind of man one would find in a commercial for razor blades, towel wrapped around his chiseled torso as he flashed a wry smile that radiated product placement. Everett wasn't buying it.

"I'm not embarrassed. I love my job... I *have* a job."

Ethics regained his composure. All right, he thought, if this was the way he wanted to play it, so be it. He would be the defending attorney then. "Well, yes. But you're not very good at it."

"What?"

"You forgot to take my order."

"And what can I get *you*, Ethics?"

"Ah — a sense of humor."

"Oh, God."

"Work with me. I'm defending myself here."

"I'm working. Consider me the bailiff. Need water?"

"And I'm sure you work yourself harder than anyone even expects of you. It's admirable. But I don't know anyone else who can do what you can do. So you should think about that." Ethics' eyebrows were raised now. He had just called out the witness on the stand and solved the murder like in an episode of *Perry Mason*, a look Everett knew well from countless youthful hours with a television as his only friend. He looked away, eye contact was something he had never been totally comfortable with. He forgot where they were in the scene and found himself without an immediate retort. Moments passed.

"So, what can I bring you, by the way?" Eyes askew, he fixed his glare on the young man's perfect earlobes.

"The cheeseburger deluxe, of course. I hear it's pretty good." He turned to rejoin the fellow elite at his table.

"Yes sir... *counsel.*"

Ethics turned back around and flashed that toothy grin again. "You really can play. You know that, right?" He shot him a glance that seemed to be at least laced with sincerity, while the beer from the tap overflowed one of the pilsners. Oh, just go back to your table with your silly pals, for Chrissakes, and let me get on with my job, he thought, mopping up the beer from the rim. Arrogant rich kids, all of them.

"Smile," was his parting word, before he was finally off to officially rejoin his own. 'Smile.' Who the fuck was he, anyway, some happy-go-lucky swell out to charm the peasants? Expecting us all to be impressed with his lineage and trillion-watt smile. He rang in the order and busied himself restocking glasses behind the counter.

Bridget's had the best piano in town. He liked to venture over there after his evening shifts. Mandy behind the bar always brought him a scotch and ginger as he sailed though ten or twenty tunes, sometimes more, tearing up the keyboard. No one ever really took notice, he was just wallpaper. But it was a release for him, an air pocket, a chance to inhale real air in oxygen-less outer space, and it was to there he would venture again this evening, just as the fever pitch of well groomed, academic nightlife was drawing to a close and that gorgeous piano sat waiting for him like an expectant lover.

Ding! Table 39's order was up.

Summer, 1978: Mason City, Iowa

It was going to be a very long afternoon. The sound of sports permeated the house, echoed through the corridors, sound waves reverberating straight from the television through the walls. Burnt popcorn pervaded the air. His mother sat next to the alien, adoringly, in the middle of the slightly worn sofa, because that was her role, even though she had always loathed sports. She would pretend. What else was there for her to do on a stale Saturday afternoon such as this, anyway?

"Jiminy Christmas!" she shrieked, one hand on his denim clad knee, a hand which crept up the mid section of his thigh, as some sort of ball, they were all basically the same no matter which game, sailed through the air. "Go! Go! GO!" yelled the alien, lunging forth from the

sofa onto his freakishly long legs, "ARGH!" he finally relented, dropping back down upon the poor cushions.

The young man sat on the last step of the staircase, Henry the sock monkey in his lap, wondering what on Earth drew the two of them, with such intensity, to the television every Saturday afternoon without fail, rain or shine, season after season.

His stepfather preferred to consume his popcorn from a brown paper grocery bag. Curious, thought the young man, for the house was well furnished with proper bowls, beautiful cream-colored porcelain bowls of various sizes, salvaged from their former life. But there was something about a brown paper grocery bag that made the wiry tall man with speckled silver hair feel more at home. Perhaps, during his youth, or whatever life he had come from before he entered the young man's, bowls had been foreign to him, having not grown up amongst nice things, therefore brown paper grocery bags settled him in a way.

A whistle sounded; half time, or "intermission," as the young man preferred to call it, if only to be obnoxious, really. This always caused a row and that was entertainment, at least for a few moments before things got bad. And they could get bad quickly: go from the usual gray to pitch black in a matter of seconds. He sometimes felt as though he were living inside a black and white movie, but not a big glamorous one like he sometimes saw on television; a dark, sinister one with bad guys and shadows. The sound of a whistle prompted them both to rise: her to refill her wine glass, and he to pop more corn for his oil-stained paper bag.

Had circumstances been different, it might have been a very pleasant house. The young man thought of this, having ventured outside into the early summer air, out to the driveway to gaze at what, from the outside, must have appeared to be a charming home to passers-by: a scant two stories of white brick with maroon shutters and well cut grass, which he tended himself. The back of the property featured a proper patio with a thin metal table and assorted thin, metal chairs, oil lamps and a large maple tree from whence a swing had once draped before it was recently decided that he was far too old to indulge in such juvenile playthings, so it had been cut down and removed. Yes, it was all one could hope for of suburbia. Of course, inside was another matter altogether. He was loathed, first by him and gradually by her. A cocoon had grown around their bond and he had been shut out of it, left to scavenger about the woods on his own.

It was a good day to sneak off to the reservoir, he decided. Not a cloud in the sky today, yet everyone locked inside of their respective homes; not a soul to be seen all the way around Windsor Court, everyone sitting, watching sports games on their own televisions he supposed, or enveloped in their own worlds and various crisis. What better time for swimming, he thought. His secret spot was just a bike ride away, not half an hour up the hill and through the woods. Sometimes, he liked to swim naked, but of course he told no one of this.

She had been so different, not just a few years ago, he recalled, as he pedaled his red dirt bike alongside the road. She had been cheerful and it had been genuine. She had laughed and it had been a real laugh, nothing artificial to it. She had worn such smart, beautiful colors and everyone had known it when she swept into a room. When she picked him up at school or ventured inside for conferences or banquets, he had always been so proud as she chatted with his teachers and the other mothers. He recalled her former smile as he turned from the sidewalk and pedaled onto the soft, worn grass and then uphill through the trees, along the dirt path, the leaves now obscuring most of the sunlight, like entering a secret land only he knew about. How confident she had been, how full of gracious instruction as she had taken him to the shopping center, to their special ice cream place where they enjoyed Rocky Road with paper cups of water, which always seemed such a perfect compliment to each other; the water unique mostly because it had been served from those very paper cones, the scent of which influenced the taste and somehow complimented the marshmallow. She had inspired in him a security, a safeness, an assurance that he stood upon solid and well tended ground. He had breathed so easily in those years, carefree and gently, excited to burst out of bed to explore the days' adventures. But that was the past, now.

The trees were clearing and the sparking blue water was just up ahead. He would soon be there. The reservoir sat peacefully at the top of the hill, silent and alone: a beautiful jewel devoid of visitors. He was grateful that nobody else seemed to know about this place he thought of as his own. Certainly none of this classmates ever ventured up this way and he was glad. This was a place where he didn't have to be different. He could just allow the water to embrace every inch of him. For the stretch of time that he was here, he lived life on a perpetual exhale.

He liked to believe that it was an ocean, as he stripped down to splash about in his own private sea, leaving his clothes draped on his bicycle which sat patiently on the bank. Henry the sock monkey stood guard, nestled in the foliage, carefully surveying the territory to ward off any potential predators. If he swam out far enough, perhaps he would touch the shore of some foreign land, where he would be welcomed to solid ground and celebrated by broad, confident smiles and he could begin a new life, never to look back.

Floating on his back, he gazed up at the sky, still not a cloud to be seen. The warm water, heated by the afternoon rays, caressed his naked body, reaching all the way up the sides of his face, submerging his ears so that he might hear only the movement of the liquid and whatever was happening down below, ensconced in another universe that was altogether his own.

Change was in the air that hung about his sanctuary. He could feel it. It had been a constant lately, distinct and nearly tangible in the base of his stomach; ever present. Yes, something would soon happen; plates were shifting. It was inevitable now. There was nothing to really rely on, he knew; the world is comprised of a series of changes, something captured that immediately evolves, experiences metamorphosis. But this particular change did not feel altogether pleasant. He feared it, knowing that it was only right that he do so in a kind of ritualistic preparation. He would prepare for the unknown as best he could, build his own shield, and soldier onward. If he had yet to learn total bravery, his own sense of self-reliance had evolved out of practical necessity.

The water easily sustained his body as he floated right through the horizon upon his back. For the immediate now, for this exact moment in history, everything was warm and pleasant, comforting and calm, a pocket of air found at the depths of an ocean. Were this a movie, quiet solo piano music would play softly, he thought. Turning his head slightly to the right and peering into the foliage to check on his monkey and his bicycle, he saw them both, perfectly still at the edge of the brush.

He was not alone. A pair of human eyes were clearly visible on the bank.

2

Autumn, 1996: West Village, New York City

THE PILLOW FACTORY closed down around three a.m., which gave them an hour to chase the drunks out before they had to legally close at four. He sat at the end of the bar, fingers throbbing from eight hours of thumping out show tunes on the tuneless monstrosity that sat in the corner. He didn't have to ask; Maria pulled out three shot glasses and filled them to the top, one by one, with straight scotch. They looked so wonderfully symmetric, sitting on the wooden bar that was stained with the spills and carved initials of the past. The liquor had an attractive, rust-colored haze to it, which he appreciated. Scotch was a sophisticated drink, something that said he'd been around, he knew his stuff and that he was a grown up. He had shrugged his own past off with a gulp. Years of gulps, in fact.

He downed the first one: "How do you solve a problem like Maria?" Then the second. "Maria... I'll never stop saying Maria." And the third. "Ave Maria." He put his head down on the bar and it wasn't even spinning. Not yet. The last of the crowd had left and it was just the two of them and the ping of the cash register as she tallied the nightly ring. He had some bills in his pocket from his tip jar, never enough, and he put a ten down on the bar, which Maria picked up and put back in his shirt pocket, just as she always did.

"Let's do this once more. You need it." Saint Maria, a tall and plain-looking woman of forty-eight with gorgeous red hair and a rosy complexion that seemed to welcome everyone, which made her an ideal bartendress, filled two shot glasses and the two of them clinked them together. "To our neighbor here in luxurious Greenwich Village, Billy fuckin' Joel and his stupid ass piano song." Salut. Maria may have been his very favorite lesbian of all the lesbians.

It was time to head home to Brooklyn. The morning rush didn't start till six, so it would be a long wait between L trains at the Union Square station with the die-hards who had just been kicked out of all the recently closed village watering holes. It was fine, he was used to it. Once home, he would make some toast and chase it down with a little more scotch, just to unwind, before, as the sun made itself known, his head hit the pillow for what he hoped would be at least six hours, but was frequently more like four or five.

4 A.M. is a good time to slump against the tiles of a subway station, as they're all hosed down around two. Closing his eyes amid the bright florescent light, thread bare black leather jacket stretched thin over his bony physique, he planned his actions as he awaited the sound of the train. Once he walked through his front door, he thought, after climbing the flight of thinly carpeted stairs, he would deliberately avoid the mirror which sat just inside, next to the RCA stereo, both of which he picked up second hand. He wasn't nearly drunk enough for his vision to be blurred and mirrors have an appalling habit of honesty. A wind from the adjacent express train blew through the station and a horn sounded... two lights down the track — home.

Fall, 2026: Malibu, CA

One thing he was not was bored. It was impossible for an artist to be bored, he decided, if he was constantly consumed with himself. No boredom there, certainly, only the fascination with that which surely bores others but never never oneself. The act of boredom, for a true artist, becomes so fascinating, introspective and all consuming, that it fills a self-absorbed soul, therefore eradicating the problem altogether. This was the thought that occupied his overactive brain that sat just beneath a layer of now mostly white hair.

The teak chair on the back porch and a cup of chamomile would do for a while, as the waves came crashing in. One can only stare at blank paper for so long before foaming at the mouth. A little sky, the breeze from the waves and some passers-by clad in cotton pants and light jackets, their children running after the gulls, would occupy a few minutes, at least. Had it not been engulfed by money, Malibu could very well have been Brighton Beach, New York with a less variable climate.

He watched the pelicans flying in and out — didn't they realize that this area was restricted? Anything would be better than thinking about the movie. The wretched thing which was the third wretched thing he would score in the span of three wretched years. Perhaps he would someday be a pelican, return to the Earth with the freedom to look down upon it all and just laugh; gobble up some fish in his chin and defecate at will.

The funny thing was that he had never much liked movies. He had learned the rules of them, of course; learned how to tailor the notes to fit the dramatic action, learned how to appease the twelve year old director, how to take the orchestra in hand on a sound stage, fire a musician, add a French horn. But actually sitting through a film, sitting in a dark room for two hours watching images of light dance around in front of him, he found interminable.

He wished it would either rain or not: choose a mood. The clouds, the agitated waves, the breeze would all indicate that a storm was at hand, yet no actual precipitation fell. How familiar. His very existence, it seemed to him, had been lived in a constant state of leaning back in his chair, eagerly awaiting inevitable terror. He had existed in that moment of utter weightlessness when it was clear he would either fall or grab onto something and pull himself to safety, that moment when the brain distinctly informs the body that danger is imminent: *that* was his life. Nature was just toying with him, as it had an annoying habit of doing. Let the storm come, see if he would care.

There he was again in an almost nonexistent yellow swim suit, the kind that hugged his ass and left little in the front to the imagination, splashing about in the surf with that big dog. Brash young man, he thought, to be out amongst such unfriendly waves, beneath a threatening sky that only grew more foreboding as the afternoon progressed. Still, he dashed through the encroaching water with — was it? Oh, no — a *Frisbee?* A Frisbee. He threw the white plastic disc at the dog who caught it in his mouth again and then again. Cold waves splashed around them and the wind most decidedly was picking up, yet they behaved as though it were a warm day in July, high summer, like this was a gum commercial with a snappy jingle and the beach were just swarming with avid sun worshipers. There was a certain bravery to that, he thought — a forced denial of reality which he admired; a kind of defiance: grey clouds met with sunny yellow swim shorts.

No matter. Young men were always coming and going at the colony — movie stars, lovers, hookers, friends, relatives, wannabe's, all swirling around the Hollywood sign, trying to believe they're a part of it all (and all too frequently, they are). There was a thud and a white plastic Frisbee appeared on his porch, knocking over one of his small potted plants and shattering its clay pot.

"Damned kid," was his first thought, but he stopped his mind before it could infect his tongue. He had, perhaps, finally become the bitter old man he always knew was his destiny. He was now the sort of man who gets annoyed when something out of the ordinary occurs, when his plan is not followed to the letter, when the path bends. Rally against it though he might, his instincts were seldom wrong; it was a change as unavoidable as nails that rust or unwatered plants that turn to mulch: he was becoming an old man. It would happen and in fact *was* happening. And wasn't this a sort of deserved finish line?

However, in an effort to lighten his own mood, perhaps, he picked up the white plastic disc and admired it. He supposed he would have to engage is some form of human contact now, some form of communication with an actual living, breathing thing. He tossed the Frisbee out toward the water with as much might as he could muster, which admittedly wasn't much as it only travelled a few feet from his property, landing dully and unaccomplished on the sand. The tan young man in the silly swimsuit approached.

"Did I break your plant?" he asked, as he picked up his toy and the dog bounced around eagerly on his hind legs, waiting for an event, for attention, for *something* to happen as his big pink tongue lagged about, raining drool down upon the sand. But then the dog looked him in the eye and he wasn't an old man, he wasn't anything other than another thing that took up space and breathed the shared air. They understood each other, they communicated, the dog and the newly old man.

"It's difficult to break a plant. A plant is a living thing, and living things, if they're worth having at all, are very, very difficult to break. Don't you agree? The pot, however, is another story altogether."

There was a pause as the chiseled young man digested this. His dress and everything about him would indicate that he was *one of those*, a silly creature whose head provided little vegetation for those blonde locks, someone who could be fully engaged for hours on a soon to be stormy beach, throwing a piece of plastic at a furry animal; yet, there was something to be admired about this, too. It had to be a full time job, maintaining a body such as his, his pectoral muscles alone were like two well developed small countries on a topography map. So he wouldn't stay for long, his muscled visitor, surely he must be on about his life and his body quite soon.

The thing was, though, he had meant his speech about his plant to be more amusing than philosophical, which of course had failed; he had come off as a second or fifth rate John Gielgud. He was decidedly out of practice with the human race, even more so when it came to attempted humor, which became more apparent with every rare human encounter. Hence, it was better to avoid these social confrontations altogether. The human race and he had never seen eye to eye, anyway, and perhaps to simply withdraw would be prudent. However, having recognized his growing curmudgeoness, would he rally against it with every remaining breath, or simply surrender and allow nature to have its way, as it surely would, eventually, anyway.

"Well, sorry I disturbed you. Nice house," and the young man turned to go. Physically, he really was a work of art. What would happen to this nice (funny how we assume that people who look as he does are *nice,* without even knowing them) young man, he wondered? Time would march across his body and his face, that which upon he seemed to have based his whole current reality would fade and he'd be left with — what? A Frisbee, maybe a dog. But oh, for the moment — how simplistic it must all seem. How running in the sun and which yellow swimsuit to don today, how wine on the patio and grilled salmon and suntan lotion. "I really like your music." And then he was gone, leaving the senior among them with a tangible shock that matriculated from his ears to his spine. It was a plainly visible hit and run.

Everett was well aware of the fact that the faces of people who score movies are not recognizable faces.

They don't hang out at the fashionable eateries, or go to the premiers of even their own movies, usually. They're not photographed by the trades. When they're hired for a film it's not even in *Variety* or spoken about over hushed tones in the valley before it's announced. There are a handful of men, mostly, who score major motion pictures and aside from the Oscar race, that annual circus, no one really pays too much attention. But this young man, clad in a ridiculous yellow swim suit that resembled a bloated rubber band and chasing a dog around on the sand under a darkening sky, knew who he was.

Impressive. But stupid, and he tried not to be flattered as he ran his wrinkled hands through his hair. He suddenly wished he had dressed better that day, not that it mattered, really, no more so than the young man's recognition. It's a small community after all, as is every community, really. Hollywood is little more than community theatre with zillions of dollars and fancy cameras. But still, the flattery was welcome, he was embarrassed to admit, as he watched the young man dash down the shore and almost out of sight. What must it be like to be so free and so young, so seemingly without care? So liberated from the confines of one's self, he wondered. So much utter weightlessness. Only footprints in the sand remained of the young man's visit now, and he gazed down upon them with jealousy.

It started to rain. Perhaps it was the adulation that had so recently been tossed his way, but he hoped the gallant young man would make it home alright before it started to pour. And it would pour; the first major deluge of the season, even. After all, should the young man avoid a lightening strike, all too common near large bodies of water, it was possible that he would even drop by again sometime... and that might be nice.

Summer, 1978: Mason City, Iowa

They were kind eyes, far from threatening. But most interesting of all, they didn't move. From his place in the water, he could make out that they were human, most likely male, but little else. The figure stood solitary at the divide of the woods and the shore and gazed at the boy's naked body, which drifted through the water as the sun poured over his pale, white skin. Intrigued yet embarrassed, the young man swum out a bit further, keeping his body submerged as best he could. He had always been just a bit chubby, and therefore, naturally, parts of his body had a tendency to float upward.

He would just keep swimming for a while, keeping himself as beneath the water as he could. What did this person want? Was he going to turn him in for swimming in the reservoir? Tell the police or worse, his mother and stepfather? Was he to be punished for running away on a warm day like today to dance with the afternoon that demanded a partner? He dared to turn around in the water and glance back: he was alone; the intruder had vanished. He looked up and down the entire coast as far as he could see, along the brief strip of land and into the woods, but there was no one. The young man breathed easily yet again but was still just that: *alone*. Floating on his back, solemnity returned; the world had righted itself if only within the freedom of the reservoir for a few hours on this most and otherwise perfect afternoon. The bright blue sky smiled down upon him as the cool water embraced his body. He went to the calm and convivial part of his imagination, his favorite spot.

A solitary existence had always suited him. He had decided not long ago, soon after the divorce, that he would need to rely upon himself for most things. He hadn't school friends nor a circle of great pals or even a pet to rely upon. He had been given a cat soon after the departure of his father, a solid gray kitten he had named Mozart. However, it had been decided by the alien force who soon entered their lives that his cat would never do, it didn't jive with his particular allergies, so Mozart had been sent to what he was told was "a farm," which he of course knew really meant otherwise. Mozart had been killed. Only his sock monkey, Henry, a gift from his father upon his tenth birthday, would serve as his witness, companion and, at times, co-conspirator now. The two were inseparable.

And so, they would create a world of their own liking and exist solely within that. When others, adults and young people alike, tried to enter the private sanctuary that they called their own, the pair would simply deny admittance, this being a world of their own creation. They liked to make believe that they were royalty, in a sense, the whole world laid out before them as though it existed only for themselves. The trees they climbed were *their* trees, the convenience stores outside of which he parked his bicycle were there merely to provide the things *they* needed, no one else. Weekly, they stopped outside of the furniture store on Washington Street and devoted a good hour to walking about amongst the staged living and dining rooms, pretending that they were all a part of their own extravagant home which sat within their own well furnished kingdom. They wandered amongst bureaus and sideboards, leather sofas and marble nightstands, giving last minute instruction to the imaginary servants who scurried about, preparing for the evening's lavish dinner party at which they would entertain royalty or perhaps a few movie stars.

He dried off on the shore, the dirt and grass from the ground sticking to his damp feet. The sun had reached its absolute peak while he was in the water and had now begun its decent. Before long, a dim sort of light would burst sideways though the trees, before extinguishing itself entirely, leaving only darkness and a hint of moonlight that would reflect off of the leaves. The woods were a magical place for him, and he so desperately needed magic.

He used his yellow t-shirt as a towel, knowing it would dry in the breeze when he put it back on. Placing Henry back into his backpack, he pedaled back to reality, something he dreaded. Glancing about for his mysterious woodland visitor who was nowhere to be found, he started up the hill and soon found the familiar dirt trail.

"You're late," she said through gritted teeth. He hadn't meant to be, but it appeared that he was. Dinner was on the faux oak table, his chair remained empty, and both of them, the stepfather and his mother, or whatever this creature who inhabited his mother's body was, sat at the oval structure, glaring at him like he were a cat who had had an accident on the living room carpet. Dinner was a major evening ritual, a religion of sorts, the table being the pulpit upon which they worshipped and indulged in whatever animal sacrifice had surrendered its life for their nourishment. His attendance at these evening services was expected, demanded, unless it was one of "those" nights. "Those" nights happened about once a week, when he was given seven dollars and asked not to return until well past nightfall, 10 P.M. at the earliest. He would spend these evenings feasting on cheeseburgers from McDonald's and roaming about town on his bicycle with Henry until well after the streetlights came on.

"That's two dollars," was his contribution to the scolding, words he was obviously quite satisfied to speak, powerful in the knowledge that it was something he could control, his icy grip around the family purse strings. Docking his stepson's allowance, petty though it was, must have been a kind of release for him. The stepfather controlled all of the finances in the house now, a task she had obediently turned over to him upon their marriage, she being so incapable, he had convinced her. "Now go and wash up," the young man turned to go, but, just for clarity, he supposed, was further directed: "Now."

The stepfather was full of little commandments like that. For example, upon Mr. Thompson's arrival at their house, a number of edicts had been established. Mr. Thompson had convinced his mother that he would take over, he was in control, and she needn't ever worry about anything again, so long as she obeyed the set of rules which he had carefully laid out for her. She relished this, as it was a complete surrender. She had left the driving to someone else, as it were, and she was free to feel the breeze from the window of the passenger's seat.

Hence, the young man was allowed an exact five minutes for bathing, once a day. Five minutes was perfectly long enough to clean one's self in the shower, and baths, which he had always enjoyed, were now strictly prohibited. Baths were not a thing a boy of his age should even contemplate, as the act of taking a bath itself was far too effete. Should he luxuriate in the shower for more than five minutes, the hot water was abruptly shut off via the switch on the hot water heater, saturating his naked body with ice cold water, like sharp daggers cutting into his skin. Try as he might to get it all in during the allotted time, he could never quite achieve it, owing mostly to the fact, said Mr. Thompson, that there was quite "a lot of him to wash." Perhaps, Jay Thompson reasoned somewhere beneath all of that thick silver hair with the cowlick, actions such as these and comments such as that would be incentive for him to lose the bothersome few pounds that he found to be quite an annoyance on his stepson. Such was the new norm in the young man's life, and he would have to dance quickly to adapt.

She had spent too many years on her own, Mr. Thompson had decided. Even when she was married, it was to an absent spouse who simply let the boy and his mother do as they pleased. Discipline was sorely needed in this household and so began a routine of appeasing the alien, adhering to the wishes of the foreigner who quickly ascended the thrown of dictatorship. What choice had she, his mother, really? A woman with a husband who had left her destitute with a young boy to raise. She should be grateful — something Mr. Thompson reminded her of daily or, it often seemed, hourly.

Along with Mr. Thompson, a grayness had taken up permanent residence in their home; a sameness, a dread, a sense that this was most certainly no longer a real home, but the result of an unfortunate twist of circumstance, a rip in the fabric of their lives. Even the walls, the floors, the windows looked different to him. With no one in his corner, as was made overwhelmingly evident to him, no one on his team except Henry, he must now be his own advocate; an army of one with little choice but to put down his rifle and succumb to his new existence as a P.O.W.

"Use your fork *correctly*," Mr. Thompson instructed. Dinner this evening consisted of Stouffer's pot pies. "You're using your fork wrong again. Someone needs to teach you to use a fork. Look —" The young man's fork was ripped out of his hands, sending morsels of food flying onto his shirt and the floor, which earned him a look of distain from the mighty Mr. T., who's bifocals were so thick, he just noticed, that it made his eyes look like huge, evil planets. He had once seen him without his glasses and his eyes were only the size of tiny marbles; he tried to remember this. The fact was that the boy was unaware that there was, indeed, an improper way to use an eating utensil unless he used it to shovel food up his nose or into his ear, for example. "Close your lips around the prongs, then remove the food and pull the fork out. You're putting the fork in your mouth and taking the food off with your teeth, that's wrong. Do it right. Another two dollars the next time I see that." At this rate, he would end up *owing* Mr. Thompson money by week's end. His allowance was only five dollars a week.

He picked up a bite of pot pie with his fork. All eyes were upon the young man now, the elder two of their trio not touching their food but rather watching as one observes a diver about to take the plunge, leaning forward in their chairs with wide eyes, scorecards at the ready. "Not so big, make it a smaller bite!" he was instructed. He readjusted, then slowly moved the fork to his mouth. It felt odd to place his lips upon the sterling silver of the fork, as though he were intruding upon its privacy, but he had little choice, his commandment was clearly to suck the fork dry like a popsicle.

"I think, so you remember, you should eat with your right hand from now on." Mr. Thompson had given his review of the play prior to its completion, the food had yet to even arrive in his mouth. The young man was certain that, had he waited for the final curtain of the task, Jay Thompson would have been more than satisfied with his newly acquired dining "skills." Or maybe not. Perhaps he had made up this whole game while awaiting his appearance at the table this evening. Sport, for Jay Thompson, was just that, and he would play it, or pretend to, when and wherever he could.

"But I'm left handed!" He'd never held a fork in his right hand.

"It'll be a way for you to remember. Rest of the month, you'll eat only with your right hand, or you won't eat at all." He tried again, this time with his right hand. It was like flying an airplane with only a vague idea of what the controls did. Pot pie fell from the utensil again, crashing back down to his plate, splattering its beige creamy-ness interspersed with the occasional green pea against the white bone china.

His mother watched him from her seat, silently swirling what wine remained in her long stemmed glass.

One eye glared in anger at him for being so out of the ordinary as to be left handed, a familiar trait of his father's which she resented, and the other seemed to glaze over, if only for the briefest of flashes, communicating a kind of telepathic request. "Please forgive me someday," he was sure that's what her cornea would say could it speak. But as soon as she noticed her child's glance of helplessness, peering up at her as a cat requests a scratch, she resumed her role. "And don't think we'll forget," she proclaimed, an actress having regained full embodiment of her character, having fleetingly gone up on her lines. Having momentarily gasped the real air, she was sucked right back down beneath the rapids of a raging river. "You have to learn these things, he's trying to help you," she was slurring her words now, just a bit, a pattern that would progress throughout the evening.

They were reliant upon Jay Thompson, there was no getting around it. Elliot's father was a foundation that simply gave way one day, sucking those standing on top into the deepest recesses of the Earth. Shelia's former husband was a beautiful bubble who had one day simply burst. Jay Thompson was the one available rock amid those ferocious white water rapids. The thing about a rock is that it is always aware of its own importance. She would cling to him as steadfastly as she could, even if her own son were swept downriver to meet the inevitable falls. She would not be.

He did the dishes, scraped their left over food bits from the fine china plates, also a relic from their former lives, and immersed his hands in hot, soapy water. The house was equipped with a dishwasher, but he was forbidden to use it as it consumed too much electricity. To do each one by hand in the sink was better discipline, anyway. At least soon, he could retreat to his bedroom where he could play Ravel for the remainder of the evening and perhaps longer. After lights out were ordered, he would plug in his headphones and listen to the movements again and again, reveling in the images the music created in his imagination and feeling joy, pure joy, an emotion he could vaguely recall from those early years of his life but that now he must reserve strictly for this tiny room, while Henry looked on with his ever-present smile from atop the covers.

He had explored other composers. With the aide of his devoted library card, he had checked out records put forth by the great symphonies of the world who performed the compositions of artists whose work he quickly came to know by heart. But it was Ravel — always Ravel to whom he returned. It was an escape, his music, yes. But it was also unexpected. Ravel's compositions were quiet and tender, frequently not unlike a lullaby, yet they could turn suddenly with great flourish into sharp movements that conjured destruction, despair, chaos, before sorting themselves out again and finding clear sailing — something he hoped to emulate for himself. Best of all, there was order to it all; moments of glorious abandon, of course, but always returning to a theme that built and grew and progressed. It was stunning, his music, it was a portal to another land, exotic color set against the backdrop of everything else that was so gray.

Still, as he lay back upon his Charlie Brown sheets with Henry on his chest, jet black hair swept over his ears to accommodate his headphones, he thought of the future.

Fall, 1996: West Village, New York City

People move to New York, by and large, to prove something, either to themselves or their families, people they know, or sometimes to completely reinvent themselves. They generally leave the city for one of three reasons: 1) They've proved it. 2) They no longer feel the need to prove it. 3) They surrender.

But there's that strange fourth category, too: those who have surrendered yet remain in New York anyway, slugging it out day to day, caught on the carousel of survival and unable (unwilling, really) to see any of the blur that zooms past them as the years progress. They lie to the world and proclaim their love for the city that never sleeps despite how much they secretly complain about it. Or, in private, they focus on the carrot that must, *must* be just around the corner, although they'd never admit this to anyone, certainly not to the masses of acquaintances who politely wrote their chances off years prior. It would be too embarrassing to admit that one still held out hope. It's brilliant to proclaim the ambitions of your youth if you're successful, but after you're not and those days have passed, it's just sad, or so he had always thought. Everett had watched it all from behind the safety of his piano — seen the young boys come in all bright and eager, and watched as they faded into the ordinary or worse, become bartenders at this very watering hole.

It had turned frigid that night. Seventh Avenue was almost at a stand still, the village deserted, everyone guarding themselves against the cold in their own homes in their own beds, wrapped up in blankets and socks. Only a few regulars congregated at the bar, drinking their way through the night while he banged out some Andrew Lloyd Weber and then a little Carole King just to shake the inclement night up a bit. The rusty radiator did little to warm the room despite its hisses, and his fingers began to go numb as he plunked out *"so far away... doesn't anybody stay in one place anymore?"* The lyrics were ironic, because the fact of the matter was that yes, just about everyone entrapped in this little room was staying in precisely the very same place, likely forever.

The door opened and the wind that blew through the room was audible. Little white paper napkins and the pages of cheap complimentary gay magazines which sat in stacks by the door flickered in the arctic blast, not to mention the Xeroxed sheet music from which he was reading, which he artfully steadied with one hand while maintaining the melody with the other.

Three men in full-length cashmere coats, which only partially masked dark suits and subtle ties, seated themselves at the bar as they continued their conversation. Oh dear, the grown-ups had joined the party, the men in suits, the mob, the real people. Every now and then, gentlemen of their ilk wafted through, businessmen who, after closing a big deal or exchanging millions of dollars on Wall Street, banded together for a celebratory evening out, The Pillow Factory usually being their last stop. Usually it was the homosexuals of the deal, representatives from both the seller and the buyer, the prosecution and the defense, the guilty and the innocent. And then sometimes it was the straight bosses trying to impress a potential new hire by showing them the "uniqueness" of the city. They were mostly a gaggle of suits come to stare at the animals through the bars of the cage, laughing over cognac and cigars, gazing upon the locals which allowed them the knowledge that they were in-the-know and terribly chic New Yorkers who could at any time escape this dark urban den and return to the real world uptown, a world of expense accounts and tailored pants, leaving these urban bar dwellers frozen in their own primitive universe. *So far away*, indeed.

He kept playing, thinking that the more he worked his fingers, the more blood would flow and the less frozen they would be. Oh, no. One of the suits was looking at him, he could see from the corner of his sleep-deprived eye. He had left the conversation with the other two, who seemed much more interested in each other, and swiveled in his bar stool to stare at the piano as though it were Pandora's box itself. He was about to be hit on, he could feel it. Not that he minded the attention, the reminder that he was still a part of the sexual world, but experience had taught him that these things were never to be trusted. He received at least one or two numbers or AOL addresses in his tip bowl each week, all of which he threw out immediately. They were either drunk, doing it on a dare to impress their friends, or, the worst, had fallen in love with the aging "genius" at the keys who had seduced them with music, only to find out far too soon that the man and the tune were hardly one and the same.

Cashmere was approaching. Fuck. He decided he would just play louder and sing with more gusto into the microphone which, attached to the rusted silver stand, jutted right into his face. *"It would be so fine to see your face at my door, and it doesn't help to know that you're so — far away..."* his voice crackled into the archaic PA system. The suit stood directly in front of the woebegone stage, in front of the enormous rainbow flag which covered one whole side of the mostly tuneless piano. He stood there, defiant in his fabulous dry cleaned coat, eyeing the instrument and, much more so, the man who controlled it as though he were staring down a tank in Tiananmen Square.

"Jesus. I sure have missed you," said the suit, loud and for all in the establishment to hear — a proclamation in the middle of the room as though he were the town crier. He stopped playing, mid-song. Maria looked up from the bar... *Oh, you're kidding...* Silence crystallized in the frigid room so one could practically touch it... those remaining looked up from their drinks, a miraculous feat in and of itself. *Fuck.*

It was time for a song change... He diverted course and struck up a Dolly Parton tune: *"Here you come again, lookin' better than a body has a right to..."* He sang the words into the pathetic old microphone as sweat beaded upon his forehead. Continuing the song, he tried not to look up, but did so, in spite of himself. Who could ever resist those "come to my private island" eyes?

Autumn, 1989: Cambridge, MA

The crowd at Bridget's wasn't breaking up. It was well past 1 A.M., but they refused to go home. Owing to the fact that they were almost all students, perhaps it was a protest of sorts, their refusal to give in and admit that summer had passed and the Fall semester was most definitely upon them. Perhaps if they stayed out long enough, drinking the night away and flirting over cosmopolitans and grapefruit martinis, somehow the weather would revert and books and papers could be exchanged for the sandals and sun that had so recently abandoned them.

They were tan and rested, having spent the past three months abroad or summering with their families on the cape. Bridget's was minimalist in nature, just four gray walls, one of which was occupied by an odd kind of metal sculpture that clutched the stucco and another by clear glass doors which tonight opened up to invite the evening air inside. The bar itself was solid glass consumed by tiny candles in clear glass votives and clinking cocktail glasses. It was what was considered modern. Rather than a homey neighborhood pub, Bridget's definitely strove to be the premiere Cambridge watering hole for the young urban sophisticates its customers were all longing to become. Bridget herself swept through every now and then: a tall, svelte young woman no more than thirty who dressed mostly in black with large, circular glasses that masked most of her face. She always hurried through the room as though she were anxious to get to the office, eager to count the evening's receipts. She was a former law student who, upon graduation, had found her true calling as an entrepreneur and had opened a bar rather than spend her life confronting billable hours and lawsuits, codicils and prenups. He always believed that she just couldn't handle the thought of leaving the nest, what had become her home, and going out to fly on her own. So, she had settled in quaint little Cambridge for good. This was fine, he thought: she had found her way and good for her. She waltzed through the bar as though she were an adult, the no-nonsense businesswoman she hoped to become and very likely would, but wasn't quite yet. For the moment, it was just a characterization, as she greeted recent graduates and former classmates with a smirk as if to say, "can you really believe I'm doing this? Don't worry, I'm only pretending to be a grown up. Don't let the suit fool you."

A scotch arrived on the small bar stool that stood next to his piano, an impressive baby grand which was kept in faultless condition. The instrument served merely for the look, Everett being the only one who ever played it, really. Bridget was happy for him to do so, but never went so far as to offer him an actual job. Why would she pay for something that she was already getting for free? Everett didn't even pass a tip jar, it just laid there, barren and frequently empty, on the piano. He needed to play, perhaps, more than the audience needed to listen. But it did add a certain something, something unique and even classy to the ambiance of this particular watering hole; so he was always welcome.

It was a cool handed, subtle kind of jazz he played this evening. Bridget's was the one place where he could experiment, play his own work in front of an audience who only half listened. He was well versed in almost every form of music, and his nightly concerts ranged from classical to soul to even a kind of bluegrass. But tonight, a subtle kind of Miles Davis-inspired jazz seemed to fit the bill. He thanked Mandy, the waitress who always looked out for him, for his fresh cocktail and, every now and then, between measures, glanced at his glass in envy, knowing that soon, between sets, he would taste his sweet friend Scotch upon his lips. The more he played, the more he drank, and it all just got better. Drinks and music: it was all medicinal to him.

"Oh, it's not from me, honey." Everett looked up, his hands still in motion upon the keys, and watched as Mandy pointed to the corner. There he sat, over by the front wall of windows: Ethical Ethics, sipping something that looked like — good God, a lemon drop? "Looks like someone's got a fan."

He would have to go over, there was no avoiding it. What would he say? Some brilliant quip was clearly called for ("what's a nice place like this doing with a lawyer like you?"), but none came to mind and his music became faster and more intense. He was making it up as he went along now, maybe it would become a new standard in his repertoire, or maybe it was all just nervous filler. He built upon his musical theme, of course, but the piano had really just become an extension of himself, and he played it as casually as he might have brushed his black hair. None of it would have mattered amid the glasses breaking and the ice chipping and the low din of chatter. He would just keep playing, he decided. He'd play for a good long while and then perhaps his new suitor — or whatever this was all about — would simply go away. He could thank him for the drink in class next week.

He was just running free now, letting his fingers express his thoughts as they glided up and down the keyboard; staying true to the idea of the piece of his own creation, the tone, of course, but released, — *unlocked.* He glanced up as his hands continued their dance independently. There he sat over by the windows with that politician's glare, resilient and determined, watching intently and *not* giving up.

Were there lyrics to Everett's improvised notes, they would have been, *"Stay away... Stay away, handsome Republican..."* If he had learned anything in his life, he knew that he, himself, was one sticky brier patch that a dashing young ethics student with a brilliantly luminous career ahead of him and no less the son of a prominent Senator, should hop right past.

3

Summer, 1978: Mason City, Iowa

T HE MAN IN the woods was back. From the water, he observed his eyes, the same eyes from the other day, as he paddled about, this time a bit closer to the shore. Was he trying to escape something, too, he wondered? Or could he ever be an admirer? He had never experienced an admirer and the thought that someone could take an interest in him, as he was, naked and plain and gliding through the water, was as frightening as it was enthralling. Although he longed for companionship, he proceeded with caution.

He had fled to the reservoir that day, late in the afternoon, as fast as the pedals on his bicycle would carry him. He would not allow tears until he arrived in the water, where they would be camouflaged.

The first part of his day had been spent as public mockery at a department store with his mother and Jay Thompson. It had been decided that, as he had recently turned thirteen, new summer clothes were called for, he having outgrown last year's. So his mother and stepfather ordered him into the family sedan, as his mother called it, (which was a lie, the car belonged to Mr. Thompson, which he loved to emphasize by saying things such as "get into MY car," or "take your shoes off before you get into MY car, if you know what's good for you," etc.) where the three of them drove just under the speed limit to Ridgeway: one of the larger, though less expensive department stores in town. The grown ups shopped at the more exclusive stores in the larger towns that surrounded their little patch of the Midwest. But when it came time to clothe this "fat kid," the more run of the mill stores would suffice, and what would it matter anyway? "An elephant in nice clothing remains an elephant," as he was told.

It was the kind of place where one found things on racks and in bins, laid out beneath flickering, florescent light bulbs attached to tall, styrofoam ceilings. The young man had little choice but to be grateful, for what was the alternative? He was fed and he was clothed. He was a young man whose needs were being met. And it was, after all, astonishingly clear that some new clothes were called for. His tennis shoes had holes in them and his shorts, the three pair he owned, were stained and mostly ripped.

"Can I help you?" a tall, rail thin, well-dressed sales associate approached. He was mostly bald yet surely not yet mid-thirties, with his remaining hair pushed forward in a kind of, the young man supposed, disguise? It was like using a napkin to cover an entire dining room table which sat nine. Still, he had a kind face and seemed pleased to assist their unhappy little trio.

"Yes, my son here has gotten too fat for all of last year's shorts, so we need to find him some new ones, but not too expensive." Sheila's remarks were said loud and clear, just to be sure, he supposed, that Jay picked up her frequency and knew that they were connected, the two of them, united in their common cause.

"Hmmm," said the sales associate, his eyes running up and down the young man. "We should probably look in," he leaned into Sheila and said the following in a kind of whisper, as though he were speaking of some terrible disease, *"husky."*

"At least," added Mr. Thompson. "Let's get a tape measure and measure his waist, so at least we know what we're working with."

"Oh, I don't think that's necessary, I have a very good eye." The young man was thankful for the sales associate, who was clearly trying to spare him further humiliation.

"No, let's do it. I'd like to know. Go get it." Jay Thompson had issued his edict, and so it would be. So there, on the poorly carpeted sales floor, between racks of generic Izod shirts and amid cheap cotton pants, under those pale florescent lights that blared from the tall ceiling and in front of dozens of other shoppers who glanced over in amused curiosity, a tape measure was flung around the young man's waist in order to satisfy Sheila (he had taken to calling his mother by her first name, at least to himself) and Mr. Thompson (it had been requested of him that he refer to his stepfather as "Jay," rather than the formal "Mr. Thompson," but the young man flatly refused, insisting instead to address him as "Mr. Thompson," even when and especially in front of others. It suggested a kind of alienation between the two of them, which was the truth. To call him by his first name would be inferring that the two were somehow buddies or pals and besides, "Jay," as it applied to this man, seemed such a desecration of a perfectly good letter of the English alphabet).

"Oh my GOD," his mouth hung open for a while. "THIRTY-FOUR INCHES!" Mr. Thompson shrieked it across the store as the young man's face turned red.

"That's four inches — FOUR INCHES more than last year!" Sheila joined her husband's chorus of discontent.

"No problem, I have some things that will fit wonderfully, be right back," said the bald salesman, who shot a look of apology and concern to the young, red-faced boy, then vanished, regretfully exiting the battlefield before laying witness to bloodshed.

And so the afternoon went.

In the dressing room, his mother brought in a few shirts for him to try on. Upon seeing him shirtless, her only remark was "you've got bigger boobs than I do!" as she slammed the door shut. Slammed doors were getting to be the norm at home, and now here was a totally foreign door for her to experiment with. After trying on nearly every stitch of "husky" clothing in the store and exhausting the kind sales associate, it was decided that they would return home empty handed, despite the striped shorts and the white pull over shirt that fit well and would be a perfectly serviceable summer outfit, thought the boy, standing there in last year's gray shorts and stretched-out, rust-colored t-shirt.

It would be best, it was decided, that he wear ill fitting clothing for the summer, which would provide inspiration for him to reduce his weight. The entire afternoon had been merely a — what? Occupation of one's time? Experiment? Lark? Nay. — *Entertainment.* He was a monkey expected to do tricks, and he knew this. Toss a peanut at it and see what the fat boy will do — it's fun. But the oddest thing, he didn't think that even *they* realized this. It was as though there were some subconscious bond between the two of them, a conspiratorial husband and wife, like the MacBeth's (he had read most of Shakespeare last Fall). They were united in a cause, was how they explained it to themselves: it was an activity that drew them together the same way some couples bond over Scrabble or fuss over their dogs. They must save and improve, mold this young man, save him from his own ego, which was enormous (like the rest of him). But what it really was, what the young man was astonished that they could not see or at least would never admit: it was *sport.* Just another sport to occupy their minds and make up for the saddening silence that would exist otherwise. He was little more than filler between innings, contributing to their otherwise empty place in the world.

"Don't indulge him, Sheila." Hence, after two hours, forty-five minutes of scratchy shorts and shirts and more than enough humiliation, they were all back in the hot sedan on their return trip to the silent cul-de-sac which sat in the middle of nothing in particular, where scoldings would abound all afternoon over the expense of clothing his enormous girth, an expense they ultimately forewent.

But soon, as early evening was approaching, the young man decided to flee to his favorite watering hole for a solo swim. Perhaps he would even defy them and not return for dinner, the ultimate sin. He wondered if they would worry over this or secretly rejoice in the fact that it would give them a brand new subject for scolding when he finally returned. When questioned, he would reply with a simple "well, you told me to slim down, so I didn't think you'd mind my skipping a few meals," or something laced with more wit, if only it would come to him.

From the television, the afternoon baseball game reverberated throughout the house along with various sportscasters squealing in their monotonic exasperation about fouls and outs and hits and ins, various buzzers sounded and a scoreboard turned different colors. The popcorn popped, the wine glass was filled, the planet spun round. He mounted his bicycle, his escape pod, and headed for the sidewalk, which would lead to the trail which led to the woods which led to the reservoir which would arrive him at peace. And perhaps, even, his secret admirer would make an appearance, a notion not altogether unwelcome.

He rarely swam this late. The sun had just about surrendered for the day and the crickets and locusts were already starting up their nightly concert. Clouds seemed to be clearing, drifting right over him as he floated on his back, leaving a clear, soon to be nighttime sky filled with emerging stars. Stars were there all the time, he supposed, but only showed themselves with the exit of the sun; clever, mysterious things. How much clearer the stars would seem out here than at home, he was certain, without the lights of suburbia to dampen them. He thought he might just hang around long enough to see, to take a good long look for himself, perhaps even set up camp and never return. He would cook his own meals; live off the land, become a mountain man. The lake felt different with the absence of the midday sun, a coolness to the air pervaded his face, seeped into his pores, while his body remained obscured beneath the warm, crystal blue liquid that moved gently beneath what was quickly becoming a purple, early evening sky. And now there they were — the same eyes on the bank had appeared yet again, but the young man no longer minded nor made any effort to conceal himself. Indeed, in what was an entirely new sensation for him, he even felt the need to be provocative.

But for the moment, it was clear that he could remain in the water no longer. Already, his fingers and toes had turned to prunes and it was time to return to life among the creatures of the land, rather than those of the sea. The wandering eyes from the bank had made their usual retreat as he swam nearer, so he strode out of the water to dry himself upon the shore, careful to place his cherished monkey, his security detail, inside his backpack, but comfortably so, so the trip home would not be an unpleasant one for him and he could peer out the top with his eyes of black glass.

"I'm sorry." The voice had come from behind, so whomever was there was, at this moment, able to see his backside. "I'm sorry that happened." The young man was frozen, could not even continue to dry himself with his rust-colored, well-worn t-shirt. "I'm sorry." Moments passed. "Awful. It's just a-awful... S-*sorry*."

Boldly, he turned to face this mysterious person who had appeared seemingly from nowhere, a creature of the woods speaking gibberish that made no sense at all. His was a kind face, and that's all he could take in for a long while. Just a kind face surrounded by a sheath of long brown hair with a touch of gray around the edges, an unusually large nose and large ears, dressed in rumpled jeans and tattered sandals and a white t-shirt with long, black sleeves. But it was his eyes — set quite a distance away from each other and large, with almost solid black pupils, which met his own, causing him to feel something in his core, something that told him that this was important, this was a moment in his life that should be captured, recorded in his DNA — because it would stay within him always.

"Don't be afraid. I'm *sorry*. Let's get you dressed." The stranger extended his hand in introduction. "Ridgeway. Today. I was there. I s-saw it. Terrible. Terrible. I'm *so* sorry." A compassionate stranger, a solo voice here in a place where he had never before seen another human being. Perhaps he was really one of the animals, an evolved woodland creature, appearing to him now in human form — a kind of magic. The boy hesitated, his wet black hair dripping onto his pale chest, then exhaled audibly. Using his t-shirt to cover himself, he spoke:

"Hello."

Winter, 1996: West Village, New York City

Well, there really was no escaping him now, he would have to say hello and be cordial. He wished he could slink away somewhere, but he was caught mid Carole King in the midst of a dive piano bar surrounded by drunks and a trio of drag queens on their way home, finally calling it a night over watered-down cosmopolitans.

Expectation, he had decided not so long ago, was a dirty and overall frustrating word that he wished to banish from the world's vocabulary as he had stricken it from his own; but it was not to be tonight. The word was writ large upon both of their foreheads upon finding themselves in the same stretch of air once more. The maestro had fallen far from the radar and was currently swimming, drifting along the bottom of the expectation chart along with the algae, frequently finding himself tangled in the seaweed. His long lost friend, of course, was no doubt surfing a high wave, flexing his bronzed torso into the sun to the delight of sun worshippers everywhere. Everett kept his gaze focused on his shaking hands for a while.

How exactly would he play this? Would he be proud and strong and pretend that he was so content in his dream job entertaining the colorful mini-masses at The Pillow Factory? Should he explain that this was merely a side job he did to keep his musical skills in shape, and he was really a concert pianist who toured the world regularly and accompanied the great symphonies of the world? Or was that just too much energy to exert, and would he instead admit his embarrassment, let loose with his own disappointment and crawl beneath a barstool? Or would he just continue to say nothing?

"I'm gonna take a short break, ya'll, ladies and gentleman and — *others,*" stifled laughter, the last of the laughs left in the few semiconscious souls who remained at the bar, still clinging to the night. "But I'll be back real soon to close us out." No one even looked up from his or "her" drinks. It was as though they were praying over their glasses, a secret alcohol-based religion. Everett emerged from behind the piano in the suddenly silent room, stepped down from the makeshift stage, and stood, small, bare and afraid, before Jamie. The two stood looking at each other for what seemed like a whole minute, drinking in the other's familiar sent and discerning the remembered, subtle hues that had been reawakened in them both. The base, the root of each of them, remained intact. They searched each other's eyes, unsure of their next moves. After some internal debate, Jamie moved to embrace his great, good friend, the cashmere of his overcoat mingled with the cotton of Everett's plaid shirt and worn and wrinkled khakis, the uniform he wore frequently when sitting behind the piano on nights such as this. It was a hesitant kind of hug at first, cold and uncertain, unsure of who should pull away first, unsure of exactly what was happening or why they had found each other on a frigid and hostile night such as this evening, tucked away in a dimly lit hovel on Christopher and Seventh Avenue in the middle of a thriving metropolis on the Eastern seaboard. But the hug evolved as familiar points of their bodies reconnected with one another, the shape of his back and how his shoulder blades fit exactly in his palms, the precise size of his chest and how the two of them merged perfectly into one another, gears of the same clock. A sense of home was awakened; atoms, molecules of all that once was ignited and blazed.

"I love hearing you play... I've missed it."

Everett swallowed hard, trying to find some suitable words, something brilliant, but that was impossible. He needed a script. Words, unlike musical notes, had always failed him so miserably. It had been such a long time since anybody had hugged him. He was taken aback by the gesture, of the closeness of another human being, by the all too familiar scent of him. He tried to erase all emotion from his tone, but knew he had failed: "Come upstairs and we can chat. You need a drink?" He strode deliberately to the bar, like leaving the scene of an accident.

Two filled glasses later, one of scotch and one lemon drop (Everett remembered), and they both sat in the empty cabaret theatre upstairs, the dusty performance space consisting of tables and chairs and seating for no more than seventy-three, precisely. Tonight, there were no half-drunken audiences roaring with laughter to witness the play the two of them were about to perform, no waitresses and bartenders scurrying about with their trays along with the random mouse or two, and no one to operate the creaky spotlight. It was just Everett and Jamie and the deafening frequency of silence, mingled with the faint beat of music from the bar next door which snuck its way through the crevices in the brick wall. Jamie looked so well, so crisp and clean and spotless, which made Everett feel as though he had worn pajamas to a dinner party. "How long have you been in town?"

"Almost a year now. The firm transferred me almost right away. I didn't even know you — "

"I sort of let my Christmas card list lapse." More silence as Everett felt Jamie's eyes all over him, surely exploring the strands of gray that had recently presented themselves in his hair. Had Everett become horribly fat or had his face broken out in boils, it would have been one thing, but he was just exactly what he was at this precise moment, and that was more difficult for him to accept than disfigurement when confronted with this mirror from his past.

"You look great, by the way."

"Yeah. Five years in a smoke filled piano bar playing for drunks and gays does wonders for the complexion." Should he have dripped with such sarcasm? Been so self-deprecating? Surely Jamie would just see it for what it was: Everett defending himself once more, boxing gloves laced tightly and bundled up about his face. He hated that fact — there was no hiding when Jamie White was in the room. His eyes darted around tiny spaces, the empty chairs, the staked glass racks, anything — before landing on his friend's fine taupe coat — Brooks Brothers, no doubt. He suddenly despised his whole attendance in this odd little play, but he had no choice but to see it through, he owed Jamie that much, he supposed. But he had no idea how to play this particular scene.

"Do you remember the one - "

"Of course."

"Could you?" Jamie indicated the dusty and dilapidated baby grand piano which sat upon the stage, which was barely the size of a postage stamp, illuminated in the glow of a single light bulb from above, what the theatrical folk called a "work light." "What do you think?"

"What, now?"

"Please?"

It had been such a long time since anyone had asked Everett to play one of his own compositions. He wondered if his fingers would even remember how. All right, he would take this little walk down the streets of yesteryear with Jamie, if it would appease him. They shared a city now and what was worse, they both now knew it. He wondered what that meant. Could he perform this little tune for this ghostly figure in cashmere so they could both move on and be done with it before losing themselves once again in the rapids of the city? Everett could then stay comfortable in the dust and cold water of downtown while he released Jamie to the shimmering warm currents of his own life, and so be it.

He moved to the piano and turned back the hinged piece of wood that covered the keys. The song came back to him the same way one recalls old home phone numbers or the exact curvature of the trees that decorated the backyards of one's youth. The very notes themselves were written in the whites of Jamie's eyes, and Everett had only to look into them, seated alone at the tiny round table in front of the stage, solitary in an empty theatre full of stale air, a singular, adoring audience of one, and it were as though he were reading carefully printed music.

Jamie recalled the melody, of course. How often he had thirsted for it in the seven years since he had seen his friend, his confidant. He watched Everett's hands upon the keys glide from note to note, precious and precise as though he were feeding an infant. The piano literally became a part of his anatomy, an extension of himself. It was a trait he had seen in him before but had almost forgotten. Almost. He may have turned cynical, he may have met his old school friend with a certain edge of hostility, but Everett was still in there, knocking about within a shell of slight decay. It was evident in his music, clear in the way he caressed the ivory. Yes, this was the sound he had loved. It poured out of a wretched and mostly out of tune instrument in a squalid little room above Sheridan Square, but the music was most *definitely* still there. The tune brought back all of what had once been familiar, of course, but more so, it had grown, evolved, become more mature and complex — not studied, really, but rather *lived.* Everett, he knew, was incapable of ever playing any piece of music the same way twice, never a creature of routine. The person he was at that moment fed his own work, it was as inescapable for him as the way the weather fluctuated from day to day or whatever washed in with the tide.

For Jamie, the music was like rediscovering a secret underwater cave that only the two of them knew about, having drifted in from an oceanic expedition gone awry, and now they would bask inside in the dark for a while with only themselves and some blind fish for company, luxuriating in this rare pocket of air. Looking up at his old nucleus, he daren't blink.

Fall, 2026: Malibu, CA

He looked at the sky and contemplated how long he would have to lie there. Eventually, he was certain, he would burn to a crisp and his charred remains would be found by some curious passerby or wayward assembly of hungry birds. His chiropractor had failed him yet again, his back was out, and there was nothing to be done about it but lie in the sand, where he had fallen at the edge of his patio, and watch the few scant clouds drift over the colony. He closed his eyes and looked at the insides of his lids, pink, not quite able to obscure the sun that beat down upon them. What would become of him, he pondered, before drifting off to sleep for a while. Perhaps, if he concentrated hard enough, he could just die right here. It would save a lot of fuss and relieve him of his current obligations *and* it would add a certain drama to it all.

A coolness pervaded, a distinct change in temperature. "Are you alright?" Someone had come to his rescue, alas, the mass of body thankfully blocking the sun and bathing him in shade. He shook off the grogginess of sleep only to be met with the silhouette of a face staring directly down at his, framed by a collection of dirty blonde hair, disheveled. Turning his head as much as he could, the face led to a finely chiseled torso, tan, rock solid thighs and various, assorted bulges here and there. It was that boy with the dog, the one in the silly, almost non-existent swimsuits. Ah, youth. Perhaps he had reached heaven and this was his reward. Perhaps not. "How long have you been lying there?" He realized that he didn't really know by exactly how much, but the sun had definitely shifted somewhat. Perhaps he had even subconsciously thrown himself from his own patio and jacked up his back deliberately, hoping that this knight in yellow spandex would gallop to his rescue. He wondered what Freud would say about that?

The young man helped him as, slowly and with ample pain and some snapping of various limbs, the senior among them made his way to his feet, one arm slung around a smooth, tan shoulder. "Here, lean on me. That's it. Now try to straighten up." There was a yelp like a puppy whose tail got caught in the fireplace. "Ok, don't straighten up, don't straighten up. Let's get you into the house. Can you walk?"

"I can make it on my own. Thank you." The young man let go only to watch his new friend topple almost to the ground again and would have had it not been for the well placed wooden railing which lined the patio. "Fuck, I'm old." The young man flung his neighbor's arm back around his own bare shoulder and half carried him into the house, an action which was cause for the old man to feel all the older; that his well weathered, pale white hand should make contact with the chiseled, golden and youthful shoulder of this well-intentioned young man seemed somehow intrusive.

"Sofa or bedroom?" He was certain that this was not an uncommon question for him.

"Surprise me." Gently, he was laid upon the soft beige sofa like a soldier recently wounded in battle who could now die in peace in his bloodstained uniform, his body having been rescued by his younger counterpart, carried home for proper burial. He felt hands pressing into his sides, and he was pretty certain he knew what this was about. "May I ask what you are doing?"

"I need you to roll over on your stomach. Here, I'll help you."

"Excuse me?"

"Just do it. Here." And carefully, small maneuver by painful small maneuver, he was turned around with great trepidation and with more than a little protest. "I'm a masseuse. Let me."

"Now shock me. Jesus. Of course, you *would* be a masseuse. Oh, fuck, — *OW!*" Silence followed. What the hell was this in his living room, anyway? A "masseuse" indeed. He tried to reconnect with the pain, something he had a habit of doing throughout his life, but that of his back, at least, seemed to have subsided, magically removed by the hands of this young healer. The pain and discomfort simply floated up to the ceiling and then vanished altogether, evaporated.

"It's gone, isn't it?" A sly grin made its way across the bronzed face of the dog-lover. What an odd creature, this old man, he thought. Refusing help when he clearly could not help himself. He had done his good deed for the day and should make a hasty retreat. He stood to go.

"Wait." He could now swing his legs to the floor and sit up with little effort. He swiveled his torso on top of his hips — yes, he was cured. Remarkable, he was forced to admit. "I should — pay you something, I guess?"

"On the house."

"Well, — thank you. Can I offer you something? Something to drink? Scotch?"

"I don't drink."

"Of course you don't. Could I at least know your name?"

"Jeffrey. Jeff." Jeff looked about the man's sparse room of treasures, finally coming to rest his eyes upon the piano. "That's a nice piano. I hear you playing, sometimes, when I walk past with Jefferson. That's Roger's dog. It's really beautiful, whatever it is you're working on."

So, he was staying with Roger Hunt, aptly named. Roger was always on the prowl in one sense or another. He directed all of those bad movies in the 80's, those mindless flicks about teenage angst that the minions flocked to, with their acne and braces, in mini-malls throughout the world, back during the five minutes in which he was Hollywood's whiz kid. He had now surrendered himself to being a permanent resident of the jet set accompanied by the excuse "they just don't write any good scripts anymore." They had been Malibu neighbors for twenty years and never once exchanged a word, just glared from their beamers or ignored each other in driveways, the way people in California do. They didn't even know why, precisely, they disliked each other, it just seemed the simpler thing to do. So the famed director had a new boy on the side, hardly surprising. The last one must have been pushing 30, so it was time for him to go, no doubt.

"I dog sit. He spends most of his time in Santa Barbara, so…" he shrugged his shoulders.

"In Santa Barbara with his wife."

"Right."

He would grill the young stud like salmon — an afternoon's folly if nothing else. Jeff was surely one of those youngsters who, looking as he did, automatically assumed everyone was in love with him. Ah — his eyes just caught sight of the Oscar in the glass cabinet over by the staircase, and there he goes — pretending not to have seen it, averting his bulging eyes. Richard Hunt didn't have any Oscars. Maybe Jeff was in a room with a man whom he truly admired, but just didn't want to gush, or perhaps simply acting unimpressed added to what he must have thought was his naive allure. The last thing Everett needed, after all, was some giddy, soundstage struck fan — or someone who aspired to moviedom, which was far worse. His young neighbor must have known this, so he would continue with his charade of disinterest — it was a cunning game he played at. His guest gazed at the piano again, a beautiful gray baby grand that shone brightly near the glass doors that led to the patio. He had never before seen a gray piano, surely — Everett had searched up and down the seaboard for it. It matched the decor of the room perfectly, everything sort of in between — not quite white, not quite black, just varying shades of the two meeting somewhere in the middle.

"Do you play?" He was intrigued by this new, youthful creature who shared his air.

"No. Always wanted to, though," he knocked the metronome to one side and it began it's tick tock motion back and forth. Terrified he had broken it, he reset it immediately as it had been and tried to cover up his indiscretion with his oversized hands.

"If I may ask, aside from the obvious, what exactly brings you to California?" He was pretty sure he knew, but wanted an answer nonetheless. Everett waited for a response, his eyebrows raised, full of curiosity.

Again with his shoulder shrug, which he must have thought excused any need for a content-filled answer or justification. "Just hanging out."

"Really. Just hanging out as in you're an actor, just hanging out?"

"Maybe."

"Well, you either are or you aren't. These are the easy questions."

"I'm trying to be. Listen, take care of your back. I should go feed Jefferson." Interesting. One rarely meets an actor who doesn't want to talk about being an actor. But then, being an actor in Los Angeles is akin to being hot in hell. To say it out loud, to admit he was an actor, perhaps made him feel typical in a way, robbing him of his individuality. Had he been a successful actor, it would be one thing. Had he even so much as a toothpaste commercial to his name, it would be different. But he most likely didn't, which just made him common.

"And how do you know Roger? Answer a want ad for dog walkers?" He regretted saying it.

Is this what he had become? Bitter and dripping with sarcasm, an attitude of which he had seen enough having lived in Hollywood for so long. Cynicism was a posture he found dreary, yet the words left his own mouth nevertheless.

"I'm his nephew who occasionally sucks his cock. Goodbye."

"Hey —" Jeffery had wit. He admired wit, it seemed, above all else, lately. "If you still want to learn. Piano, I mean. I could make some time for lessons." It surprised Everett to think it, but it was there in his mind regardless: he wanted Jeffrey to come back. He savored having someone in his house, something that hadn't happened in a good long while, aside from various cleaning people. He liked it when the young man gazed over at his trophy case; it flattered him although he'd never say it out loud. He liked how there was a flash of brilliance on the young man's face when he looked over at his piano — he recalled that flash from a time long gone by. No, Jeffrey wasn't dumb. He lived in a beach house he didn't pay for, after all. He was doing all right for a guy with no education (he presumed) nor trust fund. He didn't want to fuck Jeffrey, he had had enough of all of that. He honestly wished he'd put some more clothing on. Beautiful though he was, it was making it difficult to maintain eye contact.

He could see by the expression on Jeff's face that he had heard all of this before. This time it was "piano lessons," sometimes it was "be a guest on my yacht," "come see my swimming pool," or most recently, "come take care of my dog." How long could this dance last, he must have wondered? Jeff paused uncomfortably, unsure of his next move. Piano lessons with Everett Crisp was not unlike learning about light bulbs from Edison. But was it just a line?

Everett searched Jeffrey's eyes for an answer and clearly saw his hesitation, or maybe it was even fear. "I make it a point never to fuck my neighbor's concubines. Totally innocent, I promise." He strained not to let it show in his voice, but he wanted a 'yes.' "Consider it a nice thing to do for a lonely old man."

It was settled. They would start tomorrow at two. Pencils sharpened, time for class to begin, the start of Mr. Crisp's final semester at Low Tide, his home at what increasingly seemed to be the edge of the world. For the first time in a long while, Everett had something to anticipate, he thought, as he watched the young man go, his perfectly round backside inflating the tight yellow suit. Everett chuckled. Oh, kids today.

His tired eyes began to close of their own accord, the wrinkles on his forehead serving as proof of a life well fought. Tomorrow he would find the music once again but for now, he would let the silence envelop him.

Autumn, 1989: Cambridge, MA

"That's one of your own, isn't it?" Everett hadn't even seen him coming. He had walked right up behind him and sat himself down on the piano bench. Bold.

"Thanks for the drink," he mumbled, searching for the easiest way out of this.

"You haven't touched it," he dared to let his knee touch the pianist's own.

"I've been a little busy," he played on, both hands occupied.

"I know. This has been, what, a twenty-two minute song?" Everett felt his face getting hot. What did he want, this dashing young squire of the law? He didn't get it. Did he feel badly about the scene in the diner, was he coming to apologize, to flaunt his wealth by plying him with drinks? What *was* it?

"Well, anyway, it's a nice song." Everett punctuated the music with three short, final chords, and, resting his hands in his lap, looked up from the keys expectantly. He blinked his eyes once, twice — okay, he'd give it a third time in an effort to hopefully spar some kind coherent speech out of the gentleman from Connecticut. He didn't expect what met his gaze; something seemed very different today.

His was a round face that accompanied an utterly clear complexion with slightly blushing, plump cheeks. His short, blonde hair framed deep-set, crystal blue eyes which looked upon the young musician/fellow student of the law as though he were a riddle to be solved. He was dressed in simple blue jeans and a light blue oxford shirt, untucked yet also utterly unwrinkled, very much the young academic. He liked to dress in costume, Everett had often noticed when seeing him in class. Sometimes he wore glasses and others not, depending entirely on the argument he had to prove that day. His role was that of the brilliant young scholar, soon to be dynamo in the courtroom, to be followed by a stellar career as a politician and then an elder statesman. It was predestined. For now, however, he remained everyone's All American. It was a role he wore well.

"Are you drinking a lemon drop?"

"What? Oh, yes. We drink them at home at dinner parties and things. I don't like beer, and it's the only drink I really know, so... What's that — whiskey?"

"Scotch." Everett swallowed a gulp for lack of anything better to do and to relieve the gap in conversation. He was never really one for small talk and anyway, this wasn't even an encounter he had requested.

"You'd think, given the work you do for them, they'd let you drink for free," he chortled, also in an effort to bring a little levity to the situation.

"They do."

"Oh. So I needn't have — "

"You got my attention."

"Good," he let the rest of his leg make contact, not just his knee anymore.

"But why?" Another swig. Bold of him, Everett thought, to send a drink over to his piano in an attempt to gain his favor. It was almost cinematic, and it seemed to have worked.

"You don't make very much easy, do you?" There was just the low din of chatter now in the absence of Everett's playing. The breeze through the open glass doors that led out to the tree-lined sidewalk picked up and flickered through the candles.

Despite his twenty-three years of age, the young man at the piano didn't much understand the ways of human beings — the prescribed rules that dictated what to say and when. He was far from a virgin, but sex, mere sex, was different and he knew, instinctively, that was not what this was.

"You know, I've never done this before." He was never one to lack courage, but it had taken him hours to work up the nerve to do what he was doing right now and he was not afraid to admit that he'd like a little credit for it, if even just from himself. "I'm Jamie, by the way," he extended his perfect hand. "And I have an offer for you." Here it came. He had seen it before. Wealthy people pursued the "help" all the time, asking them if they'd like to bartend their private parties or slice meat at the buffet table, maybe play the piano to provide background music at mommy and daddy's Spring Fling. "I'd like to learn how to play and I was wondering if you give lessons?"

This creature at the keys was the most captivating thing Jamie White had ever encountered, but he couldn't say that out loud, of course. He'd watched him in class, watched him racing from building to building all around Cambridge, always alone, watched him at his job, and had been coming to Bridgit's since the start of the semester just to watch him play, always under the pretense of socializing with his numerous friends and acquaintances whom he dragged along but were merely a shield. He had a clear motive with no idea how to execute it. This was the first time he dared come alone, to speak and make himself known. He was not like most other humans, this young maestro, this was abundantly clear. It were as though he had descended from an ancient race of people who saw only the practicality in things and never the mere enjoyment. His jet-black hair stood on end, defying gravity, which framed the palest face, highlighted by brows that formed perfect arches over weary, grey eyes that looked as though they had already seen so much.

"Piano lessons."

"We can do it at my apartment. I'll make stir fry."

"Don't you —" he remembered the blonde with the tight perm from earlier in the evening. "Are you *flirting* with me?"

"Recklessly, yes." Taking a swig of lemon drop, Jamie turned away to watch the crowd and immerse himself in their low din of chatter, partly from embarrassment and partly to see who was looking but also to feel the heat of the musician's eyes upon the back of his neck. "But I have a motive," he said, boldly turning to look at his secret crush straight on. "I'd really like to learn to play. I took lessons when I was a kid, but — we'd have to start from scratch, I'm afraid, — and I'd insist on paying you." Everett stared back.

"Look, here's the address," he scratched some numbers and words on a piece of Everett's sheet music with a dull pencil which he retrieved from behind Everett's ear. "I'll be ready to learn tomorrow at eight.

I'll be a star pupil, you'll see. And I'll have the wok going, too." He stood and retrieved his still only half-empty glass from the edge of the piano, the same glass which he'd been nursing for a good hour or so. "Show up," he downed the contents with a single gulp, just to show off and make it all that much more histrionic, as he tried to conceal the exasperated cough that followed.

"What if I don't?" Everett was intrigued now, it was almost like a game. He sat looking at the address scribbled between the notes of his own design.

Jamie looked down at him, "Then I'll never come hear you play again, and that would be a bad idea. I'm your biggest fan, you know?"

"My only fan."

"That too." Jamie let his hand land on Everett's shoulder in a gesture that stretched just beyond the boundaries of mere friendship. "See you tomorrow. Don't be late," he said, as he carefully returned the pencil to the crux of Everett's right ear, slowly and deliberately. Jamie strode out of Bridgit's without looking back and sauntered off down the sidewalk into the dying evening, accomplishment fueling his every step.

Everett looked again at the address. Sitting upon his little piano bench, the command bridge from which he liked to view the world, he was suitably impressed. He finished the scotch and contemplated his own state of affairs. Boys like Jamie don't ask boys like him out, he knew; it crossed every boundary. The Jets don't flirt with the Sharks, Beverly Hills doesn't go slumming on skid row. It's just not done and even if it were — oh the young scholar's reputation! And who wants to compete with that? Of course, it went beyond that but there would be no addressing his own particular, personal darkness just now. Besides, he would have to talk if he went, and he'd never been much good at that. He supposed he could offer piano lessons, of course, but was it worth the time? Instructing a spoiled college brat about key signatures and eighth notes and middle C. Every Good Boy Deserves Favor, blah blah. Jamie had a nice smile, he was loathe to admit, but Everett was fresh out of gold star stickers. This could not happen — or at least it shouldn't. *Get that notion right out of your head, Everett Crisp,* he scolded himself as he sat transfixed by the idea of it.

It was clear that no decision would be reached this evening. So, despite a newly formed little smile, he returned to the piano and started in with a new piece of music that had been kicking around in his head. Perhaps he'd just improvise for a while and see what came of it.

4

Summer, 1978: Mason City, Iowa

KEN MOBERLY HAD wanted to be a father his whole life. How ideal it would be, he thought, to wrap his arms around a child; to guide and mold him. Perhaps, in the eyes of a child, he wouldn't seem so incapable, so lacking, as he knew he was. The company of a child would be pleasant and, as the child grew, they would become increasingly fast friends. Ken Moberly hadn't any friends, really, and all of his family were gone now.

He pushed his new friend's bicycle along for him and the young man carried his own backpack with Henry the sock monkey hanging out of the back, who eyed this newcomer to their party with suspicion, protecting his young human friend. The two, man and boy, walked side by side through the wood that ran alongside the water with only the sounds of the crickets to provide them company for a while.

"Heat's picking up. Gonna be a hot one, this summer, I think." The young man had little to say in return. "Let's get you back to the house and maybe I have a sweatshirt for you or something." The younger of the two did not protest nor did he accept the invitation, but kept walking with this odd and curious new creature, assuming that these woods must be his home. "What's your monkey's name?"

"Henry."

Good, thought Ken. The boy had obviously been through the mill of life, even at his age, and he knew it would take time to earn his trust. He wanted to comfort the youngster, give him some of the happiness which he obviously lacked. "That's a real nice name. How are you today, Henry?" he asked to the monkey's face which looked back with only a vacant expression, if not suitable mistrust.

"You're a real good swimmer. I've seen you up here. I live just over there by the tree with the fern top? Right back there. Can you see it? It's called a silver-tree fern. You can see it from here, almost — in the clearing? ... It's not far away. I could make you something to eat." It felt strange to be walking with someone, Ken being so accustomed to walking alone. The heat of another human being next to him, the crush of the leaves beneath four feet rather than two, was a new sensation that he was enjoying. "You know, it's not supposed to be here at all: the silver-tree fern -- or *Ponga* as them in Zealand sometimes call it. Cause ya know, they're supposed to only be up in New Zealand and Australia and big places like that. But it's here just the same, how 'bout that?" He thought perhaps this small boy was the only human he could impress with a fact that he knew, he knowing so few, really. Ken had always been perplexed by the mysterious Ponga tree he had discovered as a child, playing in these very woods. Someone must have uprooted it from New Zealand or one of those distant places and brought it to live here beside the reservoir, was all he could figure. *Ponga,* as he came to call it over the years, had been his friend, even if it was out of place here just like him. Still, the tree seemed happy in the ground in which it stood, the only ground Ken had ever known well.

He would defy Sheila and Frank and damn the consequences, the young man decided. Even if he had to scrub the house for a year and even if he were denied his entire allowance for a month, he would not return for dinner this evening. Perhaps he would wait for them to be fast asleep and then silently creep into his bedroom. He only gave them ammunition for their little game of darts when he misbehaved, he knew, but there was no choice tonight. He would make them think he'd run away and see what happened. He was, after all, convinced that he was going to hell anyway. He could not tolerate another icy dinner wherein his numerous faults were sure to be exposed, and the size of his "crushing ego" deplored. They would then sit back in their faux-oak chairs and demand gratitude for all they did and continued to do for him, the roof over his head, the food that had made him fat, the exuberant effort they both put forth with the goal of shaping him into a respectable member of the world, much like themselves.

Ken Moberly's house approached: an elegant dwelling in a clearing on the edge of the reservoir surrounded by absolutely nothing. "It's my family's. They gave it to me. They're all dead now."

As they made their way across the lawn with the young man's bicycle, the young man admired the row of windows framed in iron, behind which must have sat a kitchen and a living room, Ken Moberly's own little patch of the world; he envied this. He must live such a quiet, peaceful life with the water and his special fern tree as his only companions. Looking at the house, a simple two stories with a sturdy roof, it had a calmness to it, a structure that sat solitary against sadness, against the run of the mill of everyday life, the opposite of the mini malls and grocery stores, sidewalks, schools and churches that occupied the crux of his own life. This solitary patch of serenity was a woodland storybook, a house he could perhaps escape to where none of the bothersome drudgery of reality might intrude.

"What's your name?" The grown-up asked the question shyly, not meaning to pry but full of curiosity to know every wonderful thing about this new person.

"Everett," he stopped to pick up a particularly shiny rock on the dirt trail.

"Ou! Y-You found a shiny. I have a whole collection of 'em! I'll show you!" They strolled up to a side door of the house and it opened without keys. "Come on in. Lemme make you something to eat. I can cook, a little."

Entering the little house, Everett inhaled. The smell in the air was not unlike that of a familiar friend; it had a signature to it, something distinct that identified this space as somebody's. There was an overstuffed sofa and two matching wingback's, a dining table just off the kitchen area with eight matching chairs that must have once been quite magnificent, now sitting in dust. There were old things that looked as though they had resided within these walls for many many years and were perhaps not selected by Ken Moberly himself — clocks and paintings and Tiffany lamps. The room, and, as he would learn, the house itself, possessed a kind of adultness which was altogether unlike Ken Moberly, who seemed in manner no more than a child.

Something was calling to him from the periphery of his sight. Not an audible call, of course, but much like a magnet, drawing his attention like a child in class who demands to be the star. There was a mystic quality to it all as he turned his head to the left where, directly in front of the three identical, rectangular windows with the iron frames he had admired as they approached from the outside, windows that overlooked the lawn and then beyond that, the water, sat a beautiful, shiny, light mahogany grand piano. The instrument sat as though smiling at him in a fatalistic kind of way, the same way you figure relatives might greet you when you arrive in heaven. The experience of witnessing the instrument bathed in the remaining rays of the sun that streaked through the prism of clear glass windows caught Everett so off guard that he gasped audibly at the site of it all. Despite the other objects in the room that were merely beautiful, here was something that was both beautiful and *useful*: a muse of sorts, and it beckoned him.

There was an unexpected hand on Everett's shoulder, a shoulder which was clad in the same ill-fitting, thin, rust colored t-shirt in which he had spent the day, now a bit damp following his swim. He didn't mind it, the touch. For both of them, the contact of another human being, flesh joined with flesh, was the event of the day, something neither had experienced in such a long, long while. "That's a real nice name... Everett." He said the boy's name as though it were melodious. "Here — I have some soup. Do you like soup?" He darted back into the kitchen and began rifling through cupboards. "Maybe some peanut butter and I think some cheese, maybe?"

Everett stood stone still in the middle of Ken Moberly's very comfortable living room. He hadn't the slightest idea what he was doing there and was certain that indeed he shouldn't be. But it was a new adventure; he had been given the opportunity to glimpse inside another world, another kind of existence, and the allure and attention lavished upon him was proving to be quite irresistible.

"That your piano?" He regretted saying it immediately. Who else would it belong to? He was reminded that he sometimes *did* say inane things, as he was told frequently. Better to just not speak, to retreat. The sound of his own voice was always alien to him anyway.

"Yes, do you play?" Ken called from the kitchen, excited that his prized possession might be put to use at long last.

"No." He would not inform Ken Moberly about his secret late night listening sessions with his favorite recordings from the library, how he knew entire movements, entire compositions by heart. Ken had returned from the kitchen with a tray of snacks, which he set down on a cluttered table before returning his hand to the young man's shoulder, which he gave a special kind of gentle squeeze.

"Why don't you sit? I'll bring you some iced tea and heat up the soup." Mr. Moberly left the room again and Everett was left alone in this new place, this new universe. The instrument that sat by the windows, bathed in what would soon become moonlight, was irresistible. Full of trepidation but certain of what he must do, he stepped over to the gorgeous piece of musical apparatus, as drawn to it as two magnets meeting for the first time. He ran his index finger along the shiny wood, taking in the trio of gold pedals, the slightly ajar top, perfect in its curvature, that exposed the inner workings of beautiful strings and felt-covered hammers, as intricate as the human body. A substantial layer of dust covered nearly everything around him, but the piano sat utterly spotless, a solitary beacon, the most precious utility in the room's arsenal. It seemed to Everett that perhaps the piano had existed first, solitary, and the rest of the house had been constructed around this treasure; much like ancient civilizations, he had learned in school, erected temples to house their most precious belongings.

He pushed back the hinged lid that obscured the keys, heavy and solid, as though he were opening a secret hatch that was the gateway to a forgotten treasure. The wooden panel slid back into the innards of the machine and eighty-eight glorious keys, white and black, stared back at him, soldiers ready to be called into battle. Full of trepidation yet with wide, longing eyes, as though he had seen the holy land, he sat himself upon the polished wooden bench, staring down at the keys like they were eighty-eight of the most precious jewels. He felt nervous sitting upon such a fine piece of polished wood, much like sitting himself upon a kind of cherished throne or a bed of diamonds, far too important to bear the weight of his body. He ran his hands along the tops of the glorious pieces of ivory and heard his recordings in his mind. Ravel... The high that it gave him when the music hit the crescendos, the ability that the correct notes in the correct order had to transport him out of one space, one life and thrust him into another altogether. He sat in what he now felt was a kind of pilot's seat, ready to fly his plane to at least a few thousand foreign planets.

Everett depressed one of the white keys and listened to the sound vibrate throughout the instrument, emitting its music into the air surrounding him, releasing itself into the ether. Slowly, he pushed a few more, recognizing, associating the sounds, the notes, with the same ones he heard in his mind throughout each day, the tones he had heard in his mind since before he knew how to think. When placed in the correct sequence and executed by his body, these keys, these notes, would congeal to create that which had power, that which offered him an exit. It didn't take him long to figure it out, once he had explored the piano key by key. He played an entire phrase from a Ravel composition, just the melody, slowly and with a certain hesitancy, one ivory at a time, and marveled at the rush of joy each note, each action, each depressed key, brought him. The organization of it all, the accomplishment, the aching satisfaction that came in knowing that he had released something beautiful into a world of such ugliness and finally, the gratitude; the immense solace and satisfaction. For once, he made the music himself, it emanated from his own self, his own mind, his very fingers. He was not merely listening to it coming at him from headphones, deep in the night; rather he himself was the genesis, the source, the *music*. It was the closest to nirvana, to God, he would surely ever experience. Yes, Everett Crisp had found home.

Autumn, 1989: Cambridge, MA

The least of Jamie's worries was the fact that he didn't actually have a piano, something that would be useful for piano lessons. He was nervous for the first time he could ever recall really being nervous. Not even his father and his evening lectures filled him with anxiety like this. What had he done? Had he gone and asked a boy, — a *man*, out on a date? Was it a date? Was he finally going to act upon this at long last? This hidden but hardly sleeping desire.

His little white apartment on the corner of campus was immaculate, his books and papers all put away in the other room and every surface scrubbed. He was ready for the curtain to go up, but he also dreaded it, lest he be booed off the stage. He heated the wok, drizzled olive oil, turned on the CD player softly, and slugged down an entire glass of cheap white wine, his palms damp and sweat glistening upon his brow.

The doorbell rang. Just a single bell tone like the first note of the intermission chime at the Met, a sound he had known well since childhood. His heart raced. He was about to dive head first into uncharted waters from the highest of high dives.

Without warning, an anvil had been set upon his chest. Was it too late to pretend he was out, that he had forgotten? No, the music, slow and sultry jazz that had been carefully selected, could be heard on the other side of the door, surely. Curse his "mood setting." It rang again. Jamie paused with his hand upon the doorknob. Turning the handle, he knew, was the entry to a portal, and he would likely not ever cross through again, back to this side. Was it time to put one foot in front of the other and aide the planet in its spinning? He turned the knob. He took the deepest of breaths, so much so that his eyes widened. Jamie White opened a door.

Winter, 1997: New York City

The cab driver's name was Herveriat. He tried to pronounce it in his head: Her-ver-ight? Her-ver-ate? He thought about what had brought him to this country and what his thoughts were of New York, of Eighth Avenue, of himself. There was some foreign chanting coming from Herveriat's radio and he did the best he could to block it out.

Oh God, had it come to this? Nervous about meeting his old friend for dinner, as the cab sped northward up the West side of Manhattan? Was he a teenager all over again? Thank God, he wasn't but still, he yearned for more traffic lights. When one is in no particular hurry, unlike the opposite, New York traffic will always, invariably, part for you and you'll have no trouble reaching your destination in a perfectly timely manner.

The cab pulled up a slight hill and, after passing a security desk, he soon found himself in a dimly lit elevator covered in mirrors on all four sides; even the sliding doors were mirrored. Polite music seeped out of carefully concealed speakers — it was that kind of a building. He watched himself — all four of him selves, sweating in the reflective surfaces. Despite the fact that Spring was still a good two months away, water seeped from his forehead like an uncontrollable spigot. He had washed his only pair of jeans that afternoon at the laundromat, and they now clung to his body like a second skin, the starch he had sprayed on his ironed shirt smelling of burnt sawdust. This was all happening too fast and he wished the elevator would slow its ascent. He clutched the unopened bottle of cheap red wine he had swiped from work and then realized the song he was listening to. Yes, it was definitely "Do You Know the Way to San Jose?" The same notes repeated again and again and AGAIN and he thought of Dionne Warwick and wondered why she shouldn't have a new hit, and he thought of Hal David and he watched the brows furrow upon all of his duplicates as the elevator rose higher, then higher, still far too fast, finally stopping in the upper twenties with an altogether unpleasant "ding."

Stepping off the elevator, he was surrounded by the muted carpet and the carefully placed, upholstered furniture and silk flower arrangements that accompany a building that houses the wealthy. And still more mirrors. He'd always thought that people with money absolutely love mirrors because in seeing themselves reflected, they were also visualizing their status in the world, or better yet a projection of cold, hard cash. Besides which, mirrors tended to make everything look bigger and more reputable than they actually are, a special trick that most wealthy people had perfected.

The door of number 2817 was already ajar and the faint, familiar smell of sizzling chicken and red peppers in a wok permeated the hallway — a comforting fragrance he had not known for the better part of a decade. He knocked, wiping the perspiration from his forehead with his hand. All too soon, there stood Jamie, just as he had stood all those years ago on the other side of an open doorway. A half filled, teardrop wine glass in hand and an amiable grin pasted across his face upon which sat that pair of crystal blue, deep set eyes that offered the entirety of his world to you with a mere glance. The young lawyer was effortlessly good looking, his appearance a natural part of his DNA. Every feature perfectly placed, every stitch of clothing falling in perfect symmetry with his body; the deep red of his shirt flowed effortlessly into a form fitting pair of jeans which, although casual, he somehow managed to make look formal. His natural allure was a fact which he refused to acknowledge about himself, which only added to his attractiveness. Oh yes, Everett could recall clearly what it was like to swim in the ocean called Jamie.

Autumn, 1989: Cambridge, MA

The small talk ended all too quickly with little more to say than "thanks for coming," "you're welcome," "would you like a glass of wine?" and "No." Discomfort filled the air as they both stood in the doorway just inches apart: teacher and student, employee and employer, child to child, playing in the adults only sandbox for the very first time. The two of them made their way into the dimly lit room with trepidation.

Everett looked around the finely organized apartment, white walls blaring out at him despite the dim lighting. "So where's the piano?"

"I don't have one." Jamie was pretty sure this would come up at his first piano lesson. He would have to play this full tilt, it was all or nothing.

"Then how — are we going to the student union, or —"

"I made this." Jamie reached behind the sofa and brought out a large white piece of poster board, upon which he had exactingly drawn all eighty-eight keys, going so far as to darken in the black ones with a magic marker. "I figured we could start with this, you could show me how to place my hands and what to do and then maybe we could work up to an actual piano." He searched the eyes of his aloof instructor for approval, or at least a grin. "It was the best I could do at short notice."

He looked at the cardboard construction for a good long while in utter disbelief. So... it was true. The gentleman from Connecticut was after more than lessons, after all. It *had* been a ruse, his coming here, but a creative one, certainly. Moments passed. What he did in the next moments would dictate the rest of the evening, he knew. How to handle this? He had been brought across campus under false pretenses and perhaps he would be angry had he not already suspected. But a cardboard piano? Really? He broke out in unbridled laughter. "You're kidding?"

"Well, it's a start. Right?" Jamie smiled with an air of pretend sheepishness. His first goal had been achieved — he had made his date laugh.

"Pour me some of that wine," said Everett, taking the replicated keyboard away from, as he was learning, this increasingly odd young son of the senate. He had obviously devoted a good deal of time to it, each key drawn to scale, straight lines exactingly sketched with the aid of a ruler, and here his persistent student wasn't even certain that his instructor was going to show up.

Knowing full well that he was being watched, Jamie retreated to the kitchen, separated from the living room by the thinnest of breakfast counters. He reached for the bottle of Chardonnay. "You know — there's something I need to know," he broadcast through the room, which seemed to help break the tension, while he uncorked a new bottle of wine, having finished the previous in his pre-date anxiety. He tried desperately to grasp hold of imaginary confidence while hoping his voice didn't reveal his trepidation. "I only know you as 'Mr. Crisp,' from class. Maybe we know each other well enough now to be on a first name basis?" There was an awkward pause and the filled glass was handed off to his — yes, to his date. Here they were, two newly emerged grown ups, sipping wine amid candles in a student apartment just off campus.

Mr. Crisp swirled his wine in the long stemmed glass, then gathered his courage to look Jamie in the eye.

"I promise not to tell anyone, Mr. Crisp. I know how you value your aloofness." Jamie had taken on the persona of someone with backbone, which had always been enough to fool most everyone. It was his own special brand of acting, steeped in the person he aspired to be.

There was a pause and for a moment, neither knew if anything would come out of the other's mouth. Finally, Mr. Crisp answered, sheepishly, "Everett."

"Nice to meet you, *Everett*." Jamie loved the name, as it was as unique and singular as the rest of him. "Now then, come sit down." Taking Everett by the hand, he led him to the beige sofa which sat in front of what had once been a fireplace but was now bricked over, a result of character-robbing renovation, too often the case with off-campus housing let by landlords anxious to turn the rooms over from semester to semester and take advantage of affluent families who routinely foot eight months rent plus security with a single check in September. To compensate, Jamie had placed five pillar candles of various heights upon the hearth, which glowed quietly, casting their shadows upon the exposed brick. They sat for a moment in silence, drinking it all in — the room, the candles, whatever this was they were doing. Finally, Jamie spoke: "I'm ready for my lesson."

Winter, 1997: New York City

"Rice, Fasano and Nadler foot the bill, I just sleep here." Jamie was almost apologetic, well aware of the fact that his high-rise, Upper West Side digs must be a far cry from Everett's Brooklyn dwelling.

It was immaculate, and Jamie had set the scene with slow jazz and about three thousand flickering candles. Jamie, Everett recalled, had always thought that everything looked better by candlelight, and secretly regretted the invention of the light bulb. It was a true one bedroom with hardwood floors, a kitchen with dishwasher (unheard of) and the kind of rubber-stamp furniture that comes with furnished apartments. There was a fake fir tree in one corner, and a banal sculpture in another, as though the place had been staged for photographs for a brochure, advertising the building's most "artistic" units. Standing by the dining table, which was laid out exquisitely with china plates, bowls and sterling silver flatware, were a row of floor to ceiling windows where Everett looked down over the whole of Juilliard, Alice Tully Hall, The New York State Theatre and of course, The Met, where intermission had brought opera buffs and tourists out of doors to huddle around the fountain and snap flash photos.

"Your Alma Mater," said Jamie, pointing to the lighted buildings of Julliard across the plaza, and handing the man who once consumed every breath of his interest, had once captivated him so thoroughly that he was willing to completely turn his own world inside out for him, a crisp glass of the chilled Pinot Grigio the firm had sent over as a welcome to New York gift, a good twelve months ago.

"Oh my God." Everett's eyes were drawn to the space above the sofa. "I can't believe you. You just got that out for tonight." It was like climbing into a rustic old attic and finding an artifact that was once dear, something that had been a part of everyday life, had been a constant but had been somehow lost at sea for so many years, devoured by the sea in a sunken ship and obscured by the ravages of salt water. "You framed it. You're ridiculous."

There, in a custom, matted, bright brass frame was that single piece of glaring white poster board: a relic that recalled an entire existence, a past to which only the two of them were allowed entry, like explorers with flashlights. Those precisely sketched out piano keys, the black ones filled in with magic marker, hung weathered, wrinkled, but as a testament of sorts to the simplicity of their former lives. Everett could see his own reflection in the polished glass. Even reflected in the glow of candlelight, the changes his face had undergone since he had last laid eyes upon this moniker of an ancient civilization in which he knew he had once existed but now seemed so foreign to him, were more than apparent. His skin was gradually losing its elasticity and his eyes were not the same as they had been during all of those late night sessions at Bridgit's, the glow of them replaced by a kind of deadened reality, diamonds regressed to mere rocks. Echoed in his ears and flashed across his pupils were scattered sounds, images of that which had been, back in what now seemed somehow like glory days. Only mere sound bytes remained, scattered moving images in sepia tones. Reality had smacked him harshly across the face, and he knew that this was written in the folds of his skin and even in the speckled strands of grey that salted his jet black hair.

But there it stood just the same, an artifact in a contemporary museum, weathered posterboard surrounded on four sides by a modern, brilliant, expensive frame. Jamie watched him from the kitchen, only a few feet away, both of them standing in front of this temple of their past. He sipped his wine and gazed at the back of this most curious man, this man who called to attention every familiar fiber of his being, even all of these years later, as history hung in the air. His brain searched for the next line. He had not written this particular part, only that which he knew would be the crux of the evening.

"Here, this is ready," said Jamie, trying to sound cheerful. Anything to lighten the mood.

"Stir fry?" It was a harkening back to yesteryear and Everett found it as funny as it was endearing. Their eyes met and remained like magnets for a few seconds.

"It's the only thing I know how to make."

"I know. I remember." Everett turned away to seat himself at the glass dining table, perfectly laid and ablaze with candles in the dim room overlooking Lincoln Center. He placed his carefully folded linen napkin upon his lap and looked at Jamie expectedly.

There was just short of flirtation to Jamie's voice now, almost an accusation but more genuine curiosity: "What else do you remember?"

Autumn, 1989: Cambridge, MA

"I don't think most people ever really experience love. Real love, I mean, in a way that it's tangible and honest and not just — what? Convenient." They were two bottles of wine down and well into their third. The candles flickered, casting their shadows throughout the darkened room and across their faces as the poster board piano lie on the floor, sprawled out in front of them.

"Really?" Jamie was amused by the maestro's theory, which he presented with all of the fascination of a Biology teacher dissecting an earthworm.

"No, I mean you grow to love, in a way, what you're presented with. There is no such thing as a soul mate, there is no one who's somehow *destined*; that's fiction. People talk about it like it's some mystical spell but it's not," his hands were doing much of the talking for him. Everett was well into his presentation on love now, a speech he had been dying to give for quite some time.

"And that's your experience?"

"Yes. Absolutely yes. It has less to do with kismet, as people like to talk about — you know, I saw him across a crowded room, our eyes met, all of that. It has more to do, I think, with basic familiarity. Passion is like — what? A thrill. Like getting a new toy when you're a kid — it's — if you take the amusement park home with you, eventually, all the rides will get boring and break down —." Everett Crisp's eyes closed via instinct and he was filled with a bright, warm, white light. There was something intangible from his past, perhaps even imagined, that he was trying to grab onto, but he couldn't quite place it amid the overwhelming euphoria.

Jamie had done it — seized the opportunity, leaned forward and stopped the madness. He had placed his own lips upon Everett's and two puzzle pieces had effortlessly fallen into place. In the span of one kiss, the experiences, joys and injuries, the scraped knees, the birthday cakes, rain upon open water, fragments of the past, the rays of feeling that had long ago been shut up in boxes and stored carefully away upon forgotten shelves surfaced like a militant submarine rising out of the ocean. They exchanged themselves with one another and for a blissful moment, merged. But most of all, there was the rush of now, the existing solely, completely and thankfully in this part of now, in this room with these candles, this wine, these walls and this man. It was almost more than either of them could handle. But they did.

Winter, 1997: New York City

"Random things. I remember random things."

"Like?"

"Arguments."

"Leaving. Do you remember leaving?"

"I had to."

"You could have said - something. *That*, even. You just *left*."

"No, I couldn't. I couldn't have done it. I had to go."

"A child's answer."

"Are we going to cross examine each other?"

"Let's!" Jamie stood. "There's more stir fry. Don't get up! Sit back down and let's go. Here — you like an absurd amount of pepper, it's on the table." Jamie turned back into the kitchen to retrieve another bottle of wine as the two of them, Jamie and Everett, were off to the races. Again.

Fall, 2026: Malibu, CA

Two-thirty, then three, then four came and went. Everett sat alone at the piano in his well-appointed living room. He was unable to work or devote his mind to any other activity, certainly not studio obligations. His mind had been made up that morning that the day's event would be the instruction of his eager young student. He had invented a specific lesson plan and was eager to bequeath his knowledge to Jeffrey. More so, that thrill of human contact, the desire to have a small piece of the social world for himself, was the very thing that demanded he leave his bed that morning. He had dressed in his gabardine pants and his favorite grated silk shirt for the occasion that, apparently, was not to be. Finally, and with some effort, he stood from his piano bench, the creases from his fine trousers beginning to right themselves again. Walking past the mirror near the kitchen, he paused — most unusual for him as he had avoided mirrors his whole life. "You stupid old man," he said aloud, as he acknowledged the circles under his eyes and the lines upon his forehead, the white of his hair. "A fool among fools remains a fool still." The reflection didn't answer back with words, it didn't need to.

At 3 P.M. he opened the scotch, the bottle that had stood in the cabinet for at least a year or more, a resilient solider ready to be called into battle. He had always known it was there, which brought him comfort, but he had deliberately avoided it and even took pride in his abstinence. He would just smell it for the time being.

However, as 5 P.M. came and went, the clinking of the cubes in the Waterford glass brought him, if not joy, an occupation, something which made the passing of the hours bearable. It was a disappointment, of course, a breaking of a fast as the familiar sound of the pour made his senses stand at alert. Then an old friend met his lips, his teeth and then his throat, stretching all the way down into the whole of his person, infecting his blood; and another glass was pored. It was a heavy glass, weighted right. The thrill of it all: the beautiful rust colored liquid, a substance that carried with it such power, met with the crystal clear ice in such a stylish glass; all of it a defiance against the ordinary, the expected. This glass and the contents therein would be his afternoon companion and transport.

He had little to do other than watch the four walls of his living room, occasionally running his fingers up and down the keys of the piano in the same manner one would fondle the strands of a loved one's hair or the ears of a favored pet. He had disconnected the phone for the afternoon so the hours brought with them only the tranquility of the waves, met with a welcome and ample chaser of Glenlivet.

Six o'clock found him on the patio, glass in hand, as he leaned back in the teak chair to observe the sky as it prepared to surrender the day and give way to stars. Otherwise, had it not been for his student's lack of manners, it would have been the most glorious of early evenings, the royal blue of the atmosphere scratched with wisps of scattered cloud which hung above the expanse of the sea, all just beginning to fade.

However, even out in Malibu, one could not escape Los Angeles, it was an entity in the air that permeated most of southern California. Indeed, Los Angeles infected the sky with a kind of green mystery, an interference that reminded all who dared to look upon nature that this tranquility was merely a facade, a set, and the reality which afforded it was just a stone's throw away, always beckoning and demanding the same attention demanded by an infant. Just beyond the canyon there were studios and stages, suits and agents all nestled in well appointed glass offices with sandwiches and assistants, and a great plethora of expectation. It all seeped over the trees and into the ocean like an airborne disease, or lava spewing down the side of a volcano, taking the villagers along in its grasp. "BAAAAH," cried Everett, gesturing in the vicinity of both the Pacific Coast Highway and his own telephone with the same wave of his arm.

He knew this feeling, as the alcohol reached further into his self; he recalled it with a certain joy of familiarity but even more with undeniable anger. It was the beginning of what he had once thought to be euphoria, but one day realized was as manufactured as the smog of downtown L.A. But something must be done with all of this disappointment, something must fill the aching passage of time he felt for sure, on this day, would be otherwise occupied. The substance coursed through his veins and he absented himself, for the first time in a long while, from the human race.

The sun was now entirely gone and only the breeze and the sound of the crashing waves pervaded the night air. But what was this? Raised voices — or was it just one voice? Everett was annoyed by the intrusion as he sloshed about his cubes in what remained of the contents of his glass; he was anxious for a refill. The wind blew through his clothes and they flapped like a sail. But a scene was being played, a beach side drama, and he would be the sole audience of one, it seemed. Turning to his right he could see them — boy and man, Roger and Jeffrey engaged in a heated debate as Jefferson wagged his tail, anxious to dash through the evening surf with his favorite companion. The timbre of their argument carried on the wind — phrases such as "I thought that's what you wanted!," "A momentary amusement!," "I did what you asked," "Did you think it was permanent? You're not THAT dumb," "I loved you, I did," blah blah blah…

Everett had seen this scene before in far too many movies, so he ventured inside for that refill. The ceremonial bag was slug around Jeff's shoulder, which could only mean one thing. Everett mockingly joked to himself that he had never before seen Jeff in pants. Ah, there it was: the door slam. The all too familiar "door slam heard 'round Malibu." It could be heard even from inside the confines of Everett's kitchen where he was already into the freezer in search of ice. Venturing back out to the patio as the breeze blew back his ashen hair, he witnessed Jeff and Jefferson, one filled with regret, or at least loss, and the other eager for an evening's adventure, sitting in the sand just a matter of feet away.

What would happen to them both, Everett wondered? But it was little of his concern. After all, his glass was filled and this was all that need occupy him for the time being. He took a deep sip as lightening flashed through his body and then even across the sky. The planet spun quickly now, and he wandered back into his living room, shutting the French doors tightly behind him.

5

Summer, 1978: Mason City, Iowa

H E PEDALED FEVERISHLY through the woods, despite Ken Moberly's insistence that he drive him home. He needed to escape, to try to make sense of what had been awakened in him while safely ensconced within the walls of the small house by the lake.

He had never owned a watch, but knew it was far, far past the time he was expected as he made his way to the sidewalk that ran alongside the road. Headlights from passing cars shown in his pale white face and the night air embraced his bare legs as he pedaled still faster, feeling the sweat trickle down his brow and re-wetting his rust colored t-shirt.

Everett had been so brave, defying authority as he explored what he knew he must. His bold act of aggression had only been a passing fancy though, and now it was time to crawl back to the only home he had ever known, and brace for impact.

Ditching his bicycle by the side of the house, he made his way to the back door. He pulled back the screen and turned the metal knob: it was locked. All of the lights were out in the house, of course. Sheila and Mr. Thompson observed a strict 9:30 lights out, which allowed Mr. Thompson an excuse to wake at 5 A.M. and criticize all others for their laziness.

He made his way to the front door, the door reserved for guests that he was instructed never to enter. Also locked, not so much as a porch light remained illuminated. He remembered the window in his bedroom, the one along the other side of the house. It was his special window from which he liked to gaze, imagining he was actually looking out over the brilliant city lights of a great, thriving metropolis that stared up at him in all of its bustling, golden glory, as he sat perched on the 300th floor. Or sometimes he imagined he was looking out over the tops of mountains from his palatial estate high in the Andes to which only certain, particular and vastly important persons were permitted entrance and which was accessed only by helicopter.

But this evening, the window would be his salvation as he reached past the shrubbery to place his flattened palms against the glass, spotted and dirty with a gray sort of filament brought on by the many rains of the new summer. To his great relief and after much effort, the window slowly slid open a few centimeters. Although he feared that his hands would burst through the glass at any moment from his hard pressing inward and upward, the widow crawled further and further up until finally he slide his fingers under it and tossed his backpack inside his dark room, Henry leading the way. He had to lean the whole of his body against the prickly yet perfectly maintained shrub (which he tended himself) that stuck itself into his body, but finally, standing on tip toe, he was able to glide the window up enough and at last, with a tremendous jump, heave his body through the open frame, grasping it to stop himself before he tumbled entirely onto the floor inside, the sound of which he knew would awaken the beasts who slumbered a mere hallway away.

Undressing, he reached for his pajamas in the dark (he daren't turn on a light) before turning back the covers of his bed. There was a clank. Looking closely through the darkness, he could make something out — ah, yes, of course: his bed was cluttered. The dinner dishes. He hadn't been present at dinner, which was a sin worse than death, and had therefore not been present to perform his nightly dishwashing duty. As a result, the dirty dishes, plates and silverware, glasses, butter dish, a pot full of leftover potatoes and a rusted old, food-stained baking pan, not to mention wine and water glasses, had been deposited upon his bed; a reminder of his disloyalty and an indication of what was to be expected come morning.

He stacked the dishes and silverware on the floor by his dresser, deciding he would definitely awaken before them both and clean them thoroughly. He mustn't lie awake dreaming of music this evening, an early rise was clearly called for, even before the sun. Finally settling into bed, he noted that the sheets and mattress were soggy in places from the dinner residue, which he would just have to live with. He needed to use the bathroom, but he would not. To open his bedroom door and creep to the lavatory would be to set off an alarm that would likely burn the entire house down by the time they were through with him. Instead, he'd lie in his bed staring at the ceiling, Henry nestled beside him, and contemplate the remarkable events of the day.

He had been touched by another human being, something he only now realized was a thing that he had hungered for. But more than the touch, he himself had touched white ivory keys and set his feet upon heavy brass pedals. He had heard the notes echo throughout the instrument as Ken Moberly sat himself beside him on the bench, the outsides of their bare legs touching.

"You do play," he had said, looking him directly in the eye as the young man shied away, looking down at his own hands which he had removed from the keys, as though regretting an indulgence while astonished at the ability of his own limbs. His hands possessed a kind of magic that had never before shown itself. As his hands had met the keys it were as though two parts made for each other but tragically separated had been reunited, home at last, and he marveled in the ability of his own fingers, which seemed to take on an identity of their very own. "You may not know it, but you do." His was a kind voice, the only kind voice he could ever really remember hearing in his short life. "Here. Place your hands like this, on the keys. That's right. See that — press it. That's middle C. Good. That's right."

And so the stretch of hours had passed: a piano lesson and tomato soup accompanied by some sort of crude cheese sandwich. At one point, Ken Moberly had stood behind him, still seated at the bench, and reached forward, both arms extended, instructing the young man to place his hands atop his own as he ran up a scale and back down again, instructing by example and willing his own knowledge onto his pupil, whose natural ability, it was startlingly obvious, far outweighed his own.

He should put Ken Moberly right out of his thoughts, he knew, as he clutched Henry, safe in his bed for the moment but nervous even by the sound of his own breathing. He'd never see his new friend again. He'd surely spend the rest of his days locked within this little room, his right hand used merely to clutch a fork to which he would need to practically make love in order to consume the rancid bread that was now to be his staple. But for this precise moment, he must quiet himself. He must try to put whatever he knew the morning would bring out of his thoughts. So he stared up at the bright white ceiling in the darkness and tried to allow his mind to go just as blank. He was sweating, and it wasn't even hot anymore. He took deep breaths and without trying to conjure them, the notes came to him of their own volition, lingering within his body, as he at last achieved sleep.

Spring, 1997: New York City

He actually looked forward to Wednesdays. Before leaving for work those nights, he would spritz his hair a little bit more, maybe dab a touch of cologne or even don a tie for Ms. P., who was sure to notice.

The absurdity that she would play this little village hovel was never lost on him. When she swept on stage in her fabulous designer clothes and outlandish costume jewelry, it were as though all of Hollywood and everything that was ever good had come to visit; it was caviar at a garage sale, Cristal at a trailer park. His job was to play show tunes on the creaky piano inside the tiny upstairs cabaret theatre for an hour while the audience was seated and they ordered their first few rounds. He was to furnish musical frivolity and a sense of the carefree for the seventy-three lucky patrons, crammed between the walls like an abundance of carefully packed garments stuffed into an old suitcase that threatened to burst open at any second, who had obtained these tickets weeks, even months prior and waited in anticipation of seeing this woman, a true show business legend and household name, up close and personal — not even two feet away for those seated down front. That hand they watched holding the microphone was the same hand they had seen on *The Tonight Show*, on *The Muppet*

Show, in scattered movies from the sixties till now. That wry smile was the same one, well — *almost* the same one, that had burst out of little village holes in the wall such as this one forty plus years ago to make a name for herself on the international stage. And she had, many times over. She had re-invented herself in every decade. But to here she returned, religiously, faithfully — to her roots. She never forgot where she came from and she never took for granted that she was successful nor even funny –– which, in and of itself, is funny, given her high HIGH profile, for better or for worse.

The money from these little shows went to charity, and that's how she excused it — it was all for those less fortunate. But one look at her on that stage, the way her entire body swelled with accomplishment and pride and *purpose* when she made an audience laugh, and it was all too clear to even the blind. She needed these evenings the same way her audiences needed her. It was a beautiful, symbiotic relationship, one she at no time just assumed would always be there — she worked at it. And so, to pay homage to the talents she had been granted, to keep herself at the top of her form, down to The Pillow Factory she ventured once a week, so long as she was in town, for what she called "her workout."

He had made it through "Surrey with the Fringe on Top" and "Maybe This Time," before he decided to hit them with "Skylark" — all standards that were among Ms. P's favorites. Although she strived and succeeded in being terribly cutting edge and up to date with all the latest pop culture and celebrity gossip, current affairs and fashion trends, she could not deny that she relished a good, old-fashioned show tune. Glancing at his watch as he played, he knew it was almost time. The room was crammed past capacity, and those who had arrived early were already beginning to slur their words, which he could hear above the din of exuberant chatter.

It was twelve past eight. From the stage, he heard the heavy back door, the one that led down to the alley via a set of old, rusted out steel stairs, bang open and then shut. The scent of her perfume pervaded the air. She had come alone, as she usually did. Out of the corner of his eye, Everett could see her looking at herself in the mirror: applying just a touch more lipstick, blotting, removing an Altoid from her mouth and placing it deliberately, still wet, upon a dusty ledge for the porter to find late that night. Perhaps he would hold it up to the light, she thought, and think, "This was sucked on by a *star!*" But she had met Mack (whose actual name was Mackenillanzion, which no one could pronounce) and knew full well that he had no idea who she was. After all, she had never had much of a following in Ecuador. So perhaps leaving something for him to clean up was simply punishment for not recognizing her.

She was gazing into the mirror now, which she always did for a few moments before each show, perhaps telepathically communicating with herself. What did she say to her mirrored clone during these private rituals, he wondered, as his piano and the chatter of the excited audience reached a fevered pitch? Was it a secret prayer, a reminder of why she was there, who she was and what she had set out to accomplish? Or was she just simply trying to remember her act?

Jamie was in the audience tonight. There he sat in his little navy pants and Geoffrey Beene shirt, surrounded by the loud and raucous creatures of the night, some of whom even dressed to look like Ms. P. Looking over the piano, Everett could see that he had struck up a conversation with an elderly Jewish grandmother and the emaciated teenager in a skin tight DKNY shirt, both of whom were seated at his table. Jamie White had stepped into his world again, and it remained an odd thing to see him sitting amongst these characters who crowded his current station in life. The past blurred with the present in a strange collage, as though a character from an old black and white movie had waltzed into a current one, still showing in all the theatres and full of colorful special effects, and walked around greeting everyone.

Finally, the house lights dimmed. Everett could feel Jamie's excitement as he saw him put down his Lemon

Drop and turn his chair to face the stage — he was her self-described "biggest fan," and he thought his head might explode when Everett told him she played the club regularly. There was silence now, as the random faces of the audience were illuminated only by the faint flicker of small, tabletop candles. Everett did a run up the keys to elicit great fanfare before announcing her from his microphone behind the piano.

"Ladies and gentleman, won't you welcome to the stage, America's Sweetheart, Ms. *Ruth Pickett!*" It were as though a nuclear bomb had gone off in the tiny 500 square feet that comprised the theatre. A wave of applause, whistles and cheers deafened Jamie's ears. Then, suddenly, before the audience could catch their breath, there she stood before them all, the lady herself, wrapped in dazzling, sparkly blue and earrings, earrings, earrings — accepting a good four minutes of standing ovation just for walking onto the warped floorboards of that tiny stage.

"Yeah, yeah, yeah. Let's get this done. I wanna get home in time to watch *Law and Order*." It was her way of saying thank you, I hear you, I love you, you are heard, and please sit so I may now see if I'm still capable of magic. She had not forgotten those nights of performing to an audience of six, those nights of bombing in Philadelphia or being booed off the stage in

Pittsburgh. She refined, she honed, she put every ounce of her brilliance into getting it right.

Everett had the distinction of sitting behind the piano and watching her at every performance, just as he had for the past four years, which had earned him a kind of distinct and rarely attained graduate degree. He looked out over the sea of audience who were all delighted to share the same oxygen as she, and sometimes he made believe that the adulation was really for him. He recalled how he had not wanted the job when it was presented to him. It paid hardly anything at all and what would be the point? Playing for a has-been who was sure to be an out of control diva? He wasn't up for star worship and thought he could make more in tips downstairs in the piano bar. But over the years, he had been able to put celebrity aside, allow himself to be astounded by her abilities, and realize that what he had in Ruth was really a good and very needed friend.

Tonight she had selected Oscar de la Renta from head to pointy-toe shoe. She never left the house anything but utterly made up to resemble herself with the makeup, the formal clothes, the hair, all of it — the last thing she wanted was to disappoint, as had been her mantra her entire life, even as a little girl. She was only comfortable in her own well-constructed costume anyway. Not even the mailman was permitted to see beyond the mascara and perfectly lined lips. Tonight, it was an all-black ensemble over which she donned a royal blue, sequined jacket which matched the deep blue, faux-diamond hoop earrings which dangled from her ears (behind which sat the remnants of her former face). It was likely a design from the 70's or early 80's. In private, she was always proud to say that her wardrobe was "older than the hills," and he wondered to what other glamorous functions she might have worn this particular ensemble — an appearance on *The Sonny and Cher Show*, perhaps? A cocaine-infused gala in the Hollywood Hills?

As she began her act, he recalled the night that De La Renta himself was in attendance at the show. The great man had climbed the rickety old stairs at the Pillow Factory and stepped over beer-stained carpet and years-old chewing gum to see the one and only Ruth Pickett perform live, wearing his clothes, in front of seventy-three of the most manic fans ever — before the two of them darted off in her chauffeured car to someplace far more upscale for a post-show dinner.

She had warmed up the crowd now and was really starting to fly. A small stream of sweat trickled down from the bangs of her wisp of bright blonde hair, only a few strands of which were her own, strands that had been faultlessly combed into the hairpiece, assembled in her palatial Upper East Side townhouse before stepping into the sleek chauffeured sedan that had brought her to this diminutive neighborhood watering hole to stand beneath the hot stage lights for an hour's worth of comedic calisthenics because "New York audiences are the best. They don't lie."

"Show us your tits!" There was always one drunk heckler in the crowd. This one was an effete thirty-something, slinging back amaretto sours in the third row. He'd be embarrassed in the morning but for tonight, in an alcohol haze, all he could do was look at her and yearn to share her spotlight.

"That might frighten you, my darling. Have you ever seen a pair of these?" She caught the ball with aplomb and tossed it right back, surfing the wave and arriving triumphantly on shore. She knew he didn't mean to be insulting, and she knew exactly how to deal with it. "Oh please. At my age, I can sweep the floor without a broom, all I have to do is take my bra off and sway." There was a remarkable musicianship about her performance, the timing of each joke, the exact number of syllables needed to elicit the laugh, the insertion of beats, the rests in which her eyes carried the story for a while, the extension of a punch line if the audience was already laughing too loudly to hear it. In a way, it was as though she were New York itself. In her eyes one could see the lights of Times Square and the whole Manhattan skyline stretched out beyond the Hudson River. She was akin to Manhattan as cocktails at the Plaza and matzo on the Lower East Side.

Here it came, she was into her grand finale now and the big jokes came one after another, the same way a fireworks display concludes. What was meant to be an hour show had stretched on for at least an hour and a half, as it always did. He could feel her toying with the idea of wrapping it up, the same way a symphony teases you into false endings, only to return triumphantly with two or three final phrases. As both the composer as well as the conductor, she wasn't ready to surrender the stage just yet — a few more, they deserved it and so did she. Yes, a few more, please.

"And remember — look GOOD! No one's gonna invite you on their yacht because you can quote Tolstoy." Everett knew the cue. The show ended differently every time, but he could sense precisely, from her rhythm, which joke she meant as her final punch line from night to night, and therefore struck up the rousing music that would provide her exit, which he played for a good five minutes of cheers, ovations and audible adulation until she was off the stage and back in the stage right wing, looking at herself in the dirty mirror again, back on solid ground having spent the past hour and a half flying around the stratosphere near the heavens, doing what she could to cheer the saddened planet. She gazed into the reflective glass again in a kind of gratitude, a thanks to herself and a salute to her audience.

Everett finished the song, making a big deal out of the final few chords, and slunk off stage. No one noticed, all of them busy settling their checks and repeating Ms. P's best punch lines of the night to one another. Soon, he was back in the little make shift dressing room with the lady herself.

"Hello my DARLING! What's new on the rialto?" She flung her arms around his neck and kissed both his cheeks.

"The election stuff was hilarious." He knew she always looked to him right after a show for either validation or criticism, and she would insist on grilling him about every moment.

"That was new tonight — you liked that? They were very nice to me." They bantered back and forth for a while about the highs of the performance, but Ruth saw something on her friend's face that hadn't been there ever before. This was an altered Everett, she could tell the same way women can tell that one of their own is pregnant. There had been a distinct shift, and it was written right across his pale white face. "You have something to tell me?"

"What?," Everett's eyes darted away, shyly, then he turned his head entirely. He didn't like feeling exposed.

"Don't play games with me, mister. I invented most of the games." Grabbing his chin with her hands, her spiky manicured nails digging into his cleft, she turned his face back to face her own. "Spill it... What's his name?"

"You're amazing."

"HIS NAME!" She had taken on the persona of a Nazi prison guard, one of her most famous. She was proud of Everett. In all of their time together, years now, she had never once known him to have anyone other than Ravel and Shostakovich in his life, and she was hopeful that he might find someone with whom to pass the time in between her shows, which of course took priority. She would have no trouble reminding him that when she beckoned, he belonged to she and she alone.

"His name's Jamie. I'm gonna bring him back," he said nervously, like a lion dangling her cub before a herd of wolves.

"Do that, honey." There was contempt to her voice, like she were a general ready to see if this new private was ready for inspection. "We'll just see about this now, won't we?" She was being funny of course, but the truth of the matter was that she would very happily kill anyone who tried to hurt Everett. She was a difficult woman to get to know, but once you were in, once you had earned her trust, she stretched her barrier of protection around you and pity to anyone who tried to make it past her force field.

"Be nice."

She shot him an amazed look. She was, after all, the most compassionate and easily approachable woman in the world, of course. Everett was off to retrieve his new paramour and she was alone in the primitive dressing room, turning her attentions back to the chipped mirror. 'Be nice.' Whatever that meant. She fluffed her "hair," wiped the remaining sweat from her brow, popped a mint in her mouth and suited up for meeting new people with a misting of expensive perfume which she retrieved from her designer handbag. She would play this cool, even though she was never one to share her toys.

Soon they were in the doorway, the two boys, just barely off the stage. My God, she thought — Batman had found his Robin. That chiseled face, those adorable blonde locks, the way he filled out a pair of slacks, the look of sheer terror in his eyes as he was about to be introduced to her. She loved it all.

"This is Jamie, Jamie, meet —" Oh, no. She would not make this easy. There was far too much fun to be had. And fun was always something to which she had aspired. She looked him up and down with her heavily mascaraed eyelids and let forth with her raspy voice:

"So are you the pitcher or the catcher?"

Summer, 1978: Mason City, Iowa

He tried to retrieve that split second — that early morning moment before the eyes open yet consciousness, even in a vague way, has been attained. That small space in between sleep and reality where there is calm; a peaceful serenity that fades in a moment before it all comes back, before the book is opened to the exact chapter where it all left off and all of it comes crashing down around you. He tried to grasp it, retain it, make it linger, but soon his eyes opened and he was back in his own bedroom; Dorothy had returned from the Land of Oz far too soon. An aching dread descended as he recalled the circumstances of the past 24 hours, and he would not be welcomed back to Kansas by well meaning farmhands nor aunts with cold compresses. Rather, this would be the beginning of a whole different world, into which he would tip toe with abundant caution.

Something physical was different about this morning, however. He woke on his stomach, as he usually did, but something was lacking, there was a presence that was absent, a warmth, a comfort that left him feeling not at all right. He was without, incomplete. He had felt his boyhood evaporate in the preceding few years, prematurely for a boy of just 13, but this last link to the security of his past was not to be found on this suddenly chilly morning. Compounded with the sense of doom that now confronted him upon this new day, there was a frightful sense that the whole morning had been hung crooked.

Henry was missing. His beloved sock monkey, his companion, the one true witness to not only history and the previous days' adventures but also so much that Everett chose to keep hidden, was not beneath his right arm where he always slumbered and woke, ready to greet the sun and serve as confidant and protector. In fact, he wasn't anywhere at all within the bed.

Leaving the shelter of his covers, Everett's skin chilled quickly as he raced to his backpack. Could he have forgotten to retrieve Henry before racing to sleep? But Henry was not to be found in his backpack, which lay askew amongst the filthy dishes from the night previous, the lipstick stained wine glass and the casserole pan in which lingered remnants of baked-on ham and potato casserole. At least he missed ham and potato casserole, he thought, as panic set in.

He would have to continue his investigation later. For the moment, he needed to get the plates and glasses and baking pan to the kitchen and clean them in the most stealth silence. If he could clear away the filth before "those who knew best" could be reminded of it, he might be granted a more lenient sentence.

She had appeared mid-scrub and stood watching him, silently. It was most definitely casserole, yes that damned ham and potato casserole was the most stubborn, the most welded to the pan; several years of scrubbing had taught him this. Yes, it was that putrid smelling casserole all right, a new recipe that had come with the marriage, one that he was expected to not only embrace but celebrate; as though he had been asked to sing the praises of ham and potato casserole throughout the streets of their little hamlet, and harken gratitude to the genius who had brought it to the attention of their obviously lacking diet. The scent of it made him physically gag, a sharp pang in the back of his throat that he couldn't control yet always tried to hide as it baked in the oven only too soon to appear upon their table, its pungent scent pervading the house.

This morning, he had let the pan soak for a while as he went about dipping the glasses into the soapy water, careful to cleanse them thoroughly with the sponge, paying special attention to the lip, lest he be asked to do it all again or even again after that, as had certainly happened in the past. He was fully aware that, especially on this day and for this stretch of hours, his work would be thoroughly inspected. He carefully dried them with a dishtowel before placing them gingerly in the cabinet, trying still not to make too much noise or, if possible, any at all.

Everett tried to ignore her, pretend that she was merely a guard checking up on the inmate as he went about his assigned prison duties. He would treat her as though she were an innocuous and silent movie camera while he went about his task, perfectly natural. But the more she stood with her imposing stance, arms folded, it became quite clear that she was waiting for him to turn around from the sink and give her his full attention which, of course, he finally did.

Her make-up from the previous day lingered upon her face, a face that had aged so rapidly just in the past five years — since the divorce, yes, but most especially since the remarriage. Eyeliner was smeared across her lower lids and lipstick hung, in a half fashion, in smeared blotches from her mouth. There was still the remnant of eye shadow, most of which had long since surrendered itself to her pillow. The fact that she was clothed only in her robe lent her a sense of vulnerability, as perhaps she knew it might.

"Sit down." It was hardly a request. Everett dried his hands upon his own bathrobe and moved to the kitchen table, the faux oak monstrosity with the plastic place mats they had also inherited upon the marriage, place mats that had been used to feed his own children from his previous marriage in his own previous life. Their own, beautiful glass table had long since been eschewed to the Salvation Army, and the finely woven linens that had adorned their past were now tucked away in the attic — too good for them to use. Everett braced himself for what he knew was sure to come. "I want to talk to you." It was six in the morning so she couldn't have possibly been drunk. Still, something about her demeanor insisted that she wasn't quite herself. There they sat in their bathrobes, the last vestige of their shared commonality.

Guilt overcame him. Had his absence at the dinner table caused her — what? A slap across the face? A lecture about her parenting skills followed by a swift series of smacks upon her ass? Or worse — the silent condemnation, a punishment Mr. Thompson had perfected when it came to her. It was a very literal and very subtle form of ostracizing her — casting her outside of the very circle the two of them — husband and wife, man and possession — had created. It would last for a relatively small period of time, until she had learned her lesson and he was satisfied. But even a small period of time, a period devoid of inclusion, was enough to send her into desperation, feeling the soil upon her feet give way with such unpredictability that she might very well descend into the very center of the Earth, alone and companionless.

She needn't have said a word; it was all spelled out in her eyes, as she knew it was. Her head was cast downward, but as her eyes looked up at him through the smeared Maybelline, Everett knew in an instant what she was trying to convey: there wasn't anything else for her, there never would be. This was what had been handed the both of them, mother and son, and they had best make it work. Her new husband was the only reason they were able to draw breath, to pretend to be normal. She had married a good 'ol boy with far reaching ties in the community, and financial resources to back them all up, of which he was fond of reminding them both on an everyday basis.

The boy reached for her hand, which she quickly pulled away.

"I'm so sorry. I was just angry. I won't do it again." He pleaded with her as he saw her hand tremble — whether it were with rage or withdraw of white wine, he knew not. "I'm sorry... It'll be okay. You'll see. I'll do much better."

She stared at him coldly for a long while. Then, as though a drop of water had unexpectedly burst though a damn, a single tear rolled down her face from her left eye.

"I want to be clear..." there was a long silence as she tried to find breath. "I will provide for you as I have agreed to do." He heard it; there was the shuffle of tennis-shoe clad feet in the foyer. Mr. Thompson was in the wings, monitoring the performance of his star actress. Yes, that was him, the clump of his foot in those clumsy bright white shoes was unmistakable. It was the same clump he had heard tip toeing down the hall, leaving his mother's bedroom late at night before they had been married. It was the same clump that caused his spine to shiver and his defenses to raise like a shield when he heard it coming toward him in the house, the garage, the driveway or anywhere at all. This very morning, Mr. Thompson was listening, monitoring, ready to provide criticism later or indeed, assistance, should she fail at her task altogether.

"But I will assure you, — if you ever do anything to sabotage my marriage again... and I mean *anything*..." She looked at Everett for a long while with eyes that now resembled large white stones, as though her own eyes had been plucked out and replaced with forgeries. Wife first; protect the mother ship, she must have been thinking. The one would have to be put before the other, she knew, it's just the way it had to be. She glared down at her son. "You won't *ever* find that window unlocked again." The droplets that ran down her face betrayed her, and she knew that they did. Therefore, she made a hasty retreat in her bathrobe, rising from the chair and rushing toward her exit until she was safely offstage.

"Henry!" Everett, endowed with a sudden sense of knowledge and even understanding, demanded an answer. The reason that last night's makeup remained pancaked to her face was not because she had been distraught and up worrying about Everett. No. She had been terrified regarding the circumstances of her own future, and that which the actions of her now regretful son might cost her. *Can't control your own fat son... what kind of a mother are you? I ought to leave you both to starve!* Everett could hear Mr. Thompson's typical words ringing in the air, words he had heard so many times. *You let him get away with that ego the size of Texas and you do nothing about it! That boy's got to be cut down to size and I'm the man who's gonna have to do it since you're too lazy!...* and there must have been some slaps. The slaps were for her, the punches usually reserved for himself.

"Where is Henry?" He said it loud for the whole house to hear, as loudly as he could - for the three of them, two against one.

Sheila Thompson returned to look at her son once more — right in the eye. How she would have loved to tell him the truth, to confide in him, to explain the reality about his absent father, to concede that she was now powerless to control the freight train of her life that was unstoppably intermingled with his own, to not feel obliged to cover up her right eye with so much of last night's make-up, to admit the reasons for it all and to apologize. However, for the time being and knowing full well that she was being watched from the confines of her very own home by a man she called lover but who had become her captor, all she could muster, in a zombie-like monotone, was: "I'm going to shower now. Have this mess cleaned up before your stepfather wakes up." There was a shuffling of tennis shoes in the foyer, not so well-disguised espionage from the warden. She turned to go, but stopped, her hand on the gilded knob of the double doors that separated the kitchen from the rest of the house. Her back to him, she put a period on her task: "I don't ever want to discuss this again. You understand me? Not *ever*."

And Sheila Thompson, not so formerly Sheila Crisp, walked out of his life for what Everett knew would be the final time.

Spring, 1997: New York City

They were in the Rolls Royce now, speeding up Sixth Avenue. "They have GOT to stop putting the straights in the front row. Will you tell them? Gays. Gays down front. Sit the straights in the back with the lesbians who never laugh. Now let's go home for wine and tawdry gossip." The car sped forward, missing almost every light. Something about being with Ruth deemed that fate was on your side. She had suffered enough slings and arrows in her life for six lifetimes, and therefore the Gods had declared her golden. Yes, these days, the sun and moon alike smiled down upon Ruth Pickett. Her career had hit a brand new peak, "a triumphant comeback!" as she liked to call it. Only a woman like Ruth could be a hit for five decades in a row.

The doors of the elevator sprung open to a room that was more film set than residence, just the way she liked it. Her apartment was ever evolving. One month it might have a rustic, woodsy look, only the next to be made over with an Egyptian theme, complete with rugs and draped silk that cascaded from the walls. It had been the ballroom of a Vanderbilt or a Rockefeller or some little piece of dandy American royalty at some point. When she found it in the mid 70's, it had fallen into complete disrepair and was housing several families of pigeons and a raccoon or three. A year and a half long renovation had brought it to the palace it now was, fit for a Queen, naturally.

One could always tell what was going on inside of Ms. P's mind by the way her living room was outfitted. It was clear that she had made no bold design choices lately, but rather thrown random bits from old designs together, creating a look of divine eccentricity. One found antique wooden jewelry boxes next to Tiffany blue marble eggs, sitting across from two stone Doberman Pinchers she had likely swiped from some movie set which watched over the decoupage vase she had rescued from the Chelsea Flea Market.

A remnant or two of the Egyptian theme hung from the ceiling while a silk screen, circa her phase from the Orient, stood in a corner, and a series of Indian masks outfitted with face paint and covering a far wall, examined the three of them with religious curiosity. But everywhere and unmovable was an endless display of photographs; large and small prints housed in shiny brass and silver frames. Photos of Ms. P with almost every famous person in the world — politicians, entertainers, world icons, yes. However, upon closer examination, one could also see her with her daughter, with her late husband, with her grandson, some black and white's with her parents, or sometimes just some sepia toned images from her ancestry. A sense of her own history fed her work, her purpose for being on the planet. Everett was acutely aware that just beyond the veneer, just beyond the character of herself, lie the very vulnerable and very shy lady who at this very moment was mostly concerned about whether or not his new friend Jamie would like her.

The boys settled on the rug, sipping wine in front of a large, blazing fire. Edna was apparently off tonight, so Ruth served the guests herself. "What, you think I've forgotten how to operate a cork screw? I may be a Jew, but I'm from Connecticut."

After sitting stupefied and star struck for the first half hour, Jamie finally opened up and got the prerequisite conversation about how he grew up watching her on TV, etc., etc., out of the way, to which she graciously responded with "and I'm sure your great-great-*great* grandparents enjoyed me on *The Tonight Show*... Perhaps I knew your ancestors back in Mesopotamia." Finally, she was relaxed; but she would have to play with him for a while before she could call him friend, it just went with the territory.

They were all a glass or two down as she re-poured. She had been off stage long enough now to unzip herself from her onstage persona and be with them as the real Ruth, unadorned. She was always happy to have post-show company. The audience always went home, but she was still flying up there amongst the stage lights for a good while after the applause stopped. It took some time to float back down to Earth. Friends helped. She stretched her neck along the cushions of her own overstuffed, Louis the XVI sofa and made her request: "Play for us, darling."

It was hardly an unwelcome request. In fact, every time he entered Ruth's apartment, her beautiful, gold-leaf grand piano stood like a welcome Olympic sized pool and he the anxious swimmer. She knew this; his eyes shone like diamonds at the site of the instrument, the same way hers did at the site of a solitary microphone. He brought his wine with him as he seated himself at the instrument, gazing upon the keys of the beautiful Steinway, which, over the years, he had come to know well at this party or that, or just during intimate evenings such as tonight.

It was something new this time, something neither of them had heard. He was writing it as he went along, just making it up, but they didn't know that. It seemed, to all who could hear, that it was complete, fully formed. It was slow and reposed, the musical equivalent of cognac. Whatever it was, it fit the mood, the room (as challenging as that was with all of its varied themes), the fire and the whole evening just perfectly. It were as though he were scoring a scene, a gift composed just for them, in honor of this very night — these moments by the fire.

The music was rhapsodic and, in it's clutches, it swept up both Jamie and Ruth, who, only physically, sat together upon pillows by the hearth. She leaned into this new person and said in a tone that was just louder than a whisper: "And THAT'S what you're getting involved with, my darling," she looked Jamie directly in the eye, subtly pointing, with a half crooked finger that was weighed down with jewelry and a perfectly manicured nail, at the man seated at the grand. "That's the magnitude of what you've got." It was almost a challenge, as though she were saying 'are you prepared to deal with this? Are you up for it? Can you go forty rounds? It will *never* be easy.'

"I know," said Jamie, settling himself amongst the fine fabric of Lady P's delicately upholstered pillows. "I've always known that." They both took another sip of wine, stared at the flames of Ruth Pickett's fire, and let the music seep through them.

6

Autumn, 1989: Cambridge, MA

J AMIE WHITE STARED at the ceiling. He had never slept in the nude but was enjoying the feeling of it. It made him feel grown up, just as if he were finally his own man — and a *sexy* man at that.

He had done it. Reached into what he knew was a forbidden world, and survived. There had only ever been those few dalliances back home, but they all paled in comparison to what he just experienced. It was certainly not what was expected of him, but something he knew to be correct and altogether perfect. It was much like putting on glasses for the very first time following years of nearsightedness. Turning on his side, his taught, tan, warm flesh stretched out upon the smooth sheets. He gazed at Everett, this creature who had fascinated him for such a long while, whom he had finally mustered the courage to pursue. It all felt right, and utterly effortless. Compared with everything else in his life that surrounded him in a loud whirl most of the time, the simplicity of this morning, this newfound joy, was rapturous.

What was his slumbering lover dreaming about, Jamie wondered, as he dared reach over to stroke his hair. What deep and secret dreams raced through a mind as turbulent as Everett's? The back of his hand ran across his pale cheek, and he could feel the warmth of his breath upon his own skin. None of it mattered, not one single damn thing beyond the confines of this small, luxurious piece of utopia. Jamie was fixated, and he allowed his mind to wander and even to contemplate the future, something he had always feared. Perhaps it was all more simple than he had previously thought. Perhaps he should simply take a breath and leap into blissfully uncharted waters. He had never before shared a bed with a man, but he knew in an instant that this would not be the last time.

Fall, 2026: Malibu, CA

The sand had turned cold. Heated by the sun, as it usually was, the sand was an oasis, a warm blanket into which he loved to sink his feet. But now, given the sudden turn of events and the frosty night air, his toes danced in moonlight as he sat, gazing out at the waves which seemed larger and louder than they had in a long, long while, their white caps not unlike sharp teeth. Jefferson rested his furry chin upon his thigh which was clad in faded and well worn denim, as Jeff Severin contemplated his next move. It was getting dark.

Maybe he should go home — maybe? No. He had made a swift exit from that place, from his jeep and his church and his girlfriend, from expectation, from factory work and union overtime and the life his father and everyone, really, assumed he'd pursue. Michigan was a million miles away. He had said he would make this life work, and so he would.

He didn't mind the massages. When he truly thought he was doing something good for someone, he was the most happy he could recall himself being — accomplished, satisfied. And sometimes he didn't mind the sex that accompanied it, either. It was a release, it was forward movement, it was a living.

It was panic which coursed through his blood right now, however; that familiar feeling that returns when one things ends and you're never sure if another will begin — like leaping from ice flow to melting ice flow in the Arctic, hoping that if you fall in, you can fish yourself back out before you freeze to death.

Jeff had once been in awe of Roger's movies, having seen them again and again at the various parties of his youth, at "80's nights." He had made the mistake of telling Roger all about this upon their first meeting, when he was called to the house for "some massage work on a very important client," as the voice on the other end of the line had informed him. Over the months and for some inexplicable reason, he had grown fond of Roger. He wasn't in love, but very much in like. Roger taught him things and, on occasion, was even tender. There was something about the grey of his chest hair that he even found comforting as he curled up next to him in the hot tub or beneath the silk sheets of the king sized bed.

Anyway, it was all over now, as he knew it eventually would be. His dog sitting days apparently behind him, he knew he'd better get to work. A new ad, some new clients, maybe ring up some old ones and it would all be fine for now. Somehow. There was a future that he was chasing, a future that consisted of stability and kindness and a middle ground; but for the immediate future, it would have to wait.

But Jefferson — what to do with him? Roger clearly didn't care, as they had both been out on the sand for several hours now, tossed out of Shangri-La without so much as a water bowl placed on the patio for either of them. Soon, he knew, a car would be pulling up containing either his wife or his replacement, and this was fine. It would have to be.

He would call Jillian, his former roommate. She'd take him in, surely, even though his room had most certainly been let. The couch would do. In time, the world would set itself right again. He was penniless for the moment, without money to even call a cab, but he would soon right that injustice. He rose, grabbed his bag which contained the same few items with which he had first entered this Malibu life nearly eight months ago, and stood upon his own two feet, as he had always prided himself in doing. It was past ten o'clock but he would have to face his former neighbor anyway and ask to use the phone.

Oh, Christ! Had he forgotten about their piano lesson amid the cries of "You're just a call boy, kept for fun! Did you think you would be a permanent resident of Malibu? You're a call boy, for fuck's sake! And by the way, I know you're older than you say you are — you're at least thirty, you've been bullshitting me. I'm a director; I know all the tricks. Don't you know who I AM?" YES. He was certain that his lesson with maestro Everett Crisp, the chance of a lifetime, had all but expired. But he'd have to knock on his door regardless; there was no choice.

It could have been the TV causing it — light and shadow so fast, back and forth, illuminated against the sliding glass door. Jeff wandered forth a few steps along the sand so he could see clearly, most of his worldly possessions in hand, poured into that neatly packed Prada bag (a gift from Roger from when they toured the French Riviera). Yes, flames. Most definitely. A fire! Everett Crisp's living room was ablaze. Jeff Severin's heart pounded as Jefferson began to bark, an urgent noise of distress that Jeff had never before heard from the animal. The world seemed to be in slow motion as he raced toward the house, sandy foot over sandy foot.

The French doors were locked, of course. He could see Everett lying there, asleep or even asphyxiated in the smoke, unconscious upon his own beige sofa as flames threatened to engulf first his living room, and then most certainly the entire house and perhaps even that little part of the colony. For the moment, the fire remained confined to the area just outside the hearth, but it wouldn't take long for the growing red and yellow flames to ignite everything.

Jeff hurled a flower pot, the unbroken one, through the glass door. Jefferson barked his lungs out before rushing in, jumping through the sharp, broken debris to lick Mr. Crisp awake, finally gnawing on his ear lobe with a resounding "grrrr" which was met with a muffled "auhhwha?"

Jeff spotted a water cooler near the kitchen. Yes, Evian would surely extinguish the fire in Everett Crisp's living room, which he found momentarily humorous amid his heroics. Thank whatever powers that be that Everett trusted nothing that came out of the tap and insisted upon a constant supply of filtered water. Jeff, strapping and able, pulled the cylinder of water from the mechanism and hurled its contents at the fireplace. Eventually, and after much effort and some charred brick, the fire was out. Jeff collapsed on the floor in exhaustion, dropping the plastic water container, now mostly empty, upon the wet floor.

"So, what are you, some renegade knight who comes to the rescue of little old men in Malibu?" Everett laughed at his own feeble joke, which seemed much funnier to him than it really was. He could see Jeff through a kind of haze. Everything in the room seemed slightly distant; in such a way that he was removed from reality and watching it all through a kaleidoscope.

Jeff remained silent for a bit, catching his breath. "Your house could have burned down. With you in it."

"Well, yeah, that would have been an event. You've made an awful mess there," he slurred. It all seemed oddly funny and frustrating to Everett.

"You shouldn't keep so much paper around the fireplace."

"I burnt the music! I burnt the music!" He was bragging now, proud of his accomplishment. "I'm free!" His eyes remained closed as he stretched out along the sofa. "Nag, nag, nag. Hey, have you been smoking?" he laughed again at his own humor, before drifting off again.

"I think we need to get you to bed," said Jeff. He had performed this duty plenty of times with his own father. "Come on, you'll feel better in the morning." The bottle of scotch sat empty upon the coffee table amid random paperweights and additional staff paper, saved from the flames yet containing little more than scribbles and random, angry doodles — some drawing of a boy with dreamy eyes, the things that fall out of our heads when we drink.

"You'd like that, wouldn't you, gorgeous? Hm?" Jeff picked him up off of the sofa and again slung one of Everett's pale arms around his own broad shoulder. After much effort, they managed to relocate to the downstairs bedroom, which sat next to the burnt living room. Everett sank with a thud onto the sheets before looking up at Jeff with hurt eyes. "You stood me up." There was genuine sadness to his voice, like his balloon had blown away.

"I'm sorry. Come on, lay down."

Everett's voice was playful, a sing-song kind of an accusation: "You were busy getting dumped and thrown out of *The Breakfast Club* over there, hmm? No *Sixteen Candles* for *you*." Again, Everett found his own joke far more humorous than it was, and laughed incoherently. Looking up at this blond paragon via bleared eyes, he smiled a wry kind of grin and slid his hand around Jeff's hip, letting his fingers creep just inside his pants to feel his tan torso, his well-defined hip bone, the same body he had seen running on the beach with Jefferson so many times now resting beneath his own hand. It was warm, and it was a thing of beauty. Taught. He had never been particularly attracted to Jeff, Ken dolls were never his thing, but he was beautiful, there was no mistaking it. There is so little actual beauty in the world, he thought, that when one stumbles upon it, it should be fully appreciated, drunk in, inhaled to the maximum. Furthermore, through his liquored haze, anything other than sleeping seemed like a good idea.

Jeff stood silently, feeling Everett's touch. For a moment, he absorbed the idea that the fingers that had not only written but played all of those brilliant pieces of music, note by note, now caressed his own self. The craftsmanship that gave birth to those symphonic masterpieces now lavished attention upon his own body. Finally, he clasped his own hand to Everett's, smiled down at him, and removed them both. Arranging Everett on the bed like a dutiful squire, he pulled the covers around him, and switched off the lamp.

"I'm going to clean up. Then I'm going to use your phone."

"Stay." Everett grasped one of his own hands to his head, which was starting to throb, and reached into the darkness for Jeff with the other. *"Stay."*

Autumn, 1989: Cambridge, MA

It poured down rain, saturating all of Cambridge and the whole world for all Jamie knew. It remained dark outside despite the hour, as though the night had been magically and thankfully extended. Nowhere pressing to rush off to, just the breezy wet weather that fell from a darkened sky in which they could luxuriate in their own private habitat. It was welcome. He opened the living room window to listen to the drops hitting the trees just beyond the protection of the screen. Rain would cleanse his whole history, and he had only to breathe in the newfound cleanliness of what had so recently presented itself, and let it seep down deep into his body. The smell of clean, of new, permeated the air that blew in from the open window.

Jamie White had always hoped he would fall in love. He had pursued it like a fantasy, a bird that flew just beyond his grasp. He smiled now as he scrambled eggs and fried bacon in a pan, knowing that the object of his infatuation would soon rise. It would not all have been a dream; it was indeed his new reality.

Just being in the kitchen seemed like a chore, albeit a comforting one, when he knew that Everett Crisp's warm and brilliant figure lie just in the other room, slumbering beneath his own sheets; a body he now, it seemed, had permission to caress and cherish. He had gazed into the eyes into which he had yearned to gaze, and taken the very first steps of his own evolution. He had achieved his goal, an important task for any Harvard man.

A whole different Jamie would have to emerge; he knew this. A whole new person would have to walk the lawns of the university and present himself to people with whom he was already acquainted, people who were already his confidents, and even strangers who knew him only by reputation. A great vulture of expectation from his homeland, from those who had reared him, loomed large upon his horizon, the weight and sheer hysteria of which was overwhelming and was therefore unceremoniously abandoned for the present. He would eschew all of that as he slowly forced his attention back to the delight of silence, an occasional pop from bacon grease. This morning was a morning in which he would bask in eggs and rain and the treasure that slumbered in his bed. The sun had not yet dared show itself, so neither, perhaps, would he or his newfound secret.

Eventually, lured by the fragrance of bacon-tainted air, Everett stumbled into the tiny kitchen, seating himself at the breakfast bar with his floppy, disheveled black hair, sleep lingering in his wild eyes. Seeing him there, looking perfectly askew, clad only in a t-shirt and wrinkled boxers, Jamie knew he was most definitely in love. He had heard about it, the idea of being "in love," and he was certain that he now knew exactly what it meant. The two of them were in a secret fort of sorts, a beautiful and perfectly private world known only to them, and Jamie basked in this, probably would have danced on the roof had he known anything other than cotillion. The rain seemed to come down even harder and there was the not so distant sound of thunder, the sound of which echoed throughout the white walls of his barely off campus abode that was their refuge. Candles were clearly called for, so Jamie White went about reigniting the pillars of the previous evening, which seemed particularly luminous given the darkness of the day, and the electric lamps he steadfastly refused to switch on.

"You made breakfast. That's quaint," Everett's eyes starred down at the perfectly placed food upon his plate. The storm was shining directly into his eyes. Everett could not recall the last time someone had made breakfast for him. And then he could. Ah, yes: the ancient melody that crept into his present on a routine basis.

What had he done? The events of the previous evening blurred together. There was wine, yes, but he hadn't been drunk, it couldn't have been that as he felt no hangover, no regret, no struggle to grasp the events themselves. He had been lost in — something — and he struggled to reclaim his own history.

"Eggs a la Jamie, juice, and a hearty Thomas's English muffin. I was going to make quiche, I wanted to make quiche, but I realized this morning I have no idea how to make quiche, I just like eating it. I'm talking too much, aren't I?" Jamie was nervous, and Everett had a hard time wrapping his mind around all this as Jamie made his way back to the stove, fumbling over the coffee maker.

Nervous over *him*? He was a piano player on a work study program, never certain he belonged at Harvard and questioning himself every day, not the dashing young child of royalty who stood across this breakfast bar, who, it seemed to Everett, was not-so-secretly and terribly concerned that his efforts in the kitchen weren't quite up to par. "It weird — having someone serve ME food. I'm so used to the other way around." They were the only words Everett found hanging about, the only thing to put forth into the sheer awkwardness of what they would both come to call "the morning after."

"Well, get used to it. I want to do nice things for you. I enjoy it," he said, kissing his newfound lover on the cheek. Jamie had hoped to elicit a smile, but there was none to be had from Everett. What, Jamie wondered, had he done wrong? It was his sole purpose, the destination of the morning, that his bedfellow be utterly comfortable and completely at ease. The most important thing that had ever happened to him had *happened,* and it was up to him to preserve it, treasure it.

Additional rainclouds blew in, squeezed themselves right through the pores of the screen, drifted right through Everett, and lingered in the room. *Was* it merely a plethora of wine, after all, that had caused this — what? What was this? He had awakened the sexuality of dear Mr. White, the Young gentleman from Connecticut, and it would be difficult to shake him loose, much like a newborn lamb who sees it's mother for the first time and runs for the nipple. He was a GUD, surely — Gay Until Graduation, nothing could EVER come of himself and the Senator's son and common logic told him to run as fast as he could to higher ground.

"I need to get going." He left his high seat at the bar, breakfast untouched, and scavenged about for his various articles of clothing.

"Not so fast, mister. We haven't completed our lesson just yet. Here we are." Jamie dumped more eggs, fresh from the frying pan, upon the plastic plate that had no doubt come with the apartment, and reached for the poster board piano like a proud boy showing off his homework to what he assumed were and always had been bemused adults.

Everett stood tall to face the dear boy who had occupied his night. It had been, what? Rapture? No. It had been what it was and he didn't begin to understand it, really. But honesty must rule the morning, otherwise a whole new dangerous path would present itself, a path upon which Everett knew he should not, *could* not, venture. They were the same in age, perhaps, yet light years apart in so many regards. Instead, all he could put forth was: "What *is* this?"

There was uncomfortable silence; Everett's words lingered in the air between them. It was very nearly accusatory, Everett's statement, like the closing argument of a terrific case. Jamie White did not know what to say, which was highly unusual for him. He had expected a gorgeously stormy, warm morning of breakfast and kissing, maybe a day spent totally inside removing and reapplying various scant bits of clothing, an indoor playground, exploring this new world with this mysterious new person, perhaps even a candle lit piano lesson upon the white poster board piano over which he had labored. He had even hoped and prayed for and it seemed *got* this glorious rain which would now force them indoors — all of the higher powers pointed to a perfect morning with his perfectly imperfect infatuation.

"It's eggs... It's just a plate of eggs," said Jamie, with all of the innocence of a well groomed and certainly obedient puppy.

Everett could see it in his eyes: he could really hurt this boy. He had lived his life, the adult portion of it, with a human force field powerfully in tact — anyone who ventured too near was met with a stalwart magnetic ball that kept all at a distance, the invisible resistance that divides himself and anyone else for fear that they might persist forward, get too close before they be consequently cemented to him. He was his own person and he could not and would not allow anyone to proceed beyond that safe boarder, as he himself had in his youth. He would not subject this young man who had ventured so far as to make him breakfast, no, he would not, put him through the trial and tribulation of truly knowing him. It would end badly as it always did. No, he would protect them both; it was the honorable thing to do.

Jamie stood like an aloof schoolboy in front of the cheap, electric GE stove, the kind that populate temporary student rentals such as these, shuffling from foot to foot and embarrassed. He would not allow this morning to die, he had just woken up to himself and he would defend the being he would now strive, with everything that mattered to him, to become. He would experience who he really was, as opposed to what he was expected to be. No, there was no room for this, this *vacillation*. Not now; perhaps not even ever. He knew what he wanted, and he would move full steam ahead and *get it*.

"You might as well know, I'm beyond sure that I'm in love with you." Jamie White meant it. His words formed an elaborate ice sculpture the moment they left the confines of his mouth, frozen in time and hovering above them both like an imposing tornado, ready to strike and obliterate, dependent merely upon the wants of the wind. But Jamie was glad that he had said what he had; he would not retreat, not anymore. The Earth flung itself forward, and so must he grasp hold and follow suit.

Jamie's words were like paper burning right next to Everett's ears and under his nose; "love" being such an ambiguous word, thrown about far too often in song lyrics and greeting cards. He had no idea, none at all. It had all been *more* to his classmate — something that stretched beyond Prince Charming merely extending himself to the peasant boy. It had been something profound and yet *again*, Everett Crisp had fucked it all up. He would dash this young man's awakening upon the rocks, he knew, and so be it. Get out now while the getting is good before he really ruins a fine young gentleman. "I gotta go."

"That bothers you, doesn't it? Someone loving you? Messes with your whole ascetic, your whole 'loner guy, outcast' image, the boy with the messy black hair and all? Well, I'm gonna mess with it anyway. What *is* it with you?"

"We had a night. We drank some wine, we got naked, big deal!" He knew that the unkind words he spat out like a nail gun were toxic, but toxicity was clearly called for this morning. It was the only thing that would kill the infection. He fluttered about the apartment in search of various pieces of clothing. "You're a Senator's son. Everybody's favorite young Republican. I'm a piano player in a college bar. I work for tips. I'm *nothing*."

"And you're *brilliant*. A *brilliant* nothing. And fuck you for bringing up my family. My family has nothing to do with this. *Nothing!* And WHAT are you doing that for, anyway?"

"What?" Where the hell was his coat? He fumbled about the place, searching.

"I have to ask you. WHAT are you doing?" Jamie's eyes were like lasers that pierced right into Everett's very existence, into that part of him that knew more than he dare admit to even himself. There was a long, agonizing pause during which neither of them moved a mussel, two warships facing off across a cold ocean. Everett stopped his frenzied search and there was silence.

"Grow up. What the fuck do you know about me?" The low octave of his voice betrayed him as he turned his head as quickly as he could in search of his other shoe.

"I don't know ANYONE, and you should know that every Christmas my mother hires three quarters of the New York Philharmonic to play at our holiday party — who can do what you can do. So WHAT *are you doing?*"

"I'm a lawyer."

"Anyone can be a lawyer. Anyone with a brain and the ability to memorize shit but you — you are *sensational*. WHAT are you doing trying to be *typical?*"

Jamie wasn't even arguing a case like they sometimes did in mock trials in class. His trembling hands betrayed his bravado. He needed his answer.

"I have to find my shoe. Where the fuck —" But he had already found it. The warm, domestic dream to which Jamie had grasped hold throughout the night, who had wrapped his arms around his own naked body that was made to feel safe, was, piece by piece, clothing himself and becoming the well put together soldier that inhabited the campus of Harvard. All around Everett's skin, the hard, impenetrable exterior was growing anew at an astonishing pace, like he had swallowed some potion; there was little Jamie could do to stop the infection. Floppy hair and boxers were quickly replaced by cold denim and worn Oxford penny loafers. Shirt, socks and a fast repositioning of his hair in the mirror by the door later, and Everett Crisp prepared himself to return to reality. This, right here in the rain, whatever this was, was a dreamland of which he could not ever be worthy.

Jamie closed his eyes and swallowed hard, not prepared to resign the one true thing he knew was absolute because of fear. Fear had held him back his entire life and he would no longer allow its tentacles to strangle him. "Don't go. *Don't.* Go. Don't run… Please, Everett."

"I have some place to be. I'll see you in class." He had meant it to sound as cold as he could muster, even looking into the eyes of his recent lover. Dismissive, even, but the effort it took to form the words exposed him. He could not look Jamie in the eye; each syllable was the greatest effort of his life. Everett Crisp had left the building without so much as a wink and a nod.

Jamie White starred at the heavy, red, steel, closed door for a good, long while. Finally, after realizing that he could not put the picture together, could not quite grasp the reality of what had just happened, he turned back to face his empty apartment with those banally painted, monotonous white walls, which for the first time seemed so decidedly lacking in color. He shivered. Filled with regret that pulsated within his stomach and evolved up through his fingers, mind and body, shot right out the top of his head before re-circulating and pushing him right back down into the Earth, he knelt in his own doorway, anxious for breath. He eventually came to rest upon the cold wooden floor, where he sat in utter silence, clad only in his scant shorts and robe, with only the passing storm to fill the void. The storm would pass, he knew, as all things eventually do.

Jamie White was alone, truly alone, for the first time in his life. There had always been the cacophony of social obligation, friends of his parents, girlfriends, fellow Ivy League leading Republicans of tomorrow, the grand dance that had always surrounded him. But after the splendor of the night previous, after the closeness of a period of time spent truly entwined with another human being, he faced a morning that was surely the coldest on record.

Fall, 2026: Malibu, CA

He awoke with the taste of sandpaper in his mouth. He was so out of practice at this and silently hated himself for a few minutes as that sinking dread that nearly pummels one into the core of the Earth threatened to swallow him whole. He tried to muster the courage to open his eyes and face the morning. Or was it afternoon? A full-scale high school marching band tromped through his head, clearly amateur and full of wrong notes, and for a moment he was certain he would vomit. No, he recalled from those years of monotony, years long past, that he would have done it already. Or had he? No. Now it was the duty of time to remove the transgressions of the previous night.

He could smell something... something almost comforting and familiar. Bacon? Yes, most definitely, bacon. Had he hired a housekeeper in his drunkenness? Phoned up a service and demanded a full staff? It was anyone's guess. With some effort, he swung his legs out of bed and reached for his glasses, which were nowhere to be found, of course. It would take every muscle in his neck to lift up his head, which this morning seemed to be saddled with the weight of twenty-five anvils. What was this room? This was not his usual room. He set about removing the previous days' clothes that, apparently, he had slept in, and in the guest room, at that. He donned an old robe he found in the closet, a robe he forgot he had, a robe that once belonged to someone else. Ah, yes. It retained his fragrance.

He really was too old for all of this, he realized. He would make today a small day and just get through it as best he could with dim lights, abundant silence and ample hydration. But first, he would have to see about this mysterious bacon-laden fragrance emanating from the hallway.

Making his way into the obnoxiously sunny kitchen, he squinted though the rays of sunlight that streamed in via the skylight. There was a dog in his house, and he appeared to be cooking bacon. He sat at attention, the tan, furry thing, watching a black cast iron pan that lingered, unattended, upon the stove. The smell was overwhelming and he grasped the counter to steady himself.

"I found it in the back of your freezer, thought you might be hungry," a voice came from behind Everett, the body of which proceeded to waltz into his kitchen in cut off shorts and a wife beater, which accentuated each and every nodule upon the well maintained body of that boy from next door.

A young man in shorts and a wife beater with tousled blonde hair stood in his kitchen preparing bacon. He had almost resigned himself to just go with it.

"Don't remember a thing, do you?" Jeff, having some experience with all of this, smiled broadly and did his best to put Everett at ease, who would surely be embarrassed.

"No, umm — fill me in?" he asked reluctantly. Everett's mind was fractured into puzzle pieces and it would take a few hours to sort them all out again. Gazing up and down the scantily clad body of his young chef, he hoped the facts of the night previous wouldn't come rushing back too quickly — like a barren water fall that suddenly regains its full strength with the flip of a switch. Although he sought the truth, the pleasant reality of the mostly unknown might be better for the time being.

"You were fine. Just needed a little hand. I swept up all the glass."

"Well, that was good of you. Glass from what?" There was an uncomfortable silence. Jeff and Jefferson (God, that really was annoying, Everett was just realizing), gazed into the living room where one of his French doors was now covered in bed sheets and masking tape.

"Oh," was all Everett could bring himself to say. The puzzle was filling in.

The two of them, the three of them including Jefferson, went about the morning as, piece by piece, the adventures of the evening previous returned to the forefront of Everett's mind from whence they had been previously drowned beneath a gallon or so of what he could only assume was methanol. Yes, it was all there and returned, detail by detail, to smack him wholly across the face. Regret was useless, but it loomed over him nonetheless. Regret. And disappointment. This was a song he knew. Breakfast was served.

"You know," said Everett, arranging a cloth napkin in his lap which had been perfectly set by his temporary houseguest, "you're better off without him. Roger." There we go. He was re-entering the land of the living, recalling the cast and its players. Yes, the piece of his mind that had gone dark for a while slowly awoke to find illumination.

Jeff fed Jefferson a piece of bacon, whose long, tan tail wagged rapidly in delight across the hardwood floor of the breakfast nook. "I know that. I always knew that. It was just —"

"Comfortable. Careful of that; comfort is a trap." So he was a school teacher today, would that be his new role? Talking took all of his energy, however he did feel he owed the young man something, some tidbit of fatherly advice, even though unsolicited. Once the entire storyboard of his actions from the previous night crystallized in his psyche, Everett deliberately avoided eye contact with anything other than his napkin and an occasional glance at the toaster.

So, the tapping had returned. The nagging constant he hoped buried had returned as though no time had passed, as familiar as his own skin. Tap, tap, tap — as though someone or something knocked right upon his living room window, refusing to stop until it was drowned. So easy it was to recall the games he had played with himself, back in those days of complete and under surrender. If he could limit it to once an hour, that was a good day. He would partake, a fresh pour would be had, cubes of ice would be dropped, but only once an hour, a strict regimen followed for the sake of that day's work. He would surrender to the tapping, which silenced it for the moment. He would have it, live and ingest and listen; yet too soon it would empty, it would end, like everything, and there's a certain sadness to that. But he would wait, his own way of tricking it, wait the hour, put up a brave fight.

The tapping would always come back of course, and with greater ferocity, but he would play the keys, something he loved or just something really loudly with force to it, something so complex and melodious that it was enough to silence even the loudest of taps. And soon, at last, the hour had passed and pure joy would splash itself upon the frosty, clear cubes, and all was extinguished with the swallow. He would pour a large rocks glass, make it last for twenty minutes or so, and then trick it some more with water, with cranberry juice, something that would give him the physical action, that would allow him to pretend, to fool it and in the years in which he followed that diatribe he produced the bulk of his greatest work, melodies and orchestrations en masse. He climbed right into the stories of those films and churned out music to fit the emotion, the occasion, the character of those films lickety-split and he was proud of that. But the tapping knew. Apparently, the tapping still knew. The tapping had come back up for air, daring him to push it back under the waves.

Silence followed for a good long while. Jeff watched this man, the maestro, clearly lost in his own mind, eyes glassed over, frozen in time. Where had he gone, Jeff wondered; floated right out of the room, out of Malibu altogether for that matter, flying around someplace within his own self; it was an ability Jeff admired. The true artists, he knew, possessed qualities such as these, which is what set them apart from the merely talented.

A car started next door and a vintage Corvette made its way down the drive and up the canyon with far too much noise. Everett, having re-inhabited himself, was repulsed, recalling how Roger Hunt liked everyone to know he was there, insisted upon making a mark so all within earshot would be aware of his existence, of his very prized and multi-award-winning place in the world — something he would further imprint with what he hoped would be utterly manly tire tracks on their little drive. The car was a pathetic plea for attention, and even Roger himself must have known that. Roger Hunt — the hot new kid in town, as he had been once upon a warped time, who became the pot bellied, pot infused, bourgeois bore who now resided next door. Perhaps that's what they gave him, these young men in tiny swimsuits — adoration, a throw back to those days when he himself was the golden child. When rose petals were thrown at his feet and everyone's eyes were stretched so wide as he passed by on a red carpet. Even more importantly, it must be a thrill to toss them aside as he once had, carelessly and without thought, in order to make way for the new, who increasingly cost him more and more in remuneration and otherwise. Of course, one could only be the hot new thing for about ten seconds, it was a reality of Hollywood that both Everett and Roger knew, and it pained him to know that Jeff was just this day realizing it. Everett had seen it all before: a flash in the pan could be spun out into a career for a while if one was lucky and truly talented and not just merely a reflection of someone else's glory. But then before too long, in most cases, you're just another boring, middle aged white man, tossed upon the heap of once headline-grabbing whiz-kids, all feeling around in the dark for their former immortality, for their former selves. Comfort so often trumps ambition and one trick ponies remain ponies, never graduating to full ought mares. Oh, Roger, thought Everett. And OH… *Jeff.* The day crept forward as a brazen strip of sunlight moved slowly across the room.

"So - what are your plans now?" With the exception of various cleaning people, it had been years since another breathing human being set foot inside his beachfront home. Everett shied away from visitors, having strived for the achievement of solitude for so long. He had long ago paid his dues at Hollywood soirees and studio screenings, backlot gossip and insider folklore. He had earned the right to his private meetings with the sea. But oddly, now that it had happened, now that another person had invaded his kingdom, welcome or not, he was finding that he rather enjoyed it. Hungover or not, there was a familiarity from what seemed like another lifetime in sharing the air of a morning with the breath of another.

"I called my old roommate. She's gonna come pick me up."

The thought of walking back into his old life didn't thrill Jeff Severin. It would be much like Cinderella returning home from the ball. But he had met no Prince, not this time. People reserved their own judgments about him, of course they did. On the rare occasions that he and Roger ventured out in public together, he could see the sneers, hear the stifled laughter, witness the flat out anger in the eyes of the clothing store attendant, the waiter, the woman who cut Roger's remaining hair every other Thursday. But the truth of the matter was that he was just doing what he needed to do in order to survive. So, he might be clad in form fitting, faded Levi's and a one of a kind designer shirt that hugged his abs. Everyone has to survive; everyone has to use whatever they've been given to do so. He was not without aspirations, however. But now he would return to home base for a while, trading marble bathtubs for a mildew-stained shower stall, running on the beach for working out at the YMCA on Schrader Boulevard. He would have to wake up; it was bound to happen sooner or later, before he could indulge in his next dream.

"She'll be by in about an hour. Okay if I hang around till then?"

"We can have that lesson now, if you like." The moment he said it, Everett felt pathetic and looked away, suddenly fascinated with a paperweight that sat upon the coffee table, which had thankfully not been engulfed by the fire. Although he had always prided himself on his independence, he recalled too well from days gone by what it was like to experience withdrawal alone: a decided awful-ness would soon start to consume him but that could be drowned out with a little continued company. Anything to stave off the bleakness of a day spent waiting for chemicals to depart a bloodstream.

Jeff had hoped for the offer, afraid to bring it up having welshed upon their previous date. "You up for that? You feeling okay?"

Everett imagined that this was only the beginning of what would become normalcy — people younger than himself asking after his health, how he was feeling, if he could still count to ten. It was embarrassing, this decline to infancy, and he knew it only stood to continue over the coming stretch of time. Yet, he *was* somewhat incapacitated this morning. He would have to bore a hole through his own, fierce hangover in order to be in any way functional and make this work. But something about Jeff made him want to do so.

"Sit down," Everett motioned to the piano bench. He stood behind his pupil as his own hands reached forward to place themselves on top of Jeff's. Such smooth and hairless flesh, naturally tan, met with the pale skin of the elder, cracked and wrinkled with a slight shake, weathered from many years at the front lines. Everett and Jeff's fingers depressed a single key together. "See that? That's Middle C. We'll start there."

7

Summer, 1978: Mason City, Iowa

H<small>E WOULD NOT</small> finish the dishes. Something had happened, shifted, the world had turned itself inside out in the span of what was less than an instant. Everett rose from the kitchen table, standing firm upon the orange linoleum floor, and walked quietly into his bedroom. Looking about, he realized that nothing in it truly belonged to him, just things that were on loan and could be reclaimed at any moment by the powers that be. Henry, his loyal sock monkey, a gift from his father in brighter days, was the only thing that was his, and he was nowhere to be found, taken from his possession and surely never to be seen again. If there was a tear to be shed, it was for the loss of Henry, his only defender and witness.

He understood it all. A complete and utter understanding of everything — all that had transpired, his place in the world and the reasoning for it, clarified and he could see it all as plainly as his unmade bed. He was a pawn, a plaything, a burden and sometimes amusement, swatted as a cat paws a toy mouse before burying it behind the sofa when all interest is lost.

He dressed, tied his shoes, put a comb through his thick black hair, and walked out of his bedroom, and then out of the house altogether. It was a beautiful summer morning, the sun had just awakened and a refreshing morning chill lingered. He breathed deeply for the first time in a long while and, retrieving his bicycle from the side of the house where he had left it, walked to the sidewalk. He made it to the edge of their property, to the end of their street, and finally to the main road before climbing aboard and pedaling away. He did not look back.

He picked up speed and the wind swept through his hair. He was free. He had unshackled himself and there was nothing in the world that could make him turn back; not now, not ever. He had no idea where he would go, what he would do, but it mattered little. Nothing could be worse than that which he had already endured.

It didn't take him too long before he left his tiny subdivision altogether and entered downtown, which he had always preferred to the remote outskirts he had once called home. He rode around the Main Street for a while. All of the just-opening shops in what was commonly referred to as "River City," seemed somehow new, filled with things he had never before seen. Even the people who populated the streets of the little town, awakening to this newfound splendor that could not possibly have been limited to himself, seemed like the brand new cast of a familiar television show, their clothes brighter and their smiles broader. He no longer belonged to anyone: freedom made the whole world seem far more vivid.

Parking his bicycle, he wandered through his favorite fancy furniture store for a while, once again imagining that the displays of shiny cherrywood sideboards and glistening mahogany dining tables were a part of his own kingdom. The showroom was empty, the bleary-eyed staff huddled about the hot coffee pot in the back, he knew. He lounged in a leather wingback chair for a while and envisioned the whole of his estate, laid out at his feet, a home that belonged to he and he alone, a goal he was determined he would attain. For now at least, with squinted eyes so the price tags were hidden, he could pretend. He was not afraid as he contemplated his own future. Rather, excitement filled his nearly fourteen-year-old self. He had run away. He was his own person. He answered only to himself.

Dan's Sporting Goods was across the street, a decidedly less glamorous location than his current perch. Gazing beyond the window display of the furniture store and across Washington Street, he could see the headless mannequins clad in sweatshirts belonging to various local sports teams and the randomly arranged camping equipment that populated Dan's storefront. A plan hatched.

He soon found himself wandering the aisles of the little store, a haven for the man's man and a place to whence overextended mothers flocked to obtain Boys Scouts uniforms and soccer jerseys. He was casual and contemplative in his browsing, playing the role of the educated consumer. The people who worked in the store, including Dan himself, whom this morning lingered behind the register rifling through the local newspaper, knew Everett well as he frequently passed the hours in all of the downtown emporiums, killing time but certainly never buying anything.

There had often been "special nights" when Sheila and Mr. Thompson wanted to be alone. As usual, seven dollars was stuffed in his pocket and he was given strict orders not to return until ten o'clock SHARP. They would be in bed by then, but they would be listening intently for his entrance through the side door and heaven help him were he even a minute late; he must hit the sixty second window for his arrival *precisely*. He was not permitted to use the bathroom or turn on any faucets after 10 P.M., however, as the sound of running water in the pipes might keep others in the house awake, so the bathroom was strictly off limits. Jay Thompson thought that rules such as these gave the young man *discipline*, his favorite word in all the English language.

So, given the frequency of nights such as these, Everett Crisp frequently found himself with ample time to waste; he was well practiced at it. He knew the precise amount of time it would take to pedal home from nearly every location in town. Were he ever a few minutes early, he would simply pedal around the sidewalk, humming melodies in his head, before venturing inside at the exact stroke of 10 P.M.

One thing that Dan McGregor, the longtime owner of the shop, had never contemplated, he being so intrigued by his paper or engaged with customers when Everett paid his visits, was that over the years, Everett had wandered into the storeroom on occasion. Indeed, he knew the whole layout of most of the shops, front and back. Nothing intrigued him more than venturing past a heavy swinging door marked with the delightfully inviting words, "Employees Only." Therefore, on this particular morning, Everett swept through the backroom, and, defying his own strong sense of right and wrong, made his way out the employee entrance with a stolen pup tent, making a mental note that one day he would repay Dan McGregor.

He made for his bicycle and sped out of the downtown area, fleeing the scene of the crime before he could be discovered and brought to justice. He felt a sense of guilt, for sure, but was certain that Mr. McGregor, being a decent man as he had observed him to be during the many hours he had lingered in his store, would surely understand had he been provided with all of the details. It was just a small, grey nylon tent, very compact in a cardboard box, and, if he could figure out how to put it together, as he was certain he could, it was to be Everett Crisp's new home. He pointed his bicycle in the direction of the reservoir and the thick and welcoming woods that surrounded it that was to be his new sanctuary. Yes, he would hide amongst the trees in his magical forest. This morning's task was clear: construct a new home, a space that would be completely of his own making, no matter how small or makeshift. It would be the second step in his own personal evolution.

Fall, 1998: New York City

The water hurled him downstream. The rapids were far larger than he was. On either side of him he could see them, looming dozens of feet above his own head. The rest of his body was consumed in a ferocious white river that occasionally dragged him under, choking his breath. He fought his way to the surface for quick gulps of air and to glimpse the land on either side of him passing by before he could make out where he was, furiously twisting his head in every direction. Something loomed up ahead, he could feel it; something terrible and demanding pulled all of this, himself, the water, forward. Turning his soaking wet head, he looked helplessly through the spray for something to grasp hold of: a rock, a branch; but there was nothing. His fate was unavoidable now, as the sound of the water rushing in his ears grew louder and louder still. Finally, it was deafening, a level of volume one would associate with being trapped inside of a jet engine. And now he could see himself from above. He was a dot, a floating speck swept far away by the dangerous current, clearly angry in its fixed determination to deliver him to whatever lie ahead and completely apathetic to his own pleas for survival, as nature so often is.

A glance up ahead revealed the falls — millions of gallons of powerful water swept over a sharp ledge with grand ferocity, plunging at least a mile to the basin below. The sheer magnitude of it was more than he could digest. It was in these monstrous falls that Everett would reach his end and cease to exist; the chair in which he had always cautiously leaned back in a constant state of teeter would finally hit the ground and carry his body right along with it. He looked up at the crystal blue sky, the peaceful part of nature, so unlike the violence of the crashing grey and white rapids which would drag him to his death in mere moments, beautifully soaring birds his only witness. How would it feel to be submerged and plummeting simultaneously? Once at the bottom, were he somehow to survive, the force of the falling water would pummel him deep beneath the lagoon, to the very core of the Earth perhaps. It was inevitable now, this world that surrounded him, this air, this breeze, this sky — he would see no more.

Everett Crisp shot straight up in bed with a sharp intake of air. He was saturated in sweat, it dripped from every pore of his body, yet he shivered as the cold night air met his fevered face and sent a shiver throughout the entirety of his body. A moment passed as he took in his surroundings. Yes, his own Brooklyn bedroom, his own wooden dresser from the rummage sale with the cracked mirror above it, his own things, scattered coins, an old manually wound clock he had had for years. The subway rattled the windows through which he could see the bright yellow illuminated circle identifying the N train. People were coming and going. He was not alone. He was in Brooklyn, and he was safe for the moment.

A hand grasped his shoulder but Everett barely felt it as he struggled to decipher fact from fiction. "You had it again, didn't you?" Jamie held him in a firm grasp — Everett needed most of all to feel that he was upon solid ground, safe, part of reality, as he groggily came out of his recurring nightmare. "It's okay. Tell me about it. Did you fall this time?"

"No." Part of Everett was disappointed. He usually made it to this part of the dream, only to wake right before the major event itself. He yearned, in a way, to see the rest of the story, to see what happens next. But someone had once told him that if one were to fall in a dream, jump out of the airplane, go over the falls, tango off a building, — one would, indeed, never wake up.

Jamie was sitting up now, both arms around his lover, who sat drenched in perspiration and shaking. Jamie's own cotton pajamas were joined with Everett's bare chest, which housed a heart that was beating nearly outside his skin. "You're safe." He kissed Everett on the top of his wet head, slowly and with great care. Then, gently, with the outstretched tips of his fingers upon his chin, Jamie turned Everett's scared and weary face toward his own to look directly into those watery and bloodshot eyes. "It wasn't your fault."

Autumn, 1989: Cambridge, MA

Jamie White had begun to contemplate his life alone. There was a great deal expected of him, and he would not disappoint. But were there to be no one person in particular by his side, perhaps that wouldn't be the worst thing. He was drowning in friends, acquaintances and well-wishers, and certainly more than a fair share of family. Indeed, they inundated him and seemed to thrive in the shadow of his energy, his charm, and this had always pleased him. But still, in actuality, he was every bit as lonely at Harvard as he had been growing up in Connecticut. Connecticut, he reasoned, for all of its upper-crustedness and swimming pool/cocktail hour refinement, was perhaps the loneliest state in the world, or at least that had been his experience. The boy with the blonde locks and the well defined jaw line he saw as he gazed into the mirror would eventually morph into a mature man, a man perhaps all too much like his father.

It was clear that whatever wild whim of a fantasy in which he had momentarily allowed himself to indulge was over. The pleasure of a dream is temporary, and this one had come to a screeching, cold water-in-the-face conclusion. Therefore, he would simply throw himself back into his studies and concentrate on the law, where he knew his most promising future could be found. He bit down on the eraser end of his pencil, and tried to decipher what exactly Professor Deakins was on about today.

The lecture hall sat nearly two hundred students. The Professor took special note this morning that Mr. White and Mr. Crisp could be found at opposite ends of the auditorium. He had watched throughout the semester as Jamie, even while accompanied by his entourage of scrubbed clean, young academic friends, all children of great statesmen or well to do industrialists, always seemed to find a way to settle himself in the same vicinity of young Everett Crisp, the black-haired outcast. Yet today, to his surprise, he found Jamie White all the way to his right, and Everett Crisp all the way left. He watched carefully at the conclusion of his lecture to see what would happen. As he suspected, Everett bolted for the door the moment class was adjourned. Jamie, whom the Professor observed with a keen eye, watched longingly as Mr. Crisp left the hall. In the few moments it took Mr. Crisp to gather his things and hastily make his exit, Mr. White drank in each and every movement of his body, the curvature of his spine and the ramshackle black sweater that hung loosely about his thin torso. The way Mr. Crisp aggressively clicked his ballpoint pen shut and meticulously avoided Mr. White's glance prior to his abrupt exit told Roger Deakins all he needed to know. Mr. White's careful study of Mr. Crisp lasted only moments of recorded time, on this particular day, before he returned his glance to his own notepad, head hung low. Obviously, some tremendous sea of resentment had bubbled up between his two young scholars and Roger Deakins was intrigued, certainly more so than he was by anything he had to impart about the law that day.

Professor Deakins had seen a great deal in his twenty plus years of law instruction. At times, the young love and rampant hormones that bounced off the walls of his lecture hall inspired him to surprise his wife, Emily, in the evening, returning home with flowers or just a special lilt in his step. He loved the law, it was true, but at times, the subtext that populated his own classroom was far more interesting, intoxicating, even, than double jeopardy or ex post facto.

"Mr. White, a moment?" Jamie was caught stone-faced. He had never been summoned before the judge, called to the principal, as it were. He looked up from the nearly undecipherable notes he had jotted down over the past two hours as the hall emptied, and soon it was just the two of them, professor and squire, alone in the cavernous hall.

"Sir?"

"I wonder if I might make a special request of you?" Professor Deakins studied the face of his confused young student. Heartbreak was writ large in the pupils of his eyes. Despite his gruff exterior, the Professor had always felt a certain responsibility for those placed in his care, a kind of carefully disguised guidance for the young people of his classroom. Sometimes it had been effective and others not, but it was always spoken through the code of law. He had seen all too frequently the misguided relationships; the roadblocks he knew would exist that just could not be avoided, knowing his students far better than they thought he did. Try as he might, all he could do was offer a nudge in the right direction, a peak into the last page of the court transcript.

A few moments of silence passed between them, before Professor Deakins, eyes steady, soldiered onward, knowing for sure that it was the right thing to do. The wrinkles beneath his eyes spoke volumes of his collected wisdom, and Jamie felt nervous if not flattered to be in the presence of such a great man, as though standing before the Great Owl.

"I'm taking on two new interns at my practice this semester. We have several new cases and we need some capable researchers. I thought you might be up for the job?" The professor spoke with calm yet direct intonation. A professional demeanor was of course the most effective way to break through to this particular student, he knew. He had read his papers, scored his examinations, listened as the other professors yammered on about the Senator's son at various faculty events. But today, he looked into the eyes of a young man in love, and he wanted desperately to provide instruction that could not be found in law books. He himself had once been Jamie White, dancing around his great love until she was almost beyond his reach, before coming to his senses. Loving Emily, not the law, had been the great passion of his life, the very thing that provided the motor of his existence. If he could provide that lesson to someone as mixed up and curious as young Mr. White, well then — perhaps he was the instructor he had always hoped he might be.

Jamie White smiled for the first time in what had been days. He was instantly flattered and was sure this would be just the thing to jolt him back to reality, back to B.E. — "Before Everett." Not only that, it would make his father proud. His face lit up; it seemed as though the sun were coming out.

"I'd be delighted, sir. Thank you." He was almost breathless. "But, if I may —." Jamie stopped short, fearing he might sound ungrateful.

"Yes?"

"Why *me*?" Jamie knew all too well what it was like to be sought after merely for his lineage. While he hoped this wasn't the case with the Professor, and indeed suspected it was not, if he didn't ask he would always wonder.

"Why not you? Don't you think you're a talented young lawyer?" Silence hung in the air. Jamie had never been totally sure about this. He trusted his ability to be a great student, but to actually practice real law... the thought was as overwhelming as it was intriguing.

"I have faith in you, Mr. White, it's time you got some in yourself." The Professor stood and returned his attention to his own notes, packing them up and stuffing them inside his leather briefcase while fastening the brass clasps. "Oh, and *Mr. Crisp* is joining the team, as well. You have met Mr. Crisp before? I'm never sure who knows who... I think you'll get along well, though." The warm green of his eyes met with the perplexed brilliant blue of his student's. Years of knowledge formed the numerous lines that sat also upon the professor's forehead, as opposed to the taught, tan skin that resided north of Jamie White's crystal corneas.

It all came raining down upon Jamie's head now. Of course, the professor would have noticed, someone was bound to. Courtrooms were all about the observance of *behavior*. But if he had known all along, who else had?

The Professor's job was complete — he had set the ball rolling down the lane, sure to strike at least a few pins. He had read Mr. Crisp's papers, as well, scored both of their examinations and knew, intrinsically, that the two were more than well matched. Oh, the heated debates and arguments that were sure to ensue, and this brought a slight smirk to his face that he struggled to erase. There was a white hot history just burning to happen between Mr. Crisp and Mr. White and, if it needed a little prodding, well, — that was just part of his job.

But for now: his hat, the door; there was no longer a visual acknowledgement of the young council, he had played his part. He placed his tweed cap atop his head and was almost out before turning back to Jamie. There was a shared understanding between them, a fatherly kindness that Jamie had never known. Jamie White was charmed by his professor, but it would have to go unspoken, merely *inferred*. "Thank you, sir. I won't let you down."

"I'm sure you won't, Mr. White. Good day." Professor Roger Deakins made his exit from the classroom, feeling more accomplished than usual, as though he had been a truly effective instructor upon this particular day. He turned his attentions to Emily now, whom was somewhat overdue, he reasoned.

Summer, 1978: Mason City, Iowa

He was hungry. He knew that eventually he would be, of course, and sure enough, here it was: real hunger and it was barely noon. It was too early and too far to pedal all the way back into town to scavenge for food just yet; he figured it would be easier to do so under the cover of darkness. Eventually, he realized, he would need to learn to hunt, perhaps, and identify the berries and flowers of the woods that were edible. There were, after all, no fish to be found in the reservoir.

Utter silence surrounded him, and he basked in this. Occasionally, a woodpecker bore his beak into a tree or a light breeze drifted through the leaves, but otherwise, it was perfectly silent in his new oasis. He even befriended the spiders and ladybugs, his new neighbors. There was no fear, as he was so accustomed to feeling, no dreaded sense that at any moment the bottom could fall out of everything.

He had built the tent, constructed his new home according to the directions, and it was the most beautiful thing he had ever seen. It belonged to him; it was a space in which he would create his own rules. Climbing inside, he stretched out along the nylon, beneath which he could feel the scattered twigs and roots that lie just beneath upon the hard ground. He had constructed the tent on a slight slope, so were he to lie one way, his feet would be elevated, the other, his head. It all seemed quite practical. All around him was the scent of new which, mingled with the fragrance of nature, of the pines and the air, radiated around his newly unpackaged home. He breathed it in as deeply as he could, breathed in what would be his new existence at the edge of the wood. There would be no one to answer to this summer, and beyond that, not ever again.

Later this evening, he would scout around downtown for a blanket, some essentials, some matches and water and things. When he woke from his nap, perhaps he would gather some firewood and teach himself to build a fire. But for now, he zipped up the hatch of his new dwelling and drifted off to sleep. Although he missed his monkey and his music, his warm companion and the entrancing sounds that had nightly crept through his headphones, he was at peace. He would create his own music now, drawn from his own tranquility. Everett Crisp was content for the first time in a long, long while.

Winter, 1999: New York City

Jamie White had a project in Everett Crisp. He was a complicated puzzle of a man, and he had taken it upon himself to find the pieces and put them all back together again in the correct order. He was fully aware that most other mates wouldn't have bothered, would long ago have thrown up their hands in despair. But Everett was like a good mystery novel, and Jamie demanded to know the ending. Curiosity aside, in reuniting with Everett he felt much like an archeologist upon an important dig, having unearthed the world's most important gem which he would keep private and to himself for at least a little while as he dusted it off and admired it, preparing it for public consumption, which he knew was inevitable.

What Jamie liked so much about the Brooklyn apartment was its simplicity. Just a bed, a dresser, a worn out piano, a collapsable kitchen table and a few odds and ends populated the sparse rooms with its mostly bare, grey walls. An old sofa that Everett had collected from the Salvation Army and an odd shag rug sat in the living room. Two milk crates and a warped piece of wood provided a kind of makeshift coffee table. There was a charm to it. It was a scene, a way of living, that Jamie had never in his life witnessed, and it was attractive to him. It was invitingly ramshackle. It was home.

He slept in Brooklyn most of the time now, only visiting the cold and intimidating apartment high above Lincoln Center, the one that had been provided for him by the firm, every now and then. Everett would be home from The Pillow Factory soon, and Jamie had just beat him through the door. In anticipation of Everett's arrival, he lit a few candles that would cozy up the place against the backdrop of the rainy weather that continued to deluge Brooklyn on this particular evening.

Everett was an exceedingly private man, a bottle bulging with secrets yet with a very firm and tightly placed iron cork. It was only during his drunken rants that glimpses of truth came out, so Jamie wasn't entirely displeased when a new bottle of scotch appeared in the kitchen, or he worked a double at The Pillow Factory. He was a heavy drinker, it was true, but not a constant one anymore. Jamie would never remind Everett of all he had said while drowned in alcohol and he knew that Everett had no recollection of the events ever taking place, so it hardly mattered. However, piece by piece, throughout the year or so of their rekindled relationship, the full man was revealing himself. Much like a Polaroid snapshot that develops slowly when exposed to oxygen and sunlight, the smog was vanishing from the corners.

It had been somehow impressed upon Everett Crisp at an early age that there was a certain rottenness to him: an idea gone bad, a spoiled dessert. Therefore, to his reasoning, he had grown into a rotten adult. Try as he might, some level of badness surely enveloped the core of himself, swirling about like billows of dark smoke that he could not ever eradicate. At some point early in his years, he had been stamped that way with permanent ink right across his body, impossible to cleanse. He was lost in his own, self-imposed storm, and Jamie fancied himself somewhat of a lighthouse, although he would never admit such sentimentality to his acerbic partner.

The storm saturated Brooklyn and the whole city over. Everett sloshed through the door in his worn leather jacket and the loafers Jamie knew had holes in the bottom, so his toes and socks would surely be underwater by now. Jamie could tell simply by the way he heard him walking up the stairs, the aggressive way in which he placed his key in the lock and turned the doorknob, then took his time entering the apartment, that his mind was somewhat lubricated. He had only played the early shift but Maria had surely kept him in scotch throughout the hours that followed. Pouring himself a drink, a somber Everett proceeded to reveal his elaborate plans for suicide via slurred words. Oh, tonight was sure to be a bad one.

Frightening though it was to hear, Jamie had learned not to take these episodes personally. Rather, he pressed on for details. Talking to Everett when he was in this state was like peering into a crystal ball, or struggling to see what comes next in a dream before one wakes. All the locks had been temporarily removed. Eventually, of course, Everett would simply talk in circles and it became useless, but there was a certain point, a level in his inebriation and the resulting inhibition that could prove useful.

Everett had planned it all since he was a mere child, felt the imaginary cold barrel of a pistol against his pale skin. Something about the light that went out of Everett's eyes as he gave every detail of his exit from this Earth assured Jamie that this was a carefully choreographed ballet that Everett liked to dance from time to time. Still, it must have been something of a release for him, as odd as it all was. To cast aside all that had troubled him since before he had ever met the man, the heavy, crippling load he had seen him cart about the Earth with him all this time, a weight that sometimes darkened his eyes and buckled his knees, must have been a kind of ecstasy for Everett; to simply turn the lights out once and for all and lie down, done with it, cast free from it all.

"I always had so much to do... I always had so much to accomplish. I was in such a *race.*" He slurped down what was left in his glass, an action which seemed to have an immediate effect. "But I never accomplished any of it. Not one damn thing." He refilled his glass with straight scotch and gazed out the window at the cracked sidewalk below, dimly illuminated by the street light, and at the neighboring Brooklynites scurrying through the storm, shoddy umbrellas twisted in the wind. A mighty oak tree decimated the walkway, roots bursting through the cement and reaching upward, exposed, drinking in the soothing relief of rain water. Perhaps they just wanted to be heard, or at least seen; to have staked their claim upon the world and told it, demanded validation that they, in fact, had been there. Perhaps they were just thirsty.

Silence passed as Jamie stared at the man he was certain was the great love of his life, although he'd never express it in words. Anyone else would flatly refuse to lie in his bed of pity, but there was something about climbing inside of Everett's soggy yet brilliant brain that thrilled if not flattered him. The flicker of candles crossed both of their faces as Jamie picked up stacks of paper from the lip of the worn down, upright piano, badly in need of tuning, and boldly placed them in front of Everett. "Look at all of these," he showed Everett his own scattered papers, thousands of lines of staff paper scrawled with an intricate series of notes and symbols, page after page filled with his own music. He held up the piles of half-finished compositions that populated the dilapidated instrument that sat by the window, as rain hurled itself against the glass. "This is all real. It's all real stuff. It exists. It's yours."

"You know what's real? The contents of this glass. It's real, it exists. It's not any of that. Those aren't real, they're just lead marks on some stupid paper." He downed the contents of the rocks glass in one single gulp. "And this is so real, that when it runs out, it comes back, it's reborn with the pour, and the whole damn broken train just lunges forward again." He made train noises as he reached for the bottle once more. *Wo-oh-wo!*

"Don't drink anymore. Not tonight. I like it when you just talk to me."

"It's never gonna come. For me. Never gonna come for me — the good train, the right train, the *silver bullet*, you know. Not gonna happen. It was a lark. A stupid — a stupid *nothing*... Just like me." He waltzed about the room with his glass, how blurred and altered it must all look to him, Jamie knew, perhaps even frightening. But something about the weight of a filled rocks glass grounded him, gave him an odd kind of security.

"But what do you know about that? You've done it all, haven't you? Mr. Tweed. Mr. Silk Tie," he slathered, tossing Jamie's tie over his shoulder as he was still dressed from work. Here it came: the accusations. Just when it started to get ugly was usually when Jamie called it quits for the night, but this evening he would press on.

"What *is* it, Ev? Tell me." Jamie was certain that if he could just pull out whatever enormous splinter had lodged itself so deeply within Everett that after all the blood and pain, there would be solace; at long last, there would be healing and a scar to wear with pride. But there was only silence, broken by the clinking of Everett's ice cubes, a melodious sound Everett had always loved and even caused him to grin a little when he heard it. "*Tell me.*"

"I'm gonna go to bed. Maybe I won't wake up." He made for the bedroom but was blocked by Jamie's body. "What are you doing slumming it in Brooklyn, anyway? Why don 'cha go back to your penthouse and take a dip in the indoor swimming pool or something, hmm? Get outta my way. Riffraff comin' through!"

"*Tell me.*" More silence, and for the briefest of flashes, Jamie knew that the real Everett had made an appearance. Everett stood before him, looking slightly down upon Jamie's insistent face. He was wobbly and consumed by the stench of scotch, but was the same man Jamie had first watched from afar across a grassy square in Cambridge, and followed around campus just to observe for a while. The same man whose exact scholastic schedule he had learned so that he might enroll in many of the same classes. He took Everett's hand, the first hand to touch his body with real warmth as it had so long ago. A tear welled in his eye. Everett stood utterly naked and without camouflage.

"Someone died." It was always a monumental thing for Everett to admit. Little did Jamie know that he had relived it, always and only to himself, many thousands of times throughout the past many years.

"Who?" Jamie's bright blue eyes bored into the retinas of one mysterious Mr. Everett Crisp. This was it, he was certain — this must be the key to it all and he was determined to get it. There was a long pause.

"*Me.*"

"No, you didn't. You're still right here. Everett Crisp is still *right here.*" Everett's glassy eyes gazed at his opponent and there was love — respect, even, which is frequently far greater than love. Yes, perhaps Everett had died a little bit along the way, but the core of him, the shiny diamond in the middle of so much rough, was still there and brightly illuminated, Jamie could see it so clearly. He reached out for this forlorn and deeply troubled man, but Everett resisted his touch.

"It wasn't your fault."

"What are you talking — *stop it.*"

"It wasn't your fault." In an instant, Jamie understood. Everett blamed himself for all of it. Always had. What a crushing anvil to cart around with a person. Jamie's heart broke in that moment, like he never knew that it could.

"Stop," Everett averted his eyes and was suddenly fascinated with the warped wooden floor. There was an utter starkness to the exchange as fear crossed Everett's face and for a moment, the profound hurt he always went through life trying to mask unhid itself.

"It wasn't your fault." This time, the back of Jamie's hand made gentle contact with Everett's face, where he rested it, secretly wishing that whatever pain that existed within this man could somehow flow out, transfer itself to his own body where he would dispose of it. Jamie kept his eyes locked upon Everett's, hoping that the dam might finally break.

"I'm going to bed." Everett quickly buried all of it right back where it had come from, right beneath the thin layer of his very own skin. He was finished for tonight, having turned his back on it all. "You can come to bed if you want, but remember, we all sleep alone."

"That's very profound." Jamie called after him, disappointed as he usually was after these little fireside chats. "Who said that? Proust?"

"Cher."

And the lights were out for the night.

Autumn, 1989: Cambridge, MA

Every night for a week, Everett would look up from his piano to find Jamie White perched in the corner of Bridget's, sipping his stupid lemon drop. Just like clockwork, at the start of his second set, just as he paused for a sip of scotch, he'd see him over by the door by himself, trying to fit in and act casual, and trying harder to make eye contact with the man behind the Steinway. Everett had long ago learned the art of the blind stare: looking in someone's general direction without looking them in the eye, so that it might look as though he were glancing at something else, all the while carefully exploring the vicinity. He had worn his glasses this evening, silly little Jamie. Everett had seen him wear them that unfortunate morning in his campus apartment when he flopped about in his silk robe and all but proposed marriage. He must have reasoned that his spectacles made him look sophisticated and therefore more apt to the crowd at Bridget's. And actually, Everett had to admit, they did, sitting just beneath his carefully quaffed hair and against his tan skin and utterly wrinkle-less eyes.

He quickly raced his fingers back to the piano and launched into anything; just something he could play off the top of his head and would require his immediate attention in the event that Jamie should wander over and try to make conversation. He had nothing to say to him, it had all been said. The young man had placed his heart in his hands and Everett just couldn't have that. Eventually he would fuck it up, he would hurt him terribly; it always went that way. Everett Crisp fancied himself built for the very purpose of destruction, certainly not one to be the subject of a boy's adolescent crush. He had seen far too much already and shouldn't Jamie be left alone to figure it all out on his own? It was his duty to be the grown up for one still so wet behind the ears.

And so, he would just keep playing, segue from one medley to another, terribly busy at the piano and concentrating without let up. Eventually, Jamie would leave, only to return at precisely the same time the following evening. It was very nearly infuriating.

But on this particular evening, Jamie White got up and approached the piano, much like legal council approaches the bench. Oh, fuck, here he came. Everett kept playing, keeping his eyes glued to the keys. He could smell the familiar scent of Jamie's cologne now, there was something almost comforting about the familiarity of it. He hit crescendo after crescendo upon the keys, making it all up as he went along, louder and louder still: a cacophony of complicated notes. His playing grew so intense that the patrons of Bridget's began to look up from their cocktails to stare in concern and bewilderment at the man at the keys, clearly suffering a musical attack of some sort. Bridget herself, nestled in the back of the room, looked up from her olive laden martini.

Then, suddenly, amid the hurricane of music, there was nothing. Jamie and the smell of him were gone, and Everett's hands froze upon the keys. Daring to look up, he could see Jamie's wisp of dirty blonde hair as he darted out the front door. At that very moment, Everett realized that for the first time in perhaps his entire life, he had stopped playing mid composition. Silence filled the night air of the little Cambridge bar for a good, long while. Time stood still as Everett tried to put the pieces together. It hadn't happened after all; the bomb hadn't dropped, Jamie had left. Exactly what was he playing at?

Seeing all eyes on him, Everett quickly returned to his playing with embarrassment, a calm sort of improvisational jazz now, music that could easily fade into the paneling of the walls, the same place to whence he wished he might escape just now. Within a few moments, thankfully, the crowd at Bridget's resumed their casual conversations. Bartenders crushed mint leaves, young women accompanied each other to the ladies room, young men criticized their professors and misquoted Keats, and the world spun forward.

After some time had passed and normalcy had infused the room, Everett glanced up again to look around, just to assure himself that he was no longer the subject of attention. His relief was reflected in his playing as the slow jazz morphed into something more melodic, harmonious and even slightly upbeat.

But still, something was different. Ah, yes, his glass tip jar, which usually sat at the edge of the piano empty, had a visitor. Something had been placed inside. Not currency, of course, that seldom occurred, but a small white slip of paper. As the composer of the composition, it was his right to end it abruptly, and so he did. Reaching forward for the glass jar, he of course already knew the identity of the author, he only hoped it wouldn't be written with random letters in various typefaces cut individually from magazines like a ransom note from an infatuated admirer. It read:

"Do you like me? Circle one: Yes. No. Maybe."

It was cute, there was no way to deny it, Jamie's grade-school plea for attention. Here was a person who had the attention of everyone on campus, all of his professors, the envy of the entire ivy-league, the one to watch, the boy wonder but none of that was good enough for James White. No, he craved the attention of this one, lonely piano player.

But what really infuriated Everett was that, gazing down at that slip of paper and admiring its originality and even the formality of the handwriting, he knew the answer to the question.

Summer, 1978: Mason City, Iowa

He woke in the woods with a chill. For an early summer evening, it had turned unexpectedly cold and he had not left his former residence with so much as a light jacket. No matter. His new life would require a certain amount of bravery. These would be his humble beginnings, and he was determined that, eventually, only greatness would emerge from them. However, first things were most decidedly first: survival.

He zipped up the entry to his tent and began his tentative journey back into town upon his bicycle. He hated to leave the security of the woods, the branches had become his disguise and he felt even colder outside the confines of their company, much like leaving a warm bed on a cold and unfriendly weekday morning. The wind picked up and blew across his bare legs as he pedaled, and something about it all just felt wrong. The street lamps were already ignited and could that be? Yes, the slight fall of raindrops upon his bare arms; scant, yet a precursor and a warning. He would soldier onward, storm be damned, he had little choice. Whatever was thrown at him, he would survive, and emerge all the stronger, he was certain of it.

He had boldly hoped to make a return visit to Dan's Sporting Goods. Surely his theft from earlier this morning could not be traced to him, the young man who had spent so much time lingering amongst the products throughout the years, barely tall enough to see the tops of the shelves, yet who always left empty handed. But both the main entrance and the employee door were locked. He had better luck in the alley behind the Left Bank restaurant. Years of observation had taught him that the proprietors of this establishment routinely threw out large quantities of uneaten food each evening, simply tossed into the passageway in large brown trash bags for the sanitation workers to remove to some nearby landfill.

The Left Bank was a more upscale establishment and therefore did scant business in a rural town of this size, particularly during the week. This wasn't the first time that Everett had made off with a few uneaten pieces of chicken parmesan or neglected bits of garlic bread, perfectly preserved within the plastic bags as though a packaged meal just for him. Tonight, he was particularly grateful for the nourishment as he ate quietly, a block or so away, behind the backdoor of Sally's card shop, in the event that any stray Left Bank employee might wander into the alley and discover him. He saved most of the bread for breakfast, wrapping it back in the tin foil and placing it in his pocket, as he went about seeking something that might keep him warm for what would be a rainy evening.

They must be plotting his punishment right about now. What would it be this time? What creative new scoldings were they dreaming up? He had been locked in a closet, "accidentally" burned with a cigarette, left on the side of the road and ordered to pay them back his meager allowance when he broke one of their 10,000 rules. He had promised himself that morning, as he strode away with his bicycle, that he would not ever think of them again, never allow the thought of his former captors to dance across his memory. The times he had been humiliated, hit, shoved, lectured and worst of all, ignored entirely might dissolve into the ocean of his memory one day. However, at present, they were there just the same. It bothered him to think that they would probably always be there, in a way, branded upon him. He would always look at the world in a different way having known Sheila and Jay Thompson, and this made him angry. Something about the pair of them would remain unavoidably burned into the insides of his eyelids forever.

They never would have considered that he would actually have had the courage to run away, this spineless, timid, egotistical, fat and spoiled little boy. He knew that they were certain they would find him banging on the locked front door any minute, seeking shelter from the rain, while they decided how long to let him bang before allowing him entrance to their private abode, in order to administer what would be his most severe punishment yet. It must be delighting them, right at this very moment, he thought, dreaming up what it would be, as they sat next to each other in front of the television, he with his greasy popcorn in a brown paper bag from the grocery, and she with countless glasses of white wine, as a sportscaster blared from the set about who was better than whom.

What had happened to Jay Thompson? He couldn't help but wonder as he pushed his bicycle from block to block, looking for anything that might be useful along the side of the street or in a trash receptacle. He was not yet capable of feeling remorse or sorrow for Mr. Thompson, all six feet two of him with his prematurely silver hair that sat glumly above Coke bottle thick bifocals, and doubted that he ever would. Yet, something vicious and evil had clearly destroyed him somewhere along the way, perhaps even at Everett's own very young age. Something, be it a thing that caused an immediate transformation or a something that had chipped away at him little by little, had overtaken him, made him into the monster who had grown so large that he would eventually envelope his own mother and, until recently, himself. Everett had put a stop to the infection that morning, or so he thought, by running away; a feat of which he was certainly proud. He declared himself emancipated, a sovereign nation of his own, where he would rule as King forever. He would now abandon fear and trudge boldly forward if he were to survive. Yet still he wondered, what could it have been? No one comes into the world a fully formed asshole.

A flash of lightening was followed in not so lengthy succession by a loud clap of thunder. The storm grew far closer, the sky now an unrecognizable palate of dark colors, bleeding into each other with the wants of the wind. It was time to head back to his new home, the threatening sky told him so as though it were warning him of the consequences of his own sinful actions. He had been successful in obtaining dinner, collecting some garlic bread for breakfast and confiscating a man's black trench coat which he had regretfully swiped from the unattended coat rack inside the front door of the Left Bank when the hostess had turned her back to seat a young couple. While there was a wallet in the front breast pocket, there was no money or anything at all, really, with the exception of used Kleenex, anywhere within the garment, he lamented. However, the wallet carried a small slip of identification behind a scant piece of plastic: Mr. Walter Able, 333 Windsor Ln. This small bounty would have to do for the evening. He would try again tomorrow, and God bless Mr. Walter Able for wearing a raincoat in late summer. He would not forget.

Once he had pedaled safely out of downtown and made it back to the main road that led to the woods, he donned the coat to shield himself from the rain that had begun to fall in bigger drops and with greater frequency. Soon, it was pouring; water fell from the sky in great buckets, making it difficult to see ahead of him through the grey fog that enveloped the whole town. Cars raced past him, their bright headlights illuminating what seemed like a monsoon. At last he veered his bicycle into the woods, his own sanctuary, the trails of which were now mostly mud, rendering pedaling useless. Getting off to push his bike through the storm, he slipped in the wet, black pudding of ground and fell, coating himself and Mr. Able's coat in sloppy, rain-infused mud. What's more, he landed flatly atop the garlic bread, his morning meal, which had sat safely in the dry breast pocket. Everett could feel a tear or two in his eyes, but fought them back. He would not give in, he would persevere in the face of adversity. His own self was all the comfort he would ever require.

Finally, making his way up the tree-lined hill and back down the other side, he spotted his newly erected shelter over by the large oak near the water's edge. Peering through the storm, it seemed the most welcoming thing he had seen all year. It stood strong and erect in the rain, an oasis belonging only to Everett that would shelter him. Home. Back inside his own few square feet, his personal air. He stripped himself of his muddy things, knowing he could wash them in the reservoir in the morning, when things would undoubtedly look better, and hang them from trees to dry. For this evening, he would huddle naked and chilled to the bone, wrapped beneath the inside lining of the black London Fog rain coat which had so recently belonged to the thankfully extra large Mr. Able who had been the unfortunate victim of his thievery. He would make it up to everyone whom he had wronged one day. But for tonight, he would shiver inside his tent which lay upon the hard, damp ground, protected by the fortress of his own construction, and dream of the brighter days that undoubtedly lie just ahead, nearly within reach, as the storm pounded down all around him.

8

Fall, 2026: Malibu, CA

JEFF SEVERIN'S HAIR smelled of youth. Not extreme youth, not the sickening sweetness that so many find appealing — the smell of babies, for example. But leaning into him ever so slightly, depressing the young man's hands upon the keys, Everett breathed in the scent of innocence, what's right next to cluelessness, mingled with a certain well-worn masculinity; a scent that seemed to say that Jeff Severin was his own person and danced to his own music. If his good looks could be captured in a scent, it would surely be that of the clean and golden fragrance of his dirty blonde locks of hair. He was kissed by the sun in nearly every way.

After they had gone over some basic scales, it became less of a lesson and more an interview. Everett, almost embarrassingly, was charmed by the young man's interest in his work, in the films of his past of which he had nearly succeeded in forgetting. When seated together on the bench, his finely pressed trousers rested next to his student's bare, tan calfs, the sight of which could have been a not-so-abstract painting. Eventually, of course, the conversation steered itself to his current projects, which was enough to make Everett distance himself from the piano and consider a drink, but instead he just depressed a series of bass keys. Drinking through the wretchedness of a hangover was a trick from the old days, and he remembered it well. So — here he was again.

The film. The blasted, stupid thing he regretted taking on. The phone would be ringing again soon enough, there was no avoiding it. He had signed the paper, taken the money; he was contractually obligated to do it, a ghastly bore of a flick, devoid of coherent story, starring whomever Hollywood's it people of the moment were. If only he could find an in, something relatable, something that could get him putting notes to paper; but nothing came. He had scarcely written a note of the melody, there was no theme, let alone an orchestration, and what he had managed to scribble down made its way into the fire the night previous. He was unprepared for perhaps the first time, living in real life the recurring dream that so many have of going to take the final exam without having read any of the books nor attended any of the lectures, or of appearing on stage knowing none of the appropriate lines. And he didn't care. It was meaningless work, after all, and he had composed a lifetime's worth of that.

An awkward silence filled the room as Everett settled himself on the sofa and lit a cigarette. Their conversation of the morning, which up to that point had been effortless, had run dry and a slight air of tension was present. Jeff, who remained at the piano, had been shuffling through the pages that lingered upon the lip, searching for an excuse to stay just a while longer. "This looks pretty complex. This is the film?"

"No. That's what — that's the real me," he gestured with his cigarette.

"For a new movie?" Jeff excitedly flipped through the many pages.

"It's a concerto, for a symphony," he said it almost apologetically, like revealing to his young squire his true identity. Masks off.

"I didn't know you wrote those —"

"I don't. I was going to once, but then — well. It doesn't matter." Everett, extinguishing his half-smoked cigarette in the Waterford ashtray which sat upon the glass coffee table, headed for the kitchen in search of ice, which soon found its way, clinking, into a fine crystal rocks glass. The first of the afternoon.

A lengthy lecture about the seduction of Hollywood and money would just be cliché and he had no desire to bore the boy. Besides, it all seemed clear in the silence that lingered anyway. It was the symphony — the concerto — that lately drew his attention. It was the piece he had been in training for his whole life and, just that season, amid the waves and seagulls of eroding Malibu, ironically, had begun to spill itself onto paper. Some of what he had written had also gone up in the flames of the night previous and that was all well and good. It wasn't quite good enough, not perfect enough. But the theme was strong within him and he knew that when he got it right, and he *would* get it right, it would be his greatest effort, a legacy of sorts even if no one ever heard it; which in all likelihood, they would not.

"Play me some of it." Jeff thrilled at the idea of being perhaps the first to hear a new composition, the first ears to absorb what would undoubtedly become famous. What Everett could never admit, of course, was that he felt much the same way about Jeff — he being the first to truly appreciate someone who was going to make his mark one way or another. One could say that young men such as Jeff are a dime a dozen in LA, but there was something truly captivating about this one, important and genuine, and it had taken the events of the past stretch of hours for him to realize it. Jeff was his well-kept secret for the moment. The world would surely have its way with him before too long, but for this morning, contained within his own sun-streaked living room, he was his.

Everett took the sheets of music from Jeff's youthful hands and settled himself beside him in front of the keys, his own leg once again pressed up against his pupil's on the bench. He paused, centered himself, found the pedals, then let lose with the first several notes. It was quiet and solitary at first, a simple stretch of music that cleared the slate and eloquently restarted the day. Everett glanced at his student, whom he could only see from the edges of his periphery; how silly, he thought, to feel as though he were auditioning for youth, but that was exactly what he was doing. At that moment in his history, Everett wanted nothing more than for Jeff to love his music.

Jeff looked down at the keys to watch the master caress each bit of ivory as though cradling an infant.

The piano was less an instrument and more a natural extension of his own anatomy, he was as familiar with it as his own fingers and toes and kneecaps, if not somewhat more. He didn't even look at the written music. His eyes closed during a long rest, before a grand cacophony of sounds radiated from deep within the piano. Strings and hammers united at the sound direction of their sovereign as vibrations that Jeff didn't even realize a piano could achieve filled the air. Wave after wave of brilliant music was released into the stratosphere as the piece took flight, taking them both to distant places of feeling, of regret, of joy, — rapture. Everett Crisp's concerto, what existed of it, was, indeed, a masterpiece.

Silence once again overtook the room as the last chord reverberated throughout the instrument and fizzled through the air. Reality came rushing back through the room, like the regretful end of a ride. The Ferris wheel had reached the bottom and this time, they were asked to disembark. Everett exhaled audibly, took a single moment, then opened his eyes, turning his neck to gaze at his student for secret approval.

"I don't know what to say. It's — it's the most incredible thing I've ever heard in my life." More silence. Neither of them knew quite how to respond, something so profound having clearly taken place, like the awkward silences two people experience during a tension-laced row. Only this hadn't been an argument, it had been — what? A revelation. "Well, — I should get my stuff together. Kelly will be here soon, that's my old roommate. Thank you. Really — thank you so much — for all of this."

Everett watched him rise as he headed to the other parts of the house to find whatever it was he had arrived with. As he watched him go he felt an actual pang of melancholy, which he hadn't expected, the feeling one gets when a vacation is over or a really good play ends; the lights had come up in the theatre and he was squinting as he re-entered that other world, the non-musical one that he had always found so tedious, the one he faced alone. He had forgotten what it was like, having an actual person hear his music, live and right before him. Even if he would regret it later, all he could bring himself to say, with a tired, cracked voice which permeated the soundlessness of this pristine late afternoon, was this:

"Stay."

Christmas, 1990: New London, CT

Everett had never seen a house so large. It wasn't so large that it was ostentatious. Rather, it was utterly beautiful with its vine draped walls and perfectly landscaped front drive. Covered in snow, it was very nearly a painting. He had hoped that Christmas in Connecticut would be just as cozy and pleasant as it sounded, fireplaces and real Christmas trees, cookies fresh from the oven and all that; but he had been forewarned.

"You're proceeding right into the viper pit," Jamie had said, only half jokingly, as their train sped forward, through the snow covered pines and rural inns of Massachusetts. He ran his open palm along his lover's gorgeous thigh, glad in denim, secretly fearful of a great many things, the least of which was who else might be on this train and what they might see. It was time the tide turned. Everett's hand laded squarely on top of his own, which sent a warm shiver down Jamie's spine.

"Stop," Everett didn't so much smile as he abundantly smirked, which was his A+ of emotions when wanting to comfort someone he cared about. "It's going to be fantastic."

A year into their relationship, Everett had finally decided it was time to see from just what cloth Jamie was cut, certain that it couldn't all be as monstrous as it had been described to him over the past twelve months. So, with ample trepidation, Jamie had relented. Further, he decided, if they were going to do it, they might as well jump right into the deep end and come for

Christmas. Hence, they found themselves on this snowy morning on a Connecticut bound train, hurtling past the small towns and hamlets that lined the gold coast until they had arrived in New London. As the train rolled to a stop, Everett could see the color literally drain from Jamie's face, so much so that were he to lie down in the snow, he'd have been perfectly camouflaged.

Barbara, their father's assistant, and, it was commonly known, long-time mistress, met them at the station in one of the lustrous black town cars the family had used for decades. She was a leggy woman, unusually tall with deep-set features and what seemed to be constantly blood-shot eyes. In all the years Jamie had known her, he had never once seen her wear anything but long, black pencil skirts with blank pantyhose and a sensible blouse which matched appropriate black high heels. She had once been quite beautiful but time in Washington had taken its toll and the lines on her face and the silver that now streaked her hair betrayed her age. A certain glint that had once radiated from her had vanished now. She had been somewhat bubbly and even funny, Jamie recalled from his youth, but that had all faded. She now chose her words carefully and whatever sparkle might have once graced her eyes had long ago retreated. She methodically went through the motions, albeit with perfect skill. Although there were many things she could not do well in life, her job was certainly not among them. The position had grown like vines all around her, vines which she embraced, finely tending to them like an expertly skilled horticulturalist. There was a perfect meld between she and his father but not a romantic one, it was practical and codependent; they were useful to each other and that was the extent of it, even sexually. Still, Jamie had known her for practically his whole life, and was always pleased to see her, even if she had been sent ahead to assess the situation and make certain that the two of them were scrubbed clean and ready for inspection.

The interior of the car was all black leather and smelled of old money, a smoothly running and well-maintained Lincoln in which the undeniable scent of cigarette and cigar smoke remained trapped. Jamie and Everett both piled into the backseat, which designated Barbara more of a curious chauffeur, which indeed she was, when called for. She was anything and everything Grant White needed at any given time. And today, it soon became abundantly clear, she had been dispatched to feel out this new friend that Jamie had unexpectedly decided to bring home for the annual White Family Holiday Party, a staunch affair that Jamie had, in recent years, avoided like a disease, which it was. The thought of coming down with a bad case of Connecticut that year did not thrill him; he'd have much rather found an excuse to stay in Cambridge until it had passed, as he usually did.

"So, how do you two know each other?" The inquisition had begun, launched from the rear view mirror; Jamie was all too aware what she meant. He turned to look out the window at the familiar surroundings of his youth.

"We have classes together. How have you been, Barbara?"

"Oh, just trying to keep up with your father, as always," she false-giggled. "Have you been to Connecticut before, Everett?"

"This is my first time," he muttered politely, embarrassed by the noise he made as he squirmed in his leather seat.

"Well, you're in for a treat. The Grant holiday party is the place to be — it trumps all the others. You'll see." Jamie rolled his eyes and gripped Everett's knee, which he was certain Barbara, who quickly averted her eyes, had seen. "Where did you say your family is from? Maine, did I hear?"

"Iowa," he called from the backseat.

"Charming little state, I hear. Bet you were never without a baked potato, hmm?" Everett was amused but Jamie embarrassed that his father's Chief of Staff hadn't really been listening when he told her on the phone where his friend had come from, and even more so that she appeared not to know that potatoes come from Idaho. For a woman so adept at multi-tasking, Jamie had clearly been put on the bottom of her to-do list.

"Well, I hope you'll have a wonderful time while you're with us." Barbara always spent the holidays at the Grant house. Politics didn't stop just because Christmas came. In fact, the holidays accelerated the workload. It was quite clear that she hadn't any family of her own to scurry home to, at least none that anybody knew of. "Tell me, do you boys just spend *all* of your time together, then?"

The car coasted over the smooth black asphalt of the White family's long, tree-lined, heated drive. Other vehicles lined the street for miles, it seemed. The party was in full swing. Someone emerged from the house to gather Everett's rumpled blue and white duffel bag from the trunk, and Jamie's leather suitcase with the brass plate monogram.

"Hey there Jimmy, this is Everett," there was excitement to Jamie's voice yet his face turned as red as Jimmy's hair. Ah, Everett had heard all about *Jimmy*. Jimmy this, Jimmy that, Jimmy the tall, strapping servant who had introduced young Jamie to all sorts of things.

Jimmy the first man Jamie had ever seen totally naked, apart from boyhood locker rooms following lacrosse practice. Too many times, Everett had been reminded of the shower in the stables and the bubble-butted servant who had changed everything. If only the Senator knew. It was their little secret. Jimmy and Jamie: it was straight out of a trashy romance novel and enough to curdle milk. He was handsome enough, Everett had to admit, robust and burley in a field hand kind of way, well put together in his formal uniform, but substantially older than both of them. He looked a little dejected at the site of Everett, seeing clearly that his "duties," which he had been looking forward to, would not be necessary this trip. He smiled at them both, the kind of knowing smile that one exchanges when a shared secret exists, and disappeared into the house with Barbara, his muscular arms laden with luggage.

"Careful in there," were Barbara's parting words to the boys, emitted through a poisonous smile, pointing toward the sound of the cheery holiday music that reverberated through the walls. Jamie knew only too well what she meant.

"I was beginning to think there was paper work or something I needed to fill out," Everett whispered to Jamie. He had never been much of a hand holder, it just wasn't his nature; but his attraction, what had become even a kind of devotion to Jamie even though he'd never admit it out loud, was unmistakable to anyone who looked at the two of them. They were far more than two casual frat-mates home for winter break to catch up on studies and party with old high school acquaintances, there would be no mistaking it. What's more, Jamie had decided that this was for the best. He had never loved anyone out loud before and he would grasp hold of this with every muscle in his body.

It had been a year of new discoveries for them both, a lot of laughing and actual dates — nights where Jamie would sit al fresco at a local Cambridge eatery, listening to Everett rattle on to the point of exhaustion about music and his favorite composers. He drank in the wine and the man at the same time as his beau waxed poetic about the singular brilliance of Ravel.

Jamie was Everett's weight tied to the bottom of his balloon, and Jamie secretly knew this. Whenever he was overwhelmed and totally lost within himself, whenever his balloon threatened to simply leave the Earth's atmosphere and enter oxygen-less outer space where it would surely burn right up, Jamie brought his own little prodigy back home with something funny or a sly look that told Everett all he needed to know. Their arguments were legendary, but so was their making up. They had each travelled such solitary roads, and they each slowly learned what it was like to have a traveling companion along for the ride. Whatever this was between the two of them was complicated and yet effortless. Their union was a very bright, luminous globe from which they each drew strength and power. It had become the thing that each of them cherished the most.

"Into the dragon's lair. Ready?" Jamie locked arms with Everett, just to be funny, as they both stood in front of the enormous white brick house that looked to Jamie like a giant pale squid, ready to wrap it's tentacles around the two of them and thrash them about the stormy sea for a while. He took a deep breath, and they both ventured inside the labyrinth, right through the looking glass.

Spring, 2001: New York City

"That's not nice!"

Ruth Pickett had been heckled. Oh, shit. Everett Crisp clutched his hands to his knees and looked at himself in her full-length mirror in the minuscule backstage. He laughed a little upon the concrete steps, where he sat amid ample dirt, random beads of faded sequins from the drag queens that had occupied this space the night previous, and the same graffiti that had littered these walls since the mid 70's. He knew full well the firing squad before which this unfortunate and clueless heckler had just stepped. Some moron from Topeka had had the balls to challenge the Queen mid-set. Blood would be shed, he was certain of it.

"And this surprises you? I've been doing this same shtick for 3,000 fuckin' years. What did you expect? Stewardess jokes?" The crowd roared in appreciation. "You want nice? Go see Debbie fuckin' Reynolds!"

Done. Peering out from the dressing room, Everett could just make him out: slightly round and in a button down, short sleeve shirt, carefully tucked, about fifty, sipping a Coke. The gentleman slouched down in his chair, feeling all eyes in the room upon him, which, of course, they most decidedly were. He would most likely have walked out of the room, but that surely would have drawn even more attention in the little theatre that sat just seventy-three, exactly. Dance with the devil and you'd best be prepared, thought Everett. So the plump mid-westerner hadn't liked her jokes about holocaust survivors just being a big bunch of complainers. So what?

Knowing Ruth as he did, he knew that situations such as these always threw her for a split second while her nimble mind raced in panic, all of which was kept well out of site from anyone who didn't know her well. She could catch an eighty-five mile per hour dodge ball with her lone bare hand and toss back sixty or seventy more, and with far greater velocity, faster than most people could blink. Secretly, she was grateful for the occasional heckler, they kept her on her toes. What appeared to the casual onlooker as the easiest and most joyful thing in the world, a woman of a certain age standing in front of a microphone telling jokes, was actually a well orchestrated and carefully executed skill that she had spent the better part of a century perfecting.

The evening had started out normal enough. He sat onstage in the packed room for an hour or so playing show tune after show tune, the pre show she insisted geared up the crowd for her arrival. She swept through the stage door alone with her usual gusto; $2,000 shoes and a rhinestone here and there, her expensive perfume (from her own line) signaling her arrival. He announced her from his microphone with a fanfare run up the keys and she took the stage with her usual entrance of utter flamboyance. But tonight, she strode to the piano with it's chipped wood and dusty lid, and, amid the ample and exuberant applause, proceeded to hug Everett with a particular *look* in her eye, unusual even for her, which left Everett perfectly dumbfounded. Was she planning to stage her own death that night, right onstage? It hardly would have surprised him. She winked at him, then, leaving her private self behind and sewing herself firmly and instantaneously into Ruth Pickett, turned to the audience and proceeded with her standard: "Let's wrap this up, I wanna get home in time to masturbate before bed." Peels of laughter. "I don't wanna be up all night! I'm old, it takes me longer."

She had masterfully handled the silly heckler now and was launching into her usual routine about her friend Trevor whom everyone thought was great at cunnilingus but was actually a "cunning linguist," whom she went on to describe as a man who "walks with a lisp," which garnered her the biggest laughs yet. People fell out of their chairs in hysterics, partly from the brilliance of the joke and equally because it had come from her, the famous one with whom they were all charmed to share even the same air. But what was this? She stopped, mid routine. Following her biggest laugh, she broke her own rhythm and simply said to the audience with a wry grin on her face: "Ladies and gentleman, I have a special treat for you tonight. You may think I need a break, I don't, I just need to go and fuck the midget who's waiting for me in my dressing room. So at this time, I give you the brilliant song stylings of, and you be nice to him or I'll come out there, my darling Mr. Everett Crisp!"

What? She had surrendered her stage mid-show, turned it right over to Everett, who was immediately struck with white-hot terror. What was wrong? Was she ill? Faint? If only he could have afforded a cellular phone, he'd call someone and get her out of there. He hoped that Rusty, her longtime driver, had stuck around. Fuck. As she advanced in age, he wondered how long she could keep up with the break-neck pace of her own demanding schedule. She had *walked off* stage mid-show which is something that Ruth Pickett just did *not* do. She swept passed him in the make-shift dressing room before she turned around to shove him on stage, hands planted firmly on his ass, which she squeezed hard, careful not to chip a well-manicured nail.

"What are you doing? Are you all right? RUTH?" He turned around frantically, half expecting to find a frail woman gasping for air, but was met only with the same glamorous and perfectly at ease Ms. P. he had always known.

"Look, my darling," standing on tip toe directly behind him, she spoke right into his ear in hushed tones, "you just trust me and DON'T fuck this up!" She kissed him on his cheek and looked him directly in the eye. Her caked mascara only partially masked very kind, very serious and very proud eyes. She was *not* messing around. And then came the final shove, far more ferocious than one would have imagined from a seventy-seven year old woman.

Suddenly, Everett Crisp found himself in front of the quietest audience that ever existed in the history of audiences, looking back at him with sheer hatred in their eyes as a single, cold stage light trapped he and a somewhat confused mosquito in its glow. He was a sorry replacement for their bejeweled monarch. Hands went up all around as everyone ordered another round and there was a masse exodus to use the men's room and the other men's room. The silence was unbearable. There was feed back from the sound system and ten years seemed to pass as he settled himself at the piano. He could see Robbie, the tech director, holding his hands up in bewilderment from the fluorescently lit tech booth, which sat behind Plexiglas in the far reaches of the room. Robbie reopened the piano mic from the soundboard as the crowd sat chewing their ice — eyes squinted in displeasure at the stage.

"You know the one. *Play it*, kid," she whispered, as much as she was capable of whispering, from backstage. She was fighting, surely, her natural instinct to retake the stage. But tonight, she would do something purely selfless, which was not entirely unlike her, despite her fictional persona.

Everett breathed deeply as he stared down at the worn white keys. He knew this piano intimately, it was like a broken down old friend whom he liked to cheer up when he came to visit. But now he was not merely background music, the sideshow, the wallpaper. He was the big tent attraction. More silence followed as people coughed and Everett heard the familiar sound of scurrying mice in the walls. He looked down at his wrinkled khakis.

"Oh, for fuck's sake, come ON!" she slammed her high heel into the cement floor backstage, not three feet away. That was all the prodding he needed.

His hands fell upon the opening chord, the force of which bounced from the walls of the tiny room. He was off to the races. The piece that was Ms. P's favorite was the one that was filled with the most flourish, of course, the most dramatic, the one full of bells and whistles, not unlike the lady herself. His hands made their way up the keys and back down in a pattern only he could fathom, caressing the white and bowing to the black. He was a kind of musical gymnast, working that warped piano, his colleague in all of this, for everything it was worth. He was no longer afraid, wrapped up in the warm embrace of music. He forgot entirely about the one hundred and forty-six eyes watching him, and said all that he needed to in what seemed like mere seconds of playing. All too soon, the end was in sight and he barreled toward it as though riding a very tall wave, bound to crash ashore in only seconds. He reached the final cord, that tricky decrescendo before the final tease of a playoff, the song's tail, he had always called it, before hitting the end hard and removing his feet from the pedals with a sound thud. He had landed squarely back on Earth, and was quickly all too aware of where he was. His pale face turned bright red, droplets of sweat streamed from his forehead as he sat, suddenly cold, in the glare of Ruth Pickett's stage lights.

Ten full seconds of silence followed. Even the wait staff had stopped serving and stood watching from the back of the room, trays folded in front of them, a tear or two present amid wide grins. Had he just, — what? Shown himself naked in front of the lot of them? Would he need now to slink away and join the heckler at the downstairs bar for an embarrassed drink or two and common commiseration?

The most violent ovation that the tiny theatre above Sheridan Square had ever seen or heard erupted. Everett, beside himself, felt, for a split second, like the maestro he had always dreamed, in his childhood fantasies, that he might one day become; the person to whom roses were tossed onstage. He allowed himself to bask for mere moments in the triumph of what he had once set out to accomplish, the cloud of appreciation that lifts one up and carries one away before leaving one utterly abandoned with no way back. Before too terribly long, there was a carefully cared for fingernail pressing sharply into his back; Ms. P had retaken the stage, looking all too pissed.

"Get the fuck off my stage! Who told you to do that? *Marry Had a Little Lamb* or something I thought you'd play. *Twinkle, Twinkle Little Star* — something for the people to fill the time so Luigi and I could do what we needed to do, which, at my age and his height, takes some special maneuvering. Who told you to be Liber-fuckin-ace, huh? Get backstage. GET!"

Enormous gratitude, an emotion somewhat foreign to him and to which he had only recently permitted himself to feel, filled the entirely of Everett Crisp's body. He had never known such generosity. She had sacrificed her own stage, and turned it over to him. From the makeshift dressing room, he stood looking at her, bathed in the starkness of the stage lights, in utter thankfulness, his body filled with the kind of euphoria that can only come from the outrageous appreciation of applause. There she stood, dancing around the tiny stage in her gold lame and rhinestones, a carefully camouflaged saint.

"Yeah, yeah — he's so great. Please. I'm an old lady out here breaking my ass in this dump and you all give it up for Little Richard and his piece of shit piano." She could see him in the wing, just barely from the periphery of her right eye, as he knew she could. One raised eyebrow his way, and he was certain that she was up to something.

Christmas, 1990: New London, CT

"It was built in 1879 by Colonel John Jason Stroman. You can see his picture in the study, and it stayed in his family until 1974 when we bought it and turned it into Lakeside Hill, that's what we call it, as I'm sure James must have told you. Of course, we've built onto it extensively over the years. Can I get you more punch?" After polite introductions, Susan White had attached herself to Everett's arm and would not let go as she led him through the arched entryway and into the heart of the party. It wasn't just that she was a good hostess, because she was, of course, following decades or practice. But for a blessed relief, there was fresh blood at the annual fete, someone whom she could take under her wing and for whom this would all be new. For a hallowed bit of time, she might forgo looking interested in talking about primary races, the incompetence of Democrats and which ex-wife was suing which recently single CFO.

Just half an hour ago, Everett had been shown his room, a grand suite with it's own bathroom and king sized bed, located at the opposite end of the house from Jamie's. He had been instructed to slip into "festive" attire. And now, Jamie sat bemused in a corner, atop the ottoman of an overstuffed Louis XVI wingback, as his mother seized his companion and ushered him around the expansive great room, introducing him as "Jamie's school friend from Harvard. Oh, another *Harvard* man!" She was in party mode now — charming, exuberant, outgoing, always appearing slightly tipsy although she never drank. It was the side of his mother that Jamie liked most but that one could only glimpse at occasions such as these. The real Susan White preferred to hide behind eighteenth century paintings and antique lamps, shut away from the world and any obligation to plaster a smile. She was kind and she was gracious — but she was also shy, cautious and, it seemed to Jamie, always just a little bit afraid.

The house was draped in tasteful pine, hanging from every gleaming oak banister and doorframe. On the first of December, just like clockwork, the people from Haynes and Company arrived at Lakeside Hill to convert the house into a Christmas wonderland. Not that it was gaudy with flashing bulbs and inflatable reindeer, but no part of their home was left untouched by the icy hand of professional decorators. Every window reflected the glow of white lights and pine.

Three enormous Christmas tress, spread throughout the main floor, were the centerpieces, each with it's own theme.

As he watched his mother, herself clad in white to match the snow, right down to her pearl earrings, Jamie recalled last Christmas in Cambridge when Everett and he had dragged home that tiny tree from the corner vendor and decorated it with a plastic tree top and the few ornaments and multicolored lights they had picked up at the drug store. How proud he had been of it as it stood, all lit up, in their own little corner of the world. It was the first Christmas tree Jamie could recall decorating in his whole life, and it was utterly beautiful in the cozy little off campus apartment he had come to think of as "theirs."

Brass and pewter gleamed from every carefully polished cherrywood surface. Family photos that looked more like campaign adds sat in expensive looking frames of pure silver, showcasing Jamie at various ages. Apparently, Jamie White had always been gorgeous — the shining golden boy — no awkward adolescent years for him, at least none that were on display, and this surprised Everett a little. There must have been at least three hundred well dressed people crammed into the various rooms of the house, men and women of well healed Connecticut society. Lawmakers, titans of industry, and people whose sole contribution to the world was their wealth all circulated around passed trays of smoked salmon and raw shrimp, punchbowls of eggnog and champagne fountains. How these people roam the streets and roads, thought Everett, the universities and supermarkets of Connecticut and one would never think to give them a second glance, or guess that they're all secretly connected to this underworld that makes so many things tick. The healthy din of polite cocktail chatter barely rose above the innocuous sounds of boring seasonal music, which emanated from the hired piano player, huddled in the center of the room in a rented tux, sitting uncomfortably behind the well-polished Steinway Grand.

"May I cut in?" Jamie, looking beyond dashing in a deep blue suit the exact color of his eyes, had appeared at the side of his "college friend," intent on separating him from his mother, all too leery of the stories that could be told. Everett had never seen him in a suit before. It was abundantly if not embarrassingly clear that this was Jamie's world, this was a place where he fit in effortlessly, it was mere genetics and dare he say it — breeding? He hated himself for thinking it, because that was exactly the kind of pretension they both loathed, especially Jamie, but nevertheless, Everett couldn't help feel like the estranged country cousin.

"If you'll excuse me, Mr. Crisp, I think I should see to the other guests," and Susan White giggled that polite hostess giggle that everyone had come to associate with her. She smiled a motherly smile at both of them, before embracing her son. "So good to have you home, James." Then, leaning into his ear, she proceeded with "he's charming, isn't he?" before making her way into the sea of wives whom she would need to compliment and husbands whose egos were surely in need of a fluff. Every year she was a little more plump and a little more run down, but this was the natural order of things. She had her job to do, she always had. She was a professional unmatched when it came to doing what she did, and it was only with the perspective of being away and seeing this world from the opposite side of the window that Jamie had come to realize it. The boys made their way into the library — a room crafted out of solid mahogany with green glass lamps and imposing, tufted leather sofas.

"Christmas at your house is *cozy*," said Everett, tongue-in-cheek, as he admired the dead swordfish that hung above a case of gold leaf, bound books, many of them first-edition.

"Oh, this is nothing. Wait till we all gather around the Christmas tree and recite the Dow Jones averages."

"What's through there?" Everett pointed across the foyer, through the great room to an expansive sun deck which housed yet another Christmas tree, this one all in white, surrounded by a particular thrush of people.

"Oh, that's where you go to see Santa Claus."

"What?"

"My father. He holds court in there so his disciples can all come through and kiss his ring."

"Well, shouldn't we pay our respects at some point?"

"Oh, sure. Let's hurry and suck all the remaining joy out of Christmas, shall we?"

The sunroom was very nearly blinding in the late afternoon light, the gloaming beautifully situated on the thick snow that saturated the well manicured lawn and shrubbery and reflected right into the faces of the guests with its powerful burnt orange hue. Had it not made him feel more of a spectacle than he already did, Everett would have reached for his sunglasses. Little by little, they made their way closer to the man in the grey suit who situated himself between the purely white tree, devoid completely of any other sense of color and decked out in nothing but glass beads and solid white snow birds, and the constantly refilled tray of martinis. It occurred to Everett that they were actually *waiting in line* to see Jamie's father, the Senator. As they inched closer, Everett half expected to find a throne and was unsure if he should bow.

Grant White was a tall, slender man with frosty white hair and crystal blue eyes that were a precise match of his son's. His booming voice could be heard above all others in the room. Casually, words like "fourth quarter," "Japanese," "Euro," and even now and then "the holidays," issued from his narrow mouth that, when not speaking, sat at rest with thin, pursed lips. His nose was slender and his muted red tie was tied tightly about his neck. The Senator had not come from money; Everett knew the story well. Like so many wealthy people, he was part saint and part criminal, the line between the two so often blurred. But for most of Jamie's life, he had been simply "Senator White, the Gentleman from Connecticut." It was clear, watching him shake hands and flash his politician's smile in that blindingly white sunroom stuffed with holiday swag, that it was to be the defining role of his career. History is so simply rewritten if two perfect covers embrace and conceal the drab pages that lie between.

"Dad."

"Oh, James! Made it back to the 'ol homestead I see." The two of them almost hugged, but it turned into more of a firm handshake and a slap on Jamie's shoulder. The Senator raised his voice to a kind of dull call. "Look who it is everyone — my son's come home!" Applause. Honest to God *applause* erupted throughout the room as Jamie fell religiously back to form, smiling and waving. Everett Crisp looked on in utter astonishment. Wow.

"I'd like you to meet — "

"The piano player! Yes. James has told us all about you — Grant White," it was a hearty handshake. It was clear that he was one of those men who was fond of saying things like 'you can tell a lot about a man by the way he shakes your hand.' "Welcome to Lakeside Hill, you just let someone know if you need anything, anything at all," already his eyes were darting about the room in search of his next social conquest.

"Good to see you, Dad." Jamie tugged at Everett's suit jacket, knowing that their time had expired.

Grant White leaned into his son's ear. "Listen, James. Let's you and me have a good long talk later, after everyone's gone to bed. I'm going to meet some boys at the club in the morning for golf, so I won't be around, but let's you and me chat tonight, okay? Don't drink too much." A final handshake was executed, probably an act his body performed out of habit, before he turned his attention to his son's black haired companion with the skinny tie and the somewhat wrinkled shirt. "Good to meet you — ?"

"*Everett.* It's Everett, Dad, like I told you on the phone."

"The pleasure is mine, sir. Thank you for having me in your lovely home." Everett smiled broadly at Senator White, who looked back at him in a not so carefully concealed assessment, as though sizing up a challenger, after which both Everett and the Senator's son made their exit, and the Senator turned his attention to the elderly woman with the heavy red lipstick wearing an excessively festive Christmas hat.

"Impressive. You're learning WASP awfully fast."

"I play by ear. Besides, he seems perfectly nice to me," Everett lied, as one does when a guest in someone else's home. He knew precisely what had just transpired. It was clear that the two of them, Senator White and Everett, had only played the introductory scene — the plot was sure to thicken. Each had looked the other directly in the eye and acknowledged it. The games were surely about to begin.

"Of course he does. That's his job. Just wait." They had made their way back through the great room and headed for the bar; the real bar, as opposed to all the fizzy punch bowls that lay scattered throughout the house.

"Wait for what?"

"The infection. Grant White is like an infection, one you don't even know you're contracting. And, poor Evey, you haven't even had your Connecticut shots. You'll see."

"How's he gonna play golf in the snow?"

"For the kind of golf he plays at the club, it'll be just fine. Had enough party?" Jamie had come home for Christmas for no other reason than Everett had asked him to. He was not at all happy about sharing Everett, the greatest find of his short life, with Grant White. He was even more embarrassed than he thought he would be, showing this bizarre little world he came from to the one person he knew genuinely loved him. "Grab that bottle and let's head back to my room for a while. Nothing happens until the speeches and they're not until a good hour from now, after the less important people have gone."

With some trepidation, Everett grabbed two Waterford glasses and a bottle of Chivas from the bar in the study, a look of fear on his face as he read the label which stated "aged twelve years. "

"You're not stealing. I live here. Come on."

Jamie's room, situated well above the party on what could have been another planet rather than merely a separate floor, was equipped with a wood burning fireplace which had been lit and tended to in anticipation of his arrival that day. Most disturbingly, there were absolutely no traces that Jamie had grown up there. There was a bed, a dresser, a stout leather chair for reading and a mahogany desk. No ribbons of youthful triumphs, no posters, no CD collection, everything utterly unadorned. Just tasteful cream carpet and a Tiffany study lamp.

"Your room's a mess." Everett poured the scotch, hoping to lighten the mood. He knew Jamie was all tied up in a knot upon returning to what he had always referred to as "The Ice Palace."

Jamie sat on the bed, gazing up at his handsome companion. He had never had anyone hold his hand through the rigors of the Connecticut social scene, no one had ever been on his side, certainly not anyone he could invite into his own boyhood bedroom. Downstairs faded into the back of his mind, and it took no effort at all for his lips to form the words:

"Take your clothes off."

Spring, 2001: New York City

"And that is why black men give the best blow jobs. *Goodnight!*" Ruth Pickett had left them with a final bit of political incorrectness, like the last dab of brilliant icing upon an elaborate cake, before she ended the set. Just as she neared the end, Everett had slipped back behind the piano, as instructed at every performance, so he could play her off with great fanfare. Even before she said "goodnight," he could instinctively feel when she was nearing the finish line and needing to get offstage, having scratched the persistent itch that demanded so much from her. She didn't need to look at him or instruct him to play her off, he felt the precise moment when she had placed a definitive period on the evening. Tonight, he struck up a rousing rendition of "Anchor's Away!" Why not?

She took bow after bow and blew kisses to the adoring crowd. But this evening, oddly, she reached right out into the front row, caught the wrist of an usually tall, wiry gentleman with a potbelly, and dragged him onstage with her. They took a bow together, she and this stranger from God knows where, for no apparent reason, just to be odd, Everett fathomed, as he watched from behind his piano. Then, she exited the stage with this person, dragging him into the minute dressing room, stage right. Everett quickly finished playing and there was scattered applause as the house lights came back up. They had forgotten all about him by this time, following the tour-de-force finale of the one and only Ruth Pickett. Everett ventured backstage, unsure of what exactly to expect.

"There he is, the man of the hour, Mr. Piano Man himself!" She greeted him in the microscopic room, really more of a tiny hallway, with a warm hug, smearing lipstick on the side of his face with every intention of doing just that.

"*What the hell was that?*" Everett was exasperated, grateful and exhilarated, but utterly confused.

"What? The thing that we do every show? Oh, right — I put it in a different place tonight, — but I like to keep you on your toes, I'm *evil* that way!" she kicked his foot, — hard. Her eyes rolled to the left where the tall, wiry man with the potbelly stood, looking down upon the young piano man. He was nearing fifty or so with receding hair, most of it brushed forward to create the illusion of fertile vegetation upon mostly barren soil. He wore blue jeans and a tweed jacket over a very expensive looking silk shirt. His Oxfords were perfectly shined, Everett noticed. This strange gentleman stood looking down at Ruth Pickett's piano player with a wide grin on his face.

"That was brilliant, what you did up there," said the man, glancing into Everett's eyes. It was sinking in now. Ms. P. was trying to fix him up. He had been so sure that she and Jamie had hit it off all this time, what was she playing at? The man looked Everett up and down; clearly he was one of those people who are entranced by talent, little else; who fall in love with the music, rather than the man.

"Thank you very much. How are you getting home, lady? Is Rusty still here or do you want me to drop you?"

"Have you met my friend, Philip Tate?"

"A pleasure to meet you," Everett smiled politely but was reaching for his jacket at the same time.

"*Philip*, as you know, is the newly appointed conductor of the New York *Philharmonic*?" Everett put down his jacket and could feel himself turning beet red. "Perhaps we should all go someplace for drinks and get to know one another, — hm?"

"I'd like that very much," said Philip Tate.

"After you, *Phil*," she said, holding the door. Ruth turned back to Everett on her way out to shoot him one of her famous, raised eyebrow looks. One of her greatest gifts, among many, was that she could communicate anything in the world with her eyes and face and within about half a second at that. And tonight, lit in the cheap, blinking, overhead florescent light bulb of the backstage of that dirty, dilapidated theatre, her face could not have been more clear: it said, practically and in plain English: *"get it right, asshole!"*

9

Summer, 1978: Mason City, Iowa

I N HIS DREAM, he was swimming in a pool with water the color of the most perfect crystal. All was peaceful as he bathed, basking in an enormous marble basin of water, large enough for masses, various pools separated by large stone columns that seemed to lie in wait solely for his own pleasure. It appeared to go on for miles, his own private oasis filled with water as clear as oxygen; nary another living soul in sight, which suited him just fine. A gentle waterfall cascaded from a nearby opening in the rock, providing it's own soothing music as it splashed down to the flooded basin below, where his body floated gently upon the majestic swell. The water was warm and embraced him with the feeling of utter security. He hadn't a care in the world, everything worrisome from his mind had long ago leaked, poured from his ears and nose, a vile dark color which contrasted violently with his surroundings, to delude in the storybook-like natatorium, before sinking to the bottom and disappearing for good. There was nothing but space and time and he reached out to gather it all, to hold it close; it all belonged to him alone — the great release, the long awaited serenity.

When the crackling began he knew almost immediately that he was dreaming. However, in the hazy state between sleep and consciousness, he tried in vain to hold onto his bucolic, fictional world, only too soon to watch it fade, the sound of the snapping branches and the sudden chill in the early morning air calling him back home to reality. Once the dream had been properly mourned, he turned his attention instead to the source of this new sound, which seemed to be approaching with some hesitancy just beyond the confines of the tent. It wasn't an animal — he could make out the shadow of a human form through the panels of his temporary home.

Yes, it was a man — the same man from the other day no doubt, the only other soul who seemed to inhabit these woods. Everett's hiding place, his serene new home, it seemed, was in danger of exposure.

Hiding inside would never work, and he regretted this. He'd have liked to have stayed wrapped up in Mr. Able's ample coat for a bit longer, perhaps forever, serene in his home as he lay against the canvas-covered ground littered with the exposed roots of trees, rather than face the cold morning. But it wasn't to be avoided as the steps drew nearer still, only finally to be accompanied by a familiar voice: "Hello... H-hello in there?"

Christmas, 1990: New London, CT

They had both nearly fallen asleep, naked and in front of the fire, the heat of which pervaded their skin, reaching right through them. The antique lamps that some decorator had selected to adorn the room remained unlit and the sun had thankfully sunk well beyond the lake. Beautiful laziness permeated the four walls of their temporary sanctuary. For the first time that Jamie could recall, his own bedroom felt comfortable. He hadn't done it just to thumb his nose at proper Connecticut society, but then the thought that perhaps he had amused him. Still, laying there in Everett's bare arms, enraptured by the sound of his lover's heartbeat as the fire cast shadows throughout the room, Lakeview Hill seemed, astonishingly enough, warm and peaceful.

Then came the banging at the door. "Jamie! Your father's asking for you. Everyone's downstairs," and again the banging. "You in there, J?" Her harsh pounding belied her tone of voice, which she obviously went to forced effort to soften so that she might sound merely concernedly cheerful, when she was surely turning somersaults inside, determined to keep the party on its rails. She may have been at a festive social occasion, but she never ceased to be on the clock. Had Santa himself slid down the chimney, she'd have asked him to wait until she could work him into the day's schedule, volunteering to bring him something to drink in the meantime.

"Well, it had to end sometime," Jamie whispered in a casual, end of the fair kind of way. Everett, instantly alarmed like a school boy caught in the backseat of a car, leapt out of bed in search of his clothes which, thank God, he had folded neatly, arranging his shirt over the back of Jamie's desk chair. He had felt wrinkled enough as it was amongst the crowd of perfectly quaffed partygoers. He scurried about the room for his socks like an insect exposed in a flashlight, wildly making gestures to his lover as though he were starring in a silent film, Jamie looking on in bemusement from his perfect nakedness.

"Are you alone in there? Your father..." she called through the wooden door. Everett held his index finger to his lips, afraid he'd be tossed out on his ear into the cold Connecticut snow for deflowering the pride of the Gold Coast under the roof of Colonel John Jason Stroman's historic estate. "Anyway, meet us downstairs. It's time...*both* of you." Jamie looked beneath the door and, through the crack, could see her turn to go, only to watch as the tips of her just-barely-too-high-heeled high heels returned. "And Merry Christmas." Poor Barbara went to great lengths to soften herself, trying not to be the pent up schoolmarm she really, and completely by nature, was. Jamie had always found that endearing.

"I was just sleeping, Barbara. W - *I'll* be right down!" She paused, then turned to go, surely thinking it better that she leave it alone. For now.

Mr. White was speaking in front of the grand fireplace in the great room when they entered. Everett hadn't noticed that one before; another fireplace — he would come to learn that the house contained six of them in all, but this one was the size of a small apartment, or perhaps the mouth of a very overgrown dragon. Susan White turned from her perch on the arm of a well upholstered beige sofa, the fabric selected by herself and imported from Italy, as the two of them trotted in, mid remarks, and settled themselves in the back of the room near the equally oversized bay windows that looked down upon the grounds. The crowd had thinned to about a hundred or so, the rest of the rooms empty now. Everyone, servants included, crowded into the Great Room for the floorshow. With the exception of the catering staff, Jamie and Everett brought the median age down considerably.

Grant White spoke with one of his long arms draped dramatically across the mantle, right beside the largest of the decorated Christmas trees and beneath an enormous oil portrait of some terrifying looking pilgrim in a wig. Everett had heard that scenes such as these really existed, that they weren't merely reserved for movies, but to see it all unfold before him, all this Americana, was akin to stepping into a novel. Had only a pocket watch hung from Senator White's vest, thought Everett, or perhaps a monocle rested on his face, it would have somehow completed the Merchant/Ivory-ness of it all.

He was going on about what a great year it had been and something about good fortune and the sense of Christmas that should fuel them throughout each of the twelve months, politician dribble that had been handed down from generation to generation. An ear as carefully trained for bullshit like Everett's could detect his insincerity effortlessly, but he had to admit — he was not unconvincing. In fact, Everett could understand just why and how this man had navigated such tricky political waters to end up in the well appointed great room of a lavish country estate, speaking to a room full of people who were elated to consider themselves friends. It was a gracious speech, and the audience of grinning supporters, all with drinks in their hands and artificial snow in their brains, applauded with great fervor for the Senator, everybody's All American with a big, capital 'A'.

"Now tonight, ladies and gentleman," Everett's attention had waned and he occupied the time watching Jamie, set against a backdrop of pine cones and Christmas lights, gazing at his father. How elegant he looked, and how he hoped he could somehow live up to all of this. Jamie was truly beautiful, and what's more, he was somehow his. For the first time that year, the gratitude one is supposed to feel at the holidays actually flowed over him. He smiled and stood close to Jamie, shoulder to shoulder, the backs of their hands grazing each other. The touch of their flesh and the closeness of their finely suited bodies reminded them they were not alone in this sea of tweed jackets and obnoxious holiday ties.

"I have a special treat for you. He took the train up here all the way from Cambridge this afternoon with my boy, Jamie. I hear he's pretty good, too, so let's see

for ourselves, the maestro himself — *Mr. Everett Crisp!*
Everett, my boy, won't you come up here and play for us?"

Everett's eyes widened and Jamie spit up his cocktail
as two hundred eyes turned their accompanying heads
to look at the boys in the back of the room. Jamie was
used to a certain amount of attention, especially when
he was on display like this, but Everett wished for a trap
door beneath him that would plunge him into a deep
abyss. He immediately understood what Jamie had
meant about his father being a disease, as the crowd
applauded, mostly to show the Senator how much they
approved of his sound choice in entertainment but
secretly glancing at their watches.

"You don't have to. I'm so sorry. Everett, I'm sorry.
I knew he'd pull something like this," Jamie was frantic,
knowing full well that Everett could barely hear him
amid the din of polite applause. It was the thing Jamie
loathed the most about this house, not being heard
above the din of other goings-on. Everett was visibly
shaking.

Time wound itself down to slow motion, the ten
thousand clocks in the house seemed at a stand still as
all sense of sound abandoned Everett Crisp entirely.
He saw the people looking toward him in expectation,
some of the ladies were actually clad in white gloves,
a custom he had again thought merely a myth. Susan

White looked upon him with an air of sadness, even apology, and Jamie, tears forming in the corners of his eyes, was so livid and embarrassed at the same time he could hardly form words anymore. Everett gazed into those piecing blue eyes, the same as his father's, and knew instinctively what he needed to do.

"It's okay. I'll be fine," he said softly. And like the bravest warrior on the field, Everett Crisp strode through the menagerie of lace and Brooks Brothers suits to situate himself at the very fine, beautifully kept Steinway grand piano that he had of course noticed earlier that afternoon. The instrument shone so brightly, it's polished mahogany wood reflecting the holiday lights so perfectly that it almost caught him short of breath. He slid the lid back.

Jamie watched him from the back of the room, a wry kind of smile on his face, knowing full well what all of those crusty people, most of whom he had known distantly his whole life, were in for. Everett did this for him, he knew that, just as he knew that, as Everett stared at the keys and silence pervaded, the only way he would get through this was by putting invisible blinders on and blocking out everyone who surrounded him, staring him down the way a poker player prepares to call a bluff. If it could just be Everett and the keys, Jamie knew, he would be just fine.

Beethoven. He had chosen Beethoven. How safe, and how utterly unlike him. It took no time at all to win over the crowd, of course. Three chords in and they were all salivating for him, all of these "patrons of the arts," who turned to each other with raised eyebrows. This was not Bridget's, but ironically, the people who populated this room were precisely what most of the pompous young academics who inhabited that campus watering hole would grow to be.

It was a festive piece, one of the concertos, which one exactly Jamie forgot but he had heard him play it before and God knows *talk* about it endlessly. It was playful, elegant, and — as Everett performed it at the piano tonight, even the slightest bit *funny* with occasional head pops and lighthearted flourishes in the notes. It was the silly kind of Beethoven, circa the first hour of *Amadeus*. It had actually been written for a harpsichord, if he wasn't mistaken, and he knew Everett would be proud of him for remembering that little historical detail. Everett played the final notes that everyone at least pretended to know so well with their approving head nods and hands slightly in the air as though they were conducting, before polite parlor claps and a symphony of "ah's," broke out throughout the room, everyone so charmed by the young man from Harvard and, Jamie was certain, perhaps just a bit jealous of himself. Susan turned back to look at her son, a suitably impressed look upon her unmistakably tired face, which Jamie saw in plain sight yet pretended to ignore. Everett stood to give a brief nodding bow before heading back into the obscurity of the crowd, but was stopped by the aggressive arm of the senior gentleman from Connecticut, who was quickly revealing himself to be an asshole.

"Not so fast young man." He turned to his own, private assembly. "I think we need one more, don't you?" Again the applause. Oh, for Christ's sake. How many lines was this putz going to cross in one night? Fine. Settling himself once more at the piano, he knew what he would do just as easily as he knew which fingers to place on which keys. He turned to see Jamie nestled behind all of the people, standing gallantly in his blue suit, his lucent eyes focused intently upon his own. Jamie wasn't scared anymore, Everett could see it in his body language, and this made him happy. Jamie was proud. Proud of *him*, the idea of which came rushing down upon him along with gratitude. Grant White huddled in a corner with an associate, a somewhat unkempt man with a mustache in a brown suit and oversized glasses, the kind of person who plays the sidekick of the villain in movies or plays. Occasionally, they both gestured toward Everett and the piano, a subject of polite conversation. Having started the show, the Senator clearly had no need to attend to it further, and so he proceeded with his business affairs.

Everett started the song slowly, playing around with the melody for a while. It was a calm, almost beautifully stark piece of music but it was its simplicity that was its greatest strength. The charged attitude in the room reduced itself from ten to two instantaneously and Susan White swore she even felt the lights dim in her own living room. It was a classic, a standard that they had all heard before, but never quite like this perhaps, from a slightly ruffled twenty-something with a mane of thick black hair and was that — yes, an earring. Perhaps two. The melodic chords continued with a cradling gentleness, like very small waves quietly finding their way ashore on a dark beach when no one's looking but the moon; and then came the lyrics:

How much do I love you?
I'll tell you no lie
How deep is the ocean?
How high is the sky?
How many times a day do I think of you?
How many roses are sprinkled with dew?

How far would I travel
To be where you are?
How far is the journey
From here to a star?

And if I ever lost you
How much would I cry?
How deep is the ocean?
How high is the sky?

It was a song for him, Jamie knew, there was no escaping it. He had never before heard Everett sing, not in all of those times he had watched him at the piano. It was the tenderest thing he had ever encountered, as though a piece of his very soul escaped his parted lips as he gave voice to the lyric, his voice stretched out beneath what must have been a star filled sky — unadorned and simple, beautiful. The hundred or so other people faded away, absorbed right into the expensive oriental rugs, and it was just the two of them dancing around the great room, a place Jamie had always despised. Yes. Tonight, James White felt encased, held, *wanted* in his own spacious home, for the first time he could really recall. Reflected in Everett Crisp's eyes, the thousands of Christmas lights never looked so comforting.

Summer, 1978: Mason City, Iowa

"Just come back for something to eat. You could starve out here, I guess." He was a large man, taller than average and in the shape of a solid rectangle.

"I'm fine." It would take some convincing. His new tent home may have been sparse, but it was home, his own home, and he would not surrender it lightly.

"Just for an hour. We'll get you some — lunch, or breakfast, really. Some eggs. I can cook eggs. And then it'll all be okay." With only Mr. Able's coat to cover him, the morning air bit sharply into his torso as he sat straight up, talking through the half-unzipped flaps of his abode, hair askew and teeth in need of brushing. "We can wash your clothes, too. Here, I'll turn around. You get dressed. I'll wait right here."

With reluctance, young Everett Crisp, clad in only the clothes he had escaped with, now stained with mud, soon found himself, once again, walking alongside Ken Moberly, back to his cottage in the woods that stood at the edge of the reservoir. But their rendezvous did not end in an hour, or even two. The piano that sat near the window beckoned him, and a second lesson ensued. Everett Crisp thrilled when he heard the sounds he himself could make possible by the deployment of his fingers upon the keys of the beautiful instrument, the wood of which was a deep color of beauty he could scarcely describe. The dusty objects of the room looked on in welcome, as though the whole house had stood in anxious anticipation of his return. The piano itself seemed grateful to have someone caressing its keys, and Ken Moberly grew excited by the sound of the house filled with music as it once had been.

Quite unexpectedly, Ken Moberly's arm had reached around him as he sat at the piano. It was jarring, just a little bit off, a bit out of the ordinary, his own space ever so slightly intruded upon. And then the other hand, reaching around his other side, but this hand held something. Everett sensed something familiar, a scent, something that said home, something constant and comforting, pervading the air — and suddenly there sat Henry, his lone companion, in his own very lap once more, red painted smile and round, glass eyes staring up at him in greeting. Henry — who had seen it all and was the only one on his side, the only real witness, the one who would stay till the end. Instantly removing his hands from the keys, he clutched his old friend and buried his nose deep in his great good companion's sponge-like body, breathing in the familiar fragrance as a single tear made it's way down the side of his face in gratitude.

"He was in the trash — just kinda thrown on the top. I rescued him. Figured I'd see you around... Figured you needed each other."

"I do..." was all the young man could whisper, so grateful for the reunion.

Ken Moberly knew full well where the boy lived, as did most of the small town. The night previous, he had driven past the small brick house, the house that looked so peaceful from the outside. Something was off, he sensed it, and it surprised him little to learn that he had been correct. He had a talent for things such as this; a special kind of intuition.

Everett had never felt such thankfulness in all his life. His lone companion was returned to him and suddenly he did not feel so completely alone. The two of them could take on the hardship that was sure to follow, both of them official outcasts now, but outcasts together. 'Thank You' hardly seemed adequate. All Everett could really bring himself to do was to look Mr. Moberly directly in the eye, his own vision blurred from the quiet tears. Ken Moberly's eyes were kind and childlike, a dazzling shade of uncommon hazel. He looked down upon Everett, for whom he suddenly felt a kind of devotion, and smiled. Devoid of words, it was Everett Crisp's greatest wish, in that moment, that his indebtedness was apparent.

Spring, 2001: New York City

There is a spectacular week that occurs annually in New York City. Somewhere during the first fifteen days of May, the scent of the air changes. The wind blows warm instead of the biting frigidness that has tormented the city for the previous eight, long months. The trees that line the streets and occupy the parks burst open with green and the luscious, assorted colors of their own flowers — pale white, crimson, blushing pinks and lavenders.

Jamie sat sprawled on a tribal print blanket in the middle of Sheep's Meadow, gazing up at a nearly cloudless sky. He had taken the day off to dance with the new season in honor of Everett, this being his big day, whom he expected at any moment. It seemed as though most of the city had called in sick that day, the first carefree afternoon of what promised to be a very attractive season. Sun worshipers and everyday New Yorkers flooded Central Park, buying pretzels, walking dogs, throwing Frisbees, all celebrating the new air. It were as though they had all emerged from hibernation, having traded huddling about a fireplace in blankets and socks for strolling in sandals through thick blades of grass.

Everett entered the park in the East 60's. The noise and the grayness of the city, the exhaust from the cars that lined Fifth Avenue, faded quickly as they were replaced by lush vegetation, showing itself for the first time that year; above which could be seen the top halves of the same brown and silver buildings that had watched over the park for so many decades, keeping watch like proud parents, admiring their own reflection in small lakes, ponds and puddles. Making his way into Sheep's Meadow, he removed his leather shoes and his black dress socks, rolling up the pant legs of his one and only suit, somewhat disheveled and ill-fitting, the jacket of which he tossed over his shoulder as the sun unleashed it's rays directly upon him, or so it seemed. He loosened his tie.

He walked with no particular urgency amongst the park dwellers, breathing in the warm air as birds chirped and foliage rustled in the breeze. A family of four, tourists no doubt, having escaped one of the nearby hotels, cleared out of his way and there sat Jamie, basking in the weather on Everett's own blanket, looking every bit as handsome as he had all those years ago in Cambridge, and as content as he had looked on that very first Christmas morning, curled in that same blanket in the little loft just barely off campus.

The moment he caught Everett's eye, Jamie White knew the answer to his urgent question. As he raised his arm to wave, the biggest smile Everett could ever recall seeing on Jamie's handsome face, with it's chiseled features and perfectly smooth, naturally tan skin, showed itself. He removed his sunglasses as Everett approached, exposing those radiant blue pupils.

"Told ya so." Everett had refused to believe any of it until he had a signed contract in his hand which, at this very moment, he did. He clutched the papers to his chest, before dropping them onto the blanket in triumph. "So?"

"On September 24, the New York Philharmonic will feature special guest soloist, Everett Crisp, who will present his own, original compositions..." he took a dramatic pause as Jamie nearly spontaneously combusted, "at Carnegie Hall." It might as well have been writ large in bright yellow letters and flung around the ticker tape in Times Square. Jamie was positively beaming, and it very nearly broke Everett's heart to see him so proud. He had just come from the office of a mister Herb Henson, henceforth to be known as Everett's agent, acquired after Ms. P. had called in a favor at her own agency. Everett joined Jamie on the blanket. There was a prolonged kiss that said nothing further than 'I am so happy that you're here today.'

The pair just lay there for a good long while, gazing up at the clouds and silently envisioning the future. Oh, Everett — who thought this day would not ever arrive. Even if nothing came of it, even were it only one night at Carnegie Hall with the New York Philharmonic, it seemed at that moment that all of it, the intense struggle, the commitment to his calling, the voice inside of him that had always said — 'no, you're right and they're all wrong. This is your path and *trust* in that," had come to fruition. Silence passed as an enormous cumulous cloud, appropriately full and fluffy and clean, joyous, drifted past until the sky was pure blue once more. Jamie would be front row center when Everett made his Carnegie Hall debut, and nothing could be more perfect.

"I've decided something." He wasn't going to bring it up today, he had no desire to muscle in on Everett's limelight. But the moment seemed so ideal, the day so entirely exquisite, that it seemed like putting cheese upon a perfectly cooked hamburger, a thought driven home to Jamie by the barbecue tainted air. Once he said it, there would be no going back. It was his own decision to make; he hadn't been coerced. He had stood firmly upon his own two feet, resolved whatever aversions he may have had, and reached a resolution. "I've decided to run for my father's Senate seat when he steps down next year." Turning on his side, he searched Everett's eyes for approval, knowing full well that both of their lives were about to catapult. "And I can't do it alone."

Everett approached this announcement as though it were a flower he had unexpectedly stumbled upon in the woods, uncertain whether or not it was poisonous. A few moments passed as the freshly poured water permeated the soil of Everett's conscious self; this wasn't entirely unexpected.

"What does Grant have to say about that?" Everett Crisp hadn't spoken with the Senator since their last, now historic meeting at the family compound in New London. It had been made perfectly clear to him that he would never be a welcome part of the White dynasty, and only stood to be a barrier between the star son and his own legacy.

"He'll learn to love it." Everett knew how badly Jamie wanted this, it had been written in capital letters across his forehead since the day they met. Try to forego his heritage though he always had, Jamie White was born to be a leader, it was evident since those very first days at Harvard when he rallied his fellow students to protest tuition hikes, even though his family could very well afford twice his tuition and that of all of his friends. Still, he had sat outside the main administration building in torn jeans beating a drum, holding up crudely designed signs and chanting badly rhymed slogans. Grant White had, of course, expressed his outrage at his son's "tacky" choice of cause, especially after his picture had been splashed across small newspapers, a profound soiling of the family image, particularly considering that Senator Grant sat upon Harvard's Board of Trustees.

In the time that had passed and as the anger with issues that were beyond his own control had resolved themselves, Jamie White had emerged a fully formed person, every bit as sure of himself as he had ever been, but with the power of his own sense of self firmly palpable. He had been told at a very early age that there was nothing he could not accomplish; it's a common saying that parents tell their children. But after all of the years that he had survived and all that he had seen and everything that had brought him to this place, he now believed that to be true. The smoke had cleared to reveal a very clear path, one that had absolutely nothing to do with expectation, but rather a path upon which he *wanted* to embark. And he wanted to walk this path with Everett Crisp, straight through to the end. There would be numerous obstacles, but that was never a good reason for not pursuing something worthwhile.

Everett looked into Jamie's sparkling eyes which sat upon a face with a smirk that just dared him not to stride into the abyss and begin this adventure with him. He had always felt himself a burden upon others — his family, lovers, those to whom he owed his education. How could he also be a burden upon this man whom he loved above all others, above everything as it turned out. The stakes were high. He could cost Jamie his entire dream — the well laid out plan his lover now embraced as his own destiny. The burden of himself was once cause for him to abandon this man entirely, give up that which meant the most to him. He would not do it again. He would find a way to be useful this time; a help rather than a hindrance. Besides, they would be political pioneers. And what's more exciting than that?

"Are you really prepared to stand on a podium in front of all of Connecticut — with *me* by your side?" He again searched Jamie's expression, but he already knew the answer. Jamie smiled that thousand kilowatt smile of his. "Okay, then." Everett grasped Jamie's hand, holding it tight as though they were both about to jump blindly yet in tandem from a supersonic jet. *"Let's do it."*

As they sat in the park that afternoon, the wistful breeze sweeping through their hair, it all seemed so simple. The great struggles of the past had melted, just as had the snow that so recently occupied the stretch of Earth upon which they now sat. Maybe it didn't have to rain all the time. Maybe it could be sunny and maybe Everett could truly breathe in the scent of Sheep's Meadow for the very first time and maybe it wasn't all the painful crusade he had always told himself it was, this prolonged wrestle with the world. Perhaps there was good to discover, a lightness of spirit, an actual contentment and even enjoyment to be found in the passing of the hours, and dare he even venture to say the days, months — years? Had he arrived at himself and could this *possibly* be real enough to trust?

That day, as they sat amid the scent of freshly cut grass with all of New York City gazing down upon them both in approval, it seemed as though joy was something that was tangible, as readily accessible as air.

Winter, 2026: Malibu, CA

It was Jeff Severin's first ride in a convertible. The studio would have sent a car but for the first time in what had to be years, Everett had the desire to put the top down on his smoke grey Mercedes and drive himself, which he rarely did. The wind in his mostly silver hair was a welcome visitor, and even more, the look of delight that was etched across the face of his handsome young friend. It was that which made the effort entirely worthwhile. Jeff was happy to be going to a real live movie studio, of course, but even more than that, — Everett Crisp was, for once, out of that ramshackle beach house and seeing the light of day. As he sat in the passenger seat of the stylish car, this couldn't help bring a smile to the young man's face as he turned to look at his friend, the maestro, sitting at the helm of a vehicle he surely hadn't seen in quite some time. It actually brought a smile to the old man's face, too, but he tried to mask this by turning to his left whenever he could.

The Malibu Colony had changed considerably since he purchased his beach house, some twenty years prior. There was less and less beach, the people had become, mostly, younger than himself and the spirit of the place had devolved into something competitive, rather than restive. Nature was eating away at The Colony, it seemed, in so many ways, and who knew what the future might hold? It wouldn't be up to Everett Crisp to decide. But the slight smell of salt water still rode on the breeze and permeated the air, as rows of overgrown houses in varied styles competed for beachfront space. Everett had a house in Bel Air as well but he hadn't seen it in at least a year, perhaps more, preferring to spend his time near his beloved Pacific Ocean. Besides, the Bel Air house had always seemed too formal, the air stifled with the thick aroma of problems — angry directors, jilted lovers, bad investments, sticky fingered staff, nosy reporters, overpriced gardeners, too much cocaine — it was a windstorm from the past he preferred blow out to sea. Early in his days in California there had been dinner parties and late nights/early mornings out by the pool, warm water that caressed the tight buttocks of young men and their restless libidos, parties that lasted till well past dawn. But that was all beyond him now. Besides, he liked the piano in the little Malibu house the most; it was freer, more willing to follow him to unusual places, unlike the staunch rigidity he felt from the keys of the other piano, now shut up in that embarrassingly large house that he had acquired, he now realized, merely to prove a silly point to himself. He should sell it and everything in it, but that would just take up valuable time. He already had plenty of money.

For Jeff Severin, pulling up to the studio gates was akin to being in a movie itself. The California sun beat down upon his dirty blonde hair as they passed the security booth and drove onto the lot and then — the whole magical world of Hollywood was laid out right before him, like standing just inside the gates of an amusement park. As commonplace as a movie lot had become for Everett over the decades, it made him smile to experience it through Jeff's eyes, as though it were the very first time for him, too. He wouldn't say it out loud, of course, but it charmed Everett to see the wonder that engulfed this young man whom he'd come to think of as his. It was all a new experience for Jeff, like finding the shiniest toy in the box.

"Well, look who decided to show up." Jeff recognized the famous director right away, but remained silent as he felt himself scrutinized just for getting out of the car. Older men who bring young companions onto the lot, both male and female, was hardly anything new in Hollywood, but certainly uncharacteristic for Everett Crisp. "They're all waiting. The scenes are cued up," the words came from Garrett Oliver, by now easily an octogenarian and a great legend of film. His was a kind face, wrinkles exaggerated by nearly half a decade or more in the sun. Despite his age, there remained a boyishness about him. His words were slow and deliberate, father like and far from scolding, although Everett's procrastination had certainly held up production on his film.

The director grabbed Everett about the arm, as though reuniting with a long lost pal, and ushered him inside, leaving Jeff to meander along behind as the warmth of the California sun was instantly exchanged for the cold darkness of the sound stage, like entering a cool torture chamber. The two of them exchanged some small talk before parting, as Jeff's eyes struggled to readjust. "I'll be up in the booth if you need me," Everett smiled a tired smile at his old friend. "And Ev," he looked from Jeff's eyes to the maestro's, "you really do look good." The director escaped into the darkness of stage fourteen, as Everett Crisp returned his attention to his guest.

"Come on. Have a look at this." Rounding a corner and walking into the light, a small city had emerged from the darkness — an entire industrial nation sat before a small wooden box, tuning instruments, sipping coffee, flipping through pages of music, engaging in idle chit chat. Behind them all was a full sized movie screen onto which images from the film in question flashed in random sequence, a barrage of numbers and letters littering the bottom of each frame. A cello player was the first to notice that Everett had entered the room, and very quickly, a hush feel over the entire proceeding, as though a joint session of Congress had been called to order. Jeff, having been seated just out of the light, was not only proud to accompany Everett, but utterly entranced by all of it. Here was a place where Hollywood ceased being Hollywood, and could transform itself into any place in the world, the universe — a dream factory.

It had been quite a few years since Everett had dared stand upon that tiny square box. Now, with all of those silent eyes boring holes right into his body, he wondered if he'd be able to do it at all. Jamie squeezed his hand, not in any sort of intimate way, but as a transfer of courage, confidence. Everett Crisp swallowed hard and made his way to the box, picking up his old friend the baton and greeting the gargantuan symphony orchestra with a shy yet stern greeting. There were some muffled instructions before Garrett Oliver's voice came over the PA system:

"Okay, so we're cued up for 42A. Do you wanna run it first —" A simple wave of the hand from Everett was all that was required for anyone to know that Everett Crisp was ready to go; he knew exactly where he was and what he wanted. He raised his arm in the air. As he brought the baton firmly down upon the wind, the power of a sixty eight-piece orchestra was very nearly enough to cause Jeff Severin to topple backward in his folding chair.

Summer, 1978: Mason City, Iowa

He looked at his body in the dusty mirror, through the dim light that enveloped the guest room. He couldn't think of a time when he had ever enjoyed seeing his reflection, convinced of the unattractiveness of himself, assured by all those who knew him, really. But tonight, in this warm room with the window open to allow just a hint of evening breeze and the faint sound of the crickets, he surveyed his arms, his torso, his thickish middle and soft, boyish chest, the way his hips were slightly wider than most, how the soft flesh around his navel, tan from swimming on his back, quivered slightly.

Ken Moberly was there to deliver a towel for the morning but couldn't help examining the scene before him — a young man exploring his own reflection. How thrilling to have another person in his home, to have life in a structure that had become so empty over so many years. He couldn't help but smile:

"You're okay. You know?" he said, looking his young guest up and down. Silence followed as the two made eye contact in the reflection. Ken Moberly's words were enough to bring small tears to the young man's eyes, but he would not let them be seen, refusing to turn around but caught red handed by the honesty of that mirror. "I used to stand in front of that same mirror when I was your age," he laid the towel down on the bed, but his eyes never left Everett. "For the morning —." Ken looked back into the mirror now, seeing himself, so much taller but certainly no wiser, behind his young houseguest. His mind flooded with thoughts of himself at the same age. How frightened, how abandoned, how questioning he was — how much he couldn't quite comprehend and still could not. He smiled at young Everett Crisp, and his smile was even returned in the glass.

"Thank you, Ken." Everett had never called an adult by his first name before, but he felt comfortable with his new friend, Ken Moberly, who drifted down the hall to his own bedroom, the one he had occupied since his birth. Everett exhaled and saw, in the mirror, the trace of his own, lingering smile. This is what others feel regularly, he thought, it must be. Home. Peace. Comfort. He had reached through the invisible bubble that had always separated himself from the rest of the world and seen things in color for the very first time. Lying down upon Ken Moberly's guest bed, he drifted to sleep, this time to music of a different kind entirely: his own.

10

Late Summer, 2001: New York City

J AMIE WHITE ROSE, without the aide of an alarm clock, at six as he usually did. He had carefully selected his suit, shirt and tie the evening previous, hanging them neatly on his side of the closet above pre-shined shoes. Plenty of hot water in Brooklyn that morning, for some reason, so he lingered for an extra few minutes beneath the stream that fell from above with never quite enough pressure. Old Brooklyn brownstones were full or quirks, so he decided to be grateful that something emerged from the pipes at all this morning. He ate his toast while wrapped in a towel, switching on a single lamp in the kitchen, the light of which cut through the dark room and illuminated the quiet, barely spilling onto Everett's piano which stood in the corner, surrounded by messy notes strewn in every which way. He glanced through *The Wall Street Journal*, something he read casually and without much interest, more so he could say he had seen this or that article should someone ask him at the office. Glancing in the bathroom mirror as he tied his tie in a stiff Windsor knot, he saw what he could only imagine was a tiny wrinkle beneath his left eye. Well, it was bound to happen sometime. Finally, dressed and with slicked hair and his Grandfather's watch clasped securely to his wrist, he kissed Everett, still asleep in their rumpled bed following his late shift at The Pillow Factory, and made his way out the door of the apartment and down the dozen or so thinly carpeted stairs which always smelled just a bit like cat urine.

It was a crisp morning, the first sign that summer was officially in the process of abandoning them, folding itself up to be put away on a shelf to be re-birthed only after nine long months had passed. Why must the cold months outnumber the warm ones by such an unfair margin, he thought. Still, as the cool morning air seeped between the layers of his clothing and into the open pores of his freshly scrubbed skin doused with aftershave, a new scent permeated the neighborhood. The turn of seasons was not altogether unwelcome, but exciting in a way. Down the concrete steps of the subway he trotted to join others dressed as he was on the N train. No seats to be had this morning, as usual. The rusted iron wheels crept forward, and Jamie White began his journey into downtown Manhattan.

Everett woke early, for him — just past nine. He headed for the piano first, looking over the notes and measures he had agonized over the previous afternoon before he had reluctantly headed in for his shift at work to plunk out show tunes for the regulars and village tourists alike from six till four. He had given up drinking for a while as he prepared for the concert, just weeks away now. His mind was clear and he was ready to work, settled behind the keys in pajama bottoms and a wrinkled, white t-shirt; black hair askew and teeth in need of brushing. A plane sauntered across the bright morning sky, bringing with it all the rattling noise of it's turbo engines and casting a shadow across the blank white walls of the little apartment. It seemed that they were getting closer and closer lately, as they prepared for their landings at LaGuardia and JFK. He opened the living room window to let the cool air rush in. Ah, yes — there it was. Summer was in the process of extinguishing itself altogether, and something new entirely would blow into town on this clearest of mornings.

Los Angeles: Winter, 2026

Everett Crisp was masterful with an orchestra. He knew each sound, each instrument, every string and player as well as he knew his own eye color or the number of fingers and toes he possessed. Simple refinements, a crescendo for the strings, the elimination of a bass line, and it was perfect; a perfect match to the raw images that flickered across the screen. He saw the sculpture clearly, and had merely to eliminate the excess stone that surrounded it. Everything married itself seamlessly, Jeff observed, and Everett stood at the head of it all.

It had only taken him three nights to write the score. With Jeff Severin drifting between the beach and the kitchen, from whence he dutifully supplied meals and clean ashtrays, the music came just as simply as water plunging from a faucet, leaving Everett the simple task of photographing it and writing it all down. If he could just get through these stretch of days, he knew, this limited time, the phone would stop ringing and he could return his attention to the waves and more important matters.

On the first break of the day, Everett headed for the Craft Services table for fruit and coffee. Stirring Sweet and Low with a plastic stick, he could see plainly that Jeff had made a new friend with the young bassoonist. Ah, yes — the two of them had been stealing glances throughout the session, it was unmistakable. *See how they smile at each other,* he thought, as the fresh aroma of java stimulated his senses; see how easy, how relaxed, how pleasant and cordial it all is. The young musician couldn't have been more than twenty-five or so, all pulled together in tight jeans and crew cut hair as was the style nowadays (again) for the young men of Los Angeles. It was all perfectly innocent and, Everett supposed, had circumstances not been what they were, he might have been charmed by it all.

He would not allow this to break his heart; no, that would be silly and expected. He would shrug it off. Everett returned his attention to the sliced strawberries on his plate, piercing them with a plastic fork that trembled in his grasp. He tried in vane to resist the temptation to gaze wistfully at the young people. So much they did not know. Everett was jealous all right, but jealous more for the luxury of ignorance. Still, he couldn't help that sting of pain that electrified an entire side of his body. *Nothing is ours to keep,* he thought to himself. *Never has been, never will be. Close as we may feel we are to anything constant, the ground will soon enough rumble, and plates will shift.* He looked down at his trembling hand.

Christmas, 1990: New London, CT

The show was over and Susan White stood in the foyer near the door, shaking the hands of the exiting partygoers, some of whom stepped clumsily and with obvious effort. She met each guest with the same genuine smile and warm farewell, despite their slurred words or obvious bids for her husband's attention. These were mostly well-practiced politicians, no matter what line of work they might represent, and each of them knew full well that Susan White had the ear of the Senator, despite outward appearances that the couple were merely a facade. Whatever anyone might have to say about them, the White's were a unit that functioned perhaps unconventionally, but that very lack of convention seemed oddly to be their greatest source of power.

Jamie stood by his mother's side, playing his role in his perfectly cut Italian suit and flashing his three hundred kilowatt smile, the same one Everett had first noticed on campus before the two had ever exchanged a word. It was that "come to my own private island" smile again, and Everett marveled at his performance as he watched from a distance, sitting at the marble-top bar in the study as the caterers cleaned up around him and he sipped the last few drops of scotch from a Waterford glass. Jamie White was seamlessly in his element, this kind of thing simply existed in his blood. It was a side of this man, this curious young oddity whom he had come to cherish above all other things, with which Everett had never before been confronted. It was instinct, his very heritage.

There was no more music, just the clinking of empty glasses as they were hurried into racks and, from a distance, the rumbling of catering trucks. It was not unlike two a.m. at Bridget's when the lights come up and the remaining bar flies are tossed out. The glasses may have been heavier and nicer, the surroundings may have been far more lush with silk flower arrangements, grandfather clocks and fourteen foot, heartlessly decorated Christmas trees, but the sentiment was just the same.

"I wonder if I might have a word." His shoulder was grasped firmly and Senator White appeared seemingly from nowhere, as he sometimes did, or so Everett had been warned. Turning on his stool, Everett could see that Grant White had not dropped by alone. Indeed, that same odd, somewhat unkempt man in the brown suit and mustache was with him, the one with the wiry round glasses that took up most of his face and the wisp of curled hair that only half concealed his head.

"Mr. Crisp, I'd like you to meet Ronald Haff. Ronald here is Dean of the Juilliard School in New York. You're familiar with Juilliard, aren't you, son?" Six eyes all exchanged informed glances. Instantly, Grant White and Everett Crisp were on the same page; they were both practiced game players because they had to be. Dean Haff simply looked at the young Mr. Crisp and all but drooled, swirling some vile looking brown liquid around in a highball glass.

"Helluva talent you have there, young man, *helluva* talent," he said, resting his arm on Everett's other shoulder. He was half sloshed, perhaps more so. Mr. Haff was obviously one of those people who had found a life in hanging on to artists, dancing in their shadows while drowning whatever might have been for himself in drinks and pity.

"Ronald here thinks that you'd be quite an asset to Juilliard. You should think about that. Give him your card, Ron." The Senator had said it with just enough ice in his voice to make it clear that it was not a request, but rather a commandment from a high ranking officer, or what's more, a high rolling donor. Dean Haff passed his card onto Everett, who was reluctant to take it. Seizing an opportunity, Ron Haff took it upon himself to place his card in Everett's shirt pocket, lingering for a few seconds too long.

"Excuse us, Ron," said the Senator, a more subtle commandment this time, perhaps in reward for obeying his first. The Senator's request brought an imaginary cold towel across the Dean's face, as though he were a hitchhiker who had just been asked to get out of the car half way to a shared destination to be left on the side of the road. Grant White made his request of Mr. Haff while keeping his eyes fixed firmly upon his son's young friend. Ah, Everett could see it now — the family trait of opening a window and making even the most out of place feel like a welcome part of the party. But the difference between father and son was that father seemed to take personal satisfaction in slamming that window shut upon innocent or even not so innocent fingers as the situation warranted and to which Dean Ronald Haff had just fallen victim. Anyone who bathes in someone else's sunlight can expect storm clouds soon enough. Full steam ahead — that was Grant White's motto. It had served him well in the war, in politics, and certainly in the politics of life. Keep all the players moving in the same direction and never take your eye off the ball; it was spelled out in the way his eyes welcomed you one moment, and cast you aside the next.

"Sure, Grant," said Dean Haff, who, after an uncomfortable pause, downed the contents of his glass and surrendered it to the bar with a full-throttled clunk, before making his way out of the library where he stumblingly joined the receiving line to pay his respects to Mrs. White and Jamie before sloshing his way out the door, leaving the Senator and Everett alone for the first time.

"He's right you know; you *are* talented."

"Thank you, sir."

"Now then: what are we going to do about it? All of your talent?"

"I'm going to be a lawyer."

"Son," the Senator sat down right next to Everett at an adjoining stool, and it were as though they were just two old drinking buddies. "Let me tell you something. Club soda, please — " he instructed a remaining cater-waiter, obviously off the clock and anxious to close up shop but who obediently lept to the request nevertheless. "The world has enough lawyers. Thousands and thousands of them all running around and many of them are very talented. VERY talented in their own way." He was uncomfortably close now, his breath warm on the side of Everett's face. As he had many times in the past with a whole array of people who ranged from unwilling "contributors" to fellow politicians, Senator White would paint an elaborate picture which he would get this young man to see clearly if he had to force it into the boy's eye sockets himself. "But if any of them could do what you can do — ANY of them; they'd be the quickest ex-lawyers you ever met in your life. Who wouldn't surrender tortes and litigation and all that *paper* and billable hours — to make *music*?" It occurred to Everett that the most successful people in the world were really used car salesmen. Dress them up however one may, you really are what you can sell in this world. "Take Jamie for example — wonderful boy, really. A little rambunctious, — reckless, as I'm sure you've realized by now. He doesn't see things the way you and I do. He's never had to." Jamie was right; he didn't know his son at all. "But his talent is the law, that's all he can do. And he's going to do it *very* well and he wants to go into politics someday because that's who *he is* — what he was put on this Earth to *do*... It's my boy's *destiny*." He was like a wizard when he spoke, concocting some strange kind of potion that he fully expected the young musician, and everyone else, for that matter, to choke down with gratitude. Everett was certain that most folks undoubtedly did so; the charm was as severe as it was infectious.

Although Everett was too embarrassed to look the Senator in the eye throughout any of this, occupying himself with the mostly dissolved ice cubes that lingered in his crystal rocks glass, he was fully aware that the elder statesman's eyes never stopped boring holes into the side of his head. Just now, he had reached into Everett's shirt pocket to retrieve Dean Haff's card. "It's time you thought about yours... *Your* destiny... Wouldn't you say?" Senator Grant White placed the card firmly in the palm of the young musician's hand and stood to tend to the smattering of remaining guests before turning back to complete his task. "By the way, we have a rather elaborate security system here at Lakeview Hill, so — it's probably best if you stay in your room tonight once the guests have all gone — it's a real bear if it goes off in the middle of the night. Just a nuisance." The two made eye contact for the first time. "I'm sure you understand." A hearty pat on the back, and Everett was left alone with a business card.

As he watched the Senator go, he wondered how many thousands of deals, how many hundreds of political scenarios perhaps played out in this very study, had made him into the fully formed, skilled and capable bullshit artist he was. He could make just about anybody around drink shit and like it. It was certainly impressive, Everett was forced to admit, as he set his empty glass down upon the smooth stone surface of the bar. Dean Haff's stupid bit of card stock lingered in his palm like an explosive. Flipping the card over, there were two words scrawled on the back in hasty ballpoint pen, both in capital letters: "FULL RIDE."

From the foyer, Jamie caught Everett's eye. The politician's son smiled that intoxicating grin of his — not even his "own private island" smile but a more personal, even more intense one, reserved exclusively for the two of them. Jamie could see something altered in Everett, ever so slightly. Above the heads of the final guests, he mouthed to him, "What?," to which Everett simply waved him away, returning his attention to his newly replenished scotch on the rocks.

Everett Crisp divided his attention between Jamie and the card, Jamie, then the card, Jamie, card. The hall clock chimed some unknowable hour — he had lost count. His heart sped up and he could hear nothing but blood rushing through his ears.

Late Summer, 2001: New York City

Everett was at a stand still. Nothing was coming. He was never the kind to get blocked, he either switched on his abilities or switched them off, it had always been that simple. But he needed to compose the best work of his life for the Carnegie Hall concert and this morning, as he sat groggily at his piano bench, he could scarcely even hear the music in his own head. Surely it was there, buried somewhere beneath a blanket of fear and anxiety and amid a few dusty old cabinets full of doubt. It took all of his effort to play what he had already written. He second-guessed every note, every key signature, even the general theme itself. He could see only the minutia this morning, the detail in which he had always placed such importance. The entirety of the piece, all of the moving parts put together as one, he could not hear and he was only moments away from chucking the whole thing into the trash. "The finest thing you have ever written or will ever write," was what he had demanded of himself after signing the Carnegie Hall contract, words he repeated even as he slept.

It was quite clear that he would get nowhere this morning. The worn-down upright piano sat near the windows that overlooked the tired gray street and in the far distance, Prospect Park, just a hint of which could be made out beyond the fire hydrant and a row of trees, who clutched their leaves tightly in anticipation of the coming autumn and the inevitable farewell that would accompany the new season. Shutting the lid of the barely tuned instrument, which he had picked up at an estate sale in Carroll Gardens from a sympathetic regular customer at The Pillow Factory, he tiptoed across the linoleum covered floors, the same faded rust color that covered the entire apartment, chilly against his bare feet for the first time that season. Making his way into the kitchen, he turned the coffee pot on and passed time waiting for the comforting sounds that brought a fresh aroma. Jamie's bright blue mug sat in the dish rack, carefully washed and left to dry, and this brought a smile to his face as he ran his fingers over the smooth ceramic.

The coffee was ready, at last. He had confiscated his own mug from work, and the sound of the hot, brown gold splashing into it brought a sense of serenity, even if it was a decidedly ugly thing to drink from, yellow with the bar's stupid logo plastered on the side. It was just Everett, hot coffee, and what would be music that morning, and there seemed everything correct about this, even if it wasn't flowing as freely as he had hoped. He headed back into the living room and made his way to the piano. He would try again. He had to. It was simply what he did.

Halfway between the bay windows and the two upside down milk crates that suspended a piece of plywood, which served as a coffee table, Everett Crisp stopped. His legs had failed him and he stopped, perfectly still, in the center of the room. An invisible hand of sorts had grabbed his ankles and held him captive exactly where he stood. A profound sense of dread overcame his entire self, instantly and without warning, filling his entire body with doubt; but then what's more than doubt: *dread*. The blackest feeling he could ever recall feeling consumed him from foot to scalp. Something was very wrong. He had been invisibly shot directly through his body several times over, the kitchen behind him no doubt riddled with spent bullets. Everett Crisp's mug fell to the floor as hot coffee, black, ran amuck, seeping into the floorboards, unbridled and uncontrolled. He stood, terrified, in the middle of the tiny room in Park Slope, Brooklyn as something very sinister swept through the world. A dam had burst, he could feel it and it was just as real and tangible as the shattered coffee cup that littered the floor.

Summer, 1978: Mason City, Iowa

Ken Mobery had a record player and an elaborate speaker system. He called it "the Hi-Fi." Everett found it almost as beautiful to look at as the polished piano that sat in the bay windows. But best of all, hidden inside a living room cabinet were over two hundred records from all the great composers — Handel, Ravel, Brahms, Beethoven — all of the music he had memorized but had never before heard right out loud — and it *burst* through the speakers of the little stone house that stood by the reservoir, filling it with the sounds he dreamed of at night. The best thing was that no one came around to bother them. Everett had found a new home, a home where he was *wanted*, and he was more than happy there.

Ken Moberly didn't really have any idea how to cook or clean, so Everett took it upon himself to show him. What a relief not to have to scrub Jay and Sheila's dishes each night or play the music that infatuated him merely through headphones, late at night. Instead, music filled the house constantly, and he could play it just as loudly as he could stand it. It was like luxuriating in silk sheets. They went swimming, they played board games, they took Ken Moberly's canoe out around the bend to watch the birds begin their migration south. Laying back in their vessel, flat on his back, he could feel youth upon his own face, and for the first time he seriously considered the future. Not just escaping his present, but what he might do, accomplish, now that he was unleashed, set free.

Sheila and Mr. Thompson crossed his mind only slightly, on the periphery, like an old skin he had shed and abandoned someplace in the woods. No doubt they had noticed his absence, but then again, it was the start of football season. It was entirely likely that his bedroom had already been converted into a sports memorabilia room, wherein Mr. Thompson no doubt sat with his paper grocery bags full of popcorn to worship at a shrine of helmets and bats, wishing only that he himself could adorn those very walls.

School would start soon, but perhaps he would not return. He was due to begin High School that year but it could wait, surely. Ken needed him; he was lost on his own, clearly. And besides, what more education did Everett require aside from the records that resided in that magic cabinet? Although he had been grateful to formal education for getting him out of Sheila and Mr. Thompson's clutches for a stretch of time each day, Everett mostly found school to be useless and boring. Everett Crisp had more important things to do.

As for Ken, he now had the playmate he had always sought. He learned things from Everett, things he never knew he should know. Despite what he had been told were his limited capabilities, he had much to share, and was anxious to do so. He didn't see why his young friend shouldn't go on living with him forever. They had packed up his tent along with Walter Able's muddy coat, and they both found a kind of sanctuary in Ken Moberly's limestone refuge. He was the last living Moberly, a descendant from a storied local family, with funds distributed from a trust four times annually, money which Ken really had no idea how to spend. Yes, this new person was exactly the thing to wake the old house up again, give it that splash of life it so desperately needed after all of these lonely, dusty years. Ken loved it.

Christmas, 1990: New London, CT

"It's done." Grant White had a way of announcing such things to his wife as proclamations as he went on about whatever tasks to which he found himself currently committed. He had always had difficulty separating his work and private lives, mostly because they were one and the same, feeding off of each other just as the lion needs the lamb. His alabaster hair betrayed his youthful vigor.

Susan White sat at her vanity, removing the last bits of cold cream from what had been a carefully painted party face. Each time she gazed into the mirror she knew the lines about her eyes were that much deeper, the outline of her face that much more plump, despite her best efforts. This wouldn't have bothered her so much had she not known that it was such a disappointment to Grant, which he would never say out loud, of course. Like so much between them, much went unspoken. She watched him from the beveled, brass mirror as he undid his tie and carefully hung his trousers in his expansive wardrobe, just as he did every night, or at least every night that he was home or rather, "in residence," as she sometimes jokingly referred to it with the staff. By the time he entered the bedroom they shared, she was quite aware that his thoughts were already onto the following day's challenges, among other things.

"He's certainly very talented, isn't he?" She would broach the subject casually, proceeding with all of the caution that was called for. Indeed, she nearly sung the words, as though the statement were as common as commenting on the weather.

"He'll be a great asset somewhere. But not here." The Senator's words were definitive, the only language he knew. Mrs. White watched her husband don his silk, monogrammed pajamas and thought what a far cry all of this was from those wayward college days when he had actually pursued *her*. Imagine that: *he* had pursued *her*. She was an art major and on top of the world back then, ready to grab a few planets in her fists and shake them around a bit. He was so poor, attending school on a work-study program. But he was so utterly sure of himself back then, so ripe with ideas and principals. Those days had been flashing through her mind quite a bit, lately.

"And did you discuss this with Jamie?" Her lips were the final thing to de-mask. She felt better once the cosmetics were off her face; she had shed her camouflage and could now speak freely. She tossed the tissues onto the vanity and turned to look at her husband, this creature who shared her bed and whom, it seemed, she hardly knew at all yet professed to know her so thoroughly that it was very nearly terrifying.

"James will be fine. He's a tough boy; he just doesn't know it yet. This kind of thing builds character." Grant White had learned early in his life that once a decision has been made, it's been made. Come hell or high water, he would defend that decision to the grave. There was to be no swaying of the Senator's very firm convictions. Even if, in the privacy of his own mind, images of his infant son occasionally made themselves known, and even if, on private occasion, he concerned himself with the boy's personal happiness; it needn't be anything to air publicly, not even with his wife nor indeed, Jamie himself. The decision had been made. Jamie White's future had been assured and it was well worth fighting for.

The elephant had been in the room for decades and Susan White was bored to tears with it. "And if he never forgives you, — will that also *build character?*" The two of them had not arrived at their place in the world without complimenting the other, without challenging each other.

"Don't be ridiculous, Sue. We do all sorts of stupid things when we're young. It's our responsibility to steer the ship. We're his parents." Senator White had turned on his debating voice now, a well-practiced facade he unknowingly pulled out whenever he felt challenged, particularly if unsure of his convictions. Even the rhythm of his speech changed and the tenor of his voice, while sincere, was really just part of a carefully practiced pantomime.

"He's our son and he's proud of his friend and he wanted us to meet him!" She put up a fight because she thought she should. This was more than a subtle suggestion in legislative policy, which she knew backward and forward. This concerned her greatest creation. But given the web that already hung about all three of their lives, this, Susan White knew, was not an argument she could win. James White was more than her son; he was a figure straight out of central casting. Nothing would ever interfere with that, as much as she yearned to cut the tangled tentacles that would always bind Jamie to the two of them.

"He didn't want to come here, it's written all over his face. That boy wanted to come, that's who. That struggling *artist* wanted to see what this was all about up here. You can see dollar signs written all over him."

"So you gave them to him." Her voice dropped a few octaves when the two of them spoke in private.

"He need never know that. I've arranged it." Case closed. Of the many, many opponents whom he had taken on socially and politically over his decades as a public servant, his most worthy adversary, by far, sat just two feet away from him, gazing into a mirror, searching for what was simply no longer there. "Go to bed, Sue. You'll feel better in the morning. Lights out."

Susan White had cringed, every time over the past thirty years, when she had suffered the indignity of hearing her husband utter the phrase "lights out." It was an expression he had picked up in the military, of course, but there was a gross selfishness about it, as though he had proclaimed the day done, despite whatever her wishes might have been, and many were the times she found herself sitting in the dark. Grant White could order the sun itself to set, or so he thought, and few were around to debate this. Susan White chose her battles judiciously, choosing not to expend energy on the merely trite.

The absurdity that the two of them still shared a bed overcame her at that moment. It was not as though they were unwilling to admit the brazen truths of their marriage, and it was a very unique marriage, to even themselves; it just simply went unspoken. In sharing a bed, still and after all of these thousands of years, the two of them somehow proved to the public at large that they were real and could be trusted, that they were not the one dimensional couple they frequently feared they were. It was all for the greater good. All of it. Susan White was left in a nearly pitch black room, sitting still with only the tiny light of her vanity illuminating her face, which she again studied in that frustratingly honest mirror.

"You know. When the parties are all over and you're out of office and the phones have stopped ringing, — it'll just be us. You know that, don't you? Just you and me." She laughed a quiet laugh, in spite of herself, and thought of her son and the charming young man who had had the great misfortune of stepping into the Connecticut land mine.

"And isn't that sad?"

Late Summer, 2001: New York City

Nothing but static danced up and down his 19" television screen. The phone in the kitchen was dead. Sirens outside. And then silence. For a long while...

silence. An uneasy and unwelcome wind swept right through the heart of Brooklyn.

He left the apartment and headed for the Brooklyn Bridge. He walked, then ran as quickly as his legs would carry him, past the serene, tree-lined blocks of his neighborhood, streets where one might never know that the world was ripping itself apart at that very moment. There was an altered smell in the air, a kind of stench that littered the atmosphere. He finally reached the bridge and struggled against the tide of thousands pouring over it from the other direction. Shell shocked individuals, an ash of gunmetal grey coating many of their faces, business suits and glasses, walked like zombies, some crying, some frantically pushing speed dial numbers on their non-functioning cell phones, but still more utterly silent, swarmed every bit of available space. The great, frenzied parade came pouring across the structure for the safety of what must have seemed to them another continent entirely. Everett fought his way forward, only to occasionally be dragged back by the frantic crowd; before fighting his way onward yet again.

Slipping past unsupervised police barricades, he heard only the sounds of exasperated shouting and the brazen jolt of emergency sirens in the distance. The soot that circulated through the air blew it's way into his eyes, infecting him with a kind of fast-spreading disease, branding him for what he already sensed would be the rest of his life. Everett squinted to take in all that surrounded him. Once recognizable streets sat before him like foreign lands. Once proud buildings, tall and sterling additions to the shining city, the envy of the world, now stood broken and decapitated, windowless and devoid of life. Plumes of sinister smoke billowed from mere blocks away, saturating the city and, for all he could tell, the whole world over. The ground had opened up and all of hell had risen to the surface of lower Manhattan. Everett could taste the horror that surrounded him. The devil had come to play.

Christmas, 1990: New London, CT

"You'll need a scarf." Barbara had caught him, mid-stair, as though she were some kind of prep school hall monitor who had never learned to surrender her title. She looked different in a nightgown and bathrobe, her hair down and those clackety high heels replaced with silk slippers. She was softer, more human. Yet, interestingly enough, her severe makeup remained firmly attached to her face, as though just to be ready should she be called into action in the middle of the night for emergency Senatorial duties, which she often was. They spoke in whispered tones, although surely no one could possibly hear them at such an early hour, standing in the tiny servant's staircase that lead from the bedrooms to the expansive kitchen. The steam from her coffee cup was the only thing in motion, save the two of them, at 3 A.M. inside Lakeview Hill. Even the ghost of Colonel John Stevens slept soundly. The house itself stood strong, always aware of comings and goings, secretly smirking at the silliness of them all, at the shy silhouettes and shrinking shadows that adorned the walls deep into the night. The hundreds of people who had swept through that evening had all departed, and the scattered remnants mostly slumbered now.

"You're making the right decision, you know? You're a smarter man than I realized, yesterday at the station," she blinked at him through heavily mascared eyes; could she have been just slightly drunk? "Funny how people reveal themselves." It was no longer distain, judgment or even trepidation that filled the pupils of Barbara's large brown eyes now; it was envy. As she looked at him, tall and attractive and so young in so many ways, she likened him to the stronger insect that had momentarily flown into the same web as she. Only he was escaping, a heroic feat of which she knew she was now, so much time having past, incapable. The moss had grown around her, the circumstances of it all would hold her firmly and exactly where she was as nature had its gruesome way with her and she was slowly devoured. But this boy, this young man with everything in the world at his disposal — he would elude the profound absurdity of it all; he would escape the White's.

Mere moments ago, Everett had sat in the desk chair of the gentleman from Connecticut, the junior of this house, and gazed over at the most perfect sleeping body ever to grace sheets. He had contemplated a great many things as he watched Jamie's chest expand and contract with every breath of well deserved sleep, a tousle of dirty blond hair sweeping just past his eyelids which remained tightly shut, harboring those exquisite eyes that held so much presence. Thank God for Jamie's eyelids, thought Everett; they masked so much, doused a brilliantly lit lighthouse. Had they slid open, even for a moment, to reveal the treasures which they housed, the young man from Iowa would have no choice but to slide his naked body back into the warm bed beside him and grasp hold till the sun dared show itself.

But instead, Everett dutifully rose from the chair and approached his sleeping lover. Placing a kissed hand upon his pale cheek, the color of warm sand, he gazed down upon all that he would miss, all that he had never known, all that had only too briefly been his — then exited the room before he could look back.

It was gratitude he would take with him, — and *that* would most decidedly have to be *that*. This, none of this, could ever be his. He would louse it all up for everyone, sooner or later, it had certainly happened before and, left unattended, would happen again. There was a certain toxicity that came along with knowing him, Everett had always known this about himself, and it would be pure selfishness, no — pure hatred, to inflict it upon anyone else, particularly one with such a future. A loving tie would have to be severed, snipped — indeed mutilated altogether. This was a life to which he could not ever aspire.

Had he been merely complicated, had he been simply self-absorbed, as all artists are, that, he could have lived with burdening upon another. But the very core of him, he knew this absolutely, was infected, and it would bring the world of anyone to whom he dared venture too close crashing down around them. He would not be the one to shatter the perfectly maintained Waterford chandelier that was the beautiful Jamie White. He would not ruin *another* life. He would say his private farewells, take his tattered duffel bag in hand, and walk briskly to the hidden staircase that was reserved for the help.

"I can drive you, if you like. It's started to snow again. I'll just get the keys to the town car." But Barbara knew before she even articulated the words that they would fall upon deaf ears. This was a young man who lived within himself, who stood firmly upon his own two feet, who wanted no witnesses, and she admired this, even recalled a certain something of herself when she looked upon him, standing there with all of the frightened bravado of a hungry squirrel. Barbara touched Everett's hand, looked him squarely in the eye and, he couldn't quite tell, but yes, he was rather certain that she smiled at him. A real, genuine, proud smile that was full of not just relief, but profound admiration. It would last only a mere moment, this miraculous crack in her carefully maintained facade, before Barbara Pruitt, clad only in an expensive looking bathrobe, made her way back up the stairs to her own suite, the same room above the library she had occupied since Jamie was a young boy.

The wind cut through Connecticut like a knife, slicing into the flesh of whoever dared venture out into the night air. It only stood to get worse, Everett could feel it, he had a sense of such things or perhaps it was merely skills he had acquired from the brash realities of his own history. The New London train station wasn't far, he recalled the way, even through the newly fallen snow. Yes, this was for the better — it was clean and everything would mend in time. The wind picked up. Snow laden with bits of ice smacked against his own forlorn face. It was not enough to obliterate Everett Crisp, though. It would take far more. His footprints left a trail that would soon dissolve in the newly fallen flakes. Jamie White could have no future with Everett Crisp around. It had been laid out plainly for him in this cold Connecticut winter.

As he made his way through the storm, away from the warm exterior lights of Lakeview Hill and further into the accumulating darkness and weather that swallowed his leather oxford shoes and made its way under the cuffs of his jeans, soaking his socks and chilling his bare skin as all light faded entirely, his thoughts turned to how Jamie, in a few short hours, would wake more alone than he had ever been in all of his life. He slept now, through the ferocity of the storm that raged outside, warm and at peace in his boyhood bed. And this brought tears as he trudged forward, only his thin leather jacket to protect him from the bitter air. But tears dry. They must.

Fall, 2001: New York City

The smoke would not stop. It poured from the base of Manhattan, unrelentingly, as though the molten hot core of the Earth itself had selected New York City as its personal vent. Lower Manhattan was a wound that refused to heal, a flood that would only rise.

Everett spent the night and several thereafter atop a pool table at The Pillow Factory, which had transformed itself into a kind of triage center. The staff handed out bottles of water to passing workers and applauded them as debris filled trucks, overflowing with twisted metal and unending piles of wreckage, made their way up the West Side Highway. Christopher Street and Seventh Avenue South was a shell of its former self. The place where Everett and so many of his companions had spent nights of such frivolity, the great party that had always swirled about that intersection —where had it gone?

Even had he wanted to return to Brooklyn, it would be tricky, as the city was sealed, bridges and tunnels closed. No, he would not return home until he found Jamie. No answers from the hospitals, there had been few arrivals. As he sat in the waiting room at St. Vincent's that first day, awaiting an answer from an overwhelmed admittance nurse whose hands shook as she shuffled disorganized papers, he watched a mother and her two children reunite with a badly mangled husband who sat in a wheelchair, his hair still coated in white dust, and a weary looking sister rejoin her bandaged brother. Everett Crisp sat alone as bright florescent light bulbs flickered overhead, and wondered where and when the reunion for he and Jamie would take place.

Maria designed a flier with Jamie's photograph which she copied five hundred times over in the manager's office and they both canvassed the neighborhood, posting them on every available bit of empty space — fences, walls, abandoned construction sites, lamp posts, newsstands. Everett took the mission further and ventured into midtown and beyond. Standing in Times Square, he counted six people. Six. At the crossroads of the world. The ticker taped blared its yellow letters, which spun around with urgency, to its smallest audience in history. Every single person in the city jumped if a car alarm sounded randomly or a truck ran through an intersection too fast. Thus was the new world.

As darkness fell each night, scores of people like Everett roamed the streets, still in search of what they knew, in their heart of hearts, they were unlikely to find. The effort made them feel useful, if not in any way better.

Everett stared at Jamie's photograph on Maria's black-and-white flier, hanging amongst the mural of others on a Fourteenth Street bus stop shelter amid the flowers and lighted candles people had left on the pavement below, which glowed warmly as darkness enveloped the city. Those eyes — those endless eyes that one could just swim in for a few centuries — they gazed directly into his own from that stark white sheet of paper. Jamie White was sending his last communication, his final playful flirt. Unable to look any longer, Everett allowed his vision to wander out of necessity. He could see the hundreds upon thousands of sheets of paper, enough to wallpaper an entire city block and more, each one representing not only an individual, but the thousands more who searched, the multitudes of bereft left behind. They stretched forever it seemed, so much so that a person could be lost amongst them, drowned in a sea of pleading paper. Gazing down Fifth Avenue, he was unaccustomed to the gaping hole that was so out of place amid the once crowded city skyline, like a car that had been stripped of its engine.

And to think, he was only one man on one tiny block of New York. That evening, as he stood amid the stench of uncertainty and the glow of hundreds of candles, he wondered what New York City must have looked like from above.

11

Spring, 2026: Malibu, CA

THE SCENT OF scotch and cigarettes still brought joy to Everett Crisp, no matter how many times he had inhaled them. Something about the mixture of the two brought with it history, yes, a divine sense of the familiar, but what's more — a coarse reminder that despite all that might be amorphous about his own life, there was a touchstone, a pleasing reality check that came with the pleasure of a fresh pour or the happiness of a new light. It was like touching base with the bottom of the pool, comforting to feel one's feet upon an honest to god surface, rather than dangling above a bottomless pit. Scotch and cigarettes was him walking down Christopher Street in the village as a young man of twenty-two, or it was him circa Brooklyn at thirty-three, or even those long ago, naked nights in the swimming pool of his Bel Air mansion, he and the others illuminated only by a single underwater light and embraced by what he had so recently rejected as frivolity, but had come to realize were, indeed, some of the greatest events of his life. It was him now, a slight man in tweed trousers and a yellow linen shirt which sat beneath mostly white hair. Yes, scotch and cigarettes — he had forsworn both for such a long while but lately, had come to embrace them once more, just as two soul mates find their way back together, or a dog dutifully returns to its master no matter how far the chasm that's forced them apart. He had chased the smoke for such a long while, only to finally capture it in his palm for the briefest of days before both would simply evaporate.

He confined himself to the patio where he could look out at his beloved ocean and, more immediately, Jeff and Barry as they went about their frolics in the sea. So what if he had become somewhat of a voyeur? He was an old man, and that's what old men did. They were beautiful: young and full of life, ready to take on whatever got in their way but totally unprepared for it, as evidenced when a large wave caught them both off guard, knocking them into the surf. Theirs was a kind of brash arrogance that accompanied a certain charm. *How they would learn,* thought Everett, as he drew another drag and watched today's perfectly blue waves cart another load of sand to the grateful shore, if only to reclaim it hours later, which of course it would. The young people would remain at sea for a while, lost in their own utopia, and good for them. Everett would return to work before the sun extinguished itself completely into the water.

Most days, nothing came. Ninety percent of composing, he had loathsomely come to realize, is waiting for something to come, waiting for some divine inspiration that was always terribly late and even then, a frequently uninvited dinner guest. But oh, when it came — when it came God himself could take a whack at Everett's feet and he'd still stand strong amid whatever storm chose to try and strike him down. But this time he was not writing for a director, nor in answer to incessant telephone calls. He was not writing in order to fulfill the terms of a piece of paper or in anticipation of a fatter bank account. He was writing merely because he could and knew, deeply in his soul, just as he always had, that he *must.*

But on this particular day, nothing came. Another smoke, another scotch, the two mingling in his mouth. Seagulls littered the sky, noisily fighting over something, or perhaps just playing games. Old people drinking alone was sad, even though he was just a bit shy of being considered truly *old*. *We have the most amount of time in our lives to be old,* really, he thought. Young lasts until twenty-five. Used to be thirty, but in these Hollywood days the whole world was experiencing, wherein everything was sped up, it was much closer to twenty-five, no matter in what business one found oneself. He had never really imagined himself being old; the constant day-to-day became the constant year-to-year. But now Hollywoodland and its mentality had infected the entirety of the world, so age was important, at least to the vast general mentality. Really, post thirty, you're in that middle-aged category where if you haven't accomplished something that the public has lauded, haven't been profiled, haven't been noticed, it's unlikely you ever will be and that is how success shall be judged — by the opinions of others. *Why had he been so lucky?* There were others with greater gifts, surely. His own success had been nothing more than a fluke. Millions of brilliantly talented people are scattered throughout the world and most of them go unnoticed despite their cries to be heard above the rapids, above the noise of mediocrity — he had seen it. He had been plucked by lady luck for no apparent reason. And now in his fifties, he was what's considered old. And then, the worst part of it all and assuming all goes well, most people have to stay old for thirty years or so. Thirty years is a long time. You don't ask for life, you don't ask for any of it, but you're expected to pay as you go and if you don't there are consequences, aren't there? Better to just surrender, perhaps, give in, relinquish the arduousness of it all. Those thirty years would surely allude him. He wondered what he'd miss. Another glass of scotch.

There was a familiar looking man jogging along the shoreline. Nothing about him should have been remotely recognizable, people jogged along the Malibu shore all the time, but something about this man drew Everett like a magnet to him. He was older than he, perhaps in his seventies, even, or even older given all of the Hollywood gizmos that painfully preserve the illusion of youth these days. He jogged right along the waterline, tangoing with the tide, eventually making his way onto the property and, without hesitation, turning his quickly moving, aged bare feet in the direction of Everett's patio, tripping over the crude sign, stuck low and haphazardly in the sand, that identified the land as Everett's own. The naming of homes was a silly matter, but Everett had adopted this moniker when he purchased the property: "Low Tide." Everything would just be a little dialed back at this house, he had decided at the time: calm and serene, no added pressures as he had felt in Bel Air. He would retreat. If Bel Air had meant suits and ties and cocaine, Low Tide meant linen shirts and cotton shorts and the occasional brandy and cigarette to accompany the ocean breeze. Everything needed to be looser at Low Tide; in this house at the edge of the world, with the sea approaching his doorstep more and more each day, he wanted to learn what it meant to be virtually carefree — to let his worries drift out to sea. He wondered if he could accomplish that and, what's more — what it might teach him.

Summer, 1978: Mason City, Iowa

It all faded with a pounding at the door. The beautiful chalk drawing in which Everett and Ken Moberly had found themselves happily encapsulated, filled with adventures and all things wonderful, of real friendship and a temporary end to loneliness, washed right out that morning.

Two uniformed officers searched the house while Everett was taken by force into a waiting patrol car, despite his protests: "NO! I want to STAY! Let GO of me!" But it was akin to spitting into the wind. It was all over now, something that would take the better part of a lifetime for him to truly understand. Ken Moberly and his little stone house had meant kindness and stability and *home* — three things that, although he did not know it at the time, he would spend the bulk of his life searching for. Ken Moberly, restrained by the officers, watched, tears saturating his pale skin, as his friend was driven away in a patrol car, their eyes locked in sheer terror until they could no longer maintain contact. Everett would not ever see Mr. Ken Moberly, the only person to ever show him genuine kindness — again.

Everett had been thrown in jail. However, they didn't call it jail, they called it a "waiting area," but it was jail nonetheless. It would only take one night, a miserable stretch of hours, before an officer would drive him back to Sheila and Jay's, that other prison he thought he had escaped. As the patrol car approached, the rhythm of the tires were all too familiar as they passed over the stretch of street leading to that particular house, over the same bumps in the road and the pattern of distinct turns. The house that seemed so peaceful on the outside drew ever nearer as Everett felt his stomach exploding; he was certain that he would be sick all over the backseat. Officer Bradley held him by the neck, Everett's day old clothes in need of retirement and the fear on his stone white face palpable.

"Whoa, there, kid. Just take some deep breaths. That's right." He called to the front seat. "Slow down a minute, Harry." The officer had big eyes and a tired, worn face that had seen a great deal, even if not the dramatic kinds of things Everett expected from police officers based upon hours spent in front of the television. Officer Bradley lifted Everett's chin so that his eyes meet his own sparkling green pupils directly. "These people here love you and are going to look after you." He was perfectly well intentioned and ignorant.

As the car pulled into the driveway of the little house in the seemingly bucolic neighborhood, Officer Bradley was the first to notice. "*Harry!* Just leave it on the street. Lemme go in first. Talk to my friend Ev, here." He had shielded the eyes of his new, young friend from what littered the porch of the happy little brick home, and exited the patrol car with a compassionate pat upon Everett's arm in a one-two motion, a male to male salute that was surely meant to be reassuring.

It had been the rumor about town and the police reports confirmed it: the runaway child and the more than willing retarded surrogate father. Everyone in the house and in the patrol car were certainly aware of it, not to mention the prying eyes that peered out from behind drawn blinds all around the street.

Officer Bradley rang the bell. Then again. And once more. The house was clearly occupied, the sounds of a football game emanated from within. It was then that he acknowledged that which he simply did not want to see: a packed suitcase and a small trunk, placed deliberately upon the porch. Everett could see plainly from the back of the patrol car. The cases surprised him little. He would not ever be welcome back. He had not been welcome *ever*, actually.

And so began a series of horrifying military schools, terrifying places all where he would learn little other than the ability to acquire the proper stockpile of defenses necessary to protect himself. Indeed, he would come to attain an entire arsenal. Everett Crisp would be tossed about like a fish trying in vane to get upstream, but repeatedly smacked backward by an unrelenting current of inhumanity and gross unkindness. He had recently turned fourteen-years-old.

It would be a long stretch of years, indeed.

September 24, 2001: New York City

Random notes from arbitrary instruments hung in the air as The New York Philharmonic tuned. A cacophony of sounds issued forth from piccolos, French horns, flutes and violins as the lobby bar issued last call prior to curtain and the throngs made their way through the granite atrium and into the auditorium. The plush red cushioned seats of Carnegie Hall unfolded as, gradually, the orchestra and all four tiers filled.

Everett gazed at his own reflection in a full-length mirror in the stage right wing. Soon, the double doors would swing open and he would stride out onto the stage where, under some of the brightest light ever to exist, his life would change. He was not nervous. He was not excited, sorrowful nor anxious. He was numb. The events of the past thirteen days had left him completely devoid of feeling. Staring back at him from the glass was merely the silhouette of a man, dimly lit by a single overhead light, who existed more as a ghost now than flesh and blood.

Finally, the house lights dimmed and soon, the full power of the Philharmonic filled all available space with music. There was an audible exhalation of relief from the still shell-shocked audience. Finally, a familiar sound, familiar notes, something constant that they could attend and take comfort therein, something from before the world had turned itself inside out. For a blissful few hours, they would immerse themselves in melodic patterns that might just drown whatever was waiting for them on the other side of those West 57th Street doors.

The program inched forward until finally, Philip Tate turned around on his conductor's platform to face the audience. "Ladies and gentleman, every season at the Philharmonic we make a point of recognizing new talent that appears on the music scene, and this year is no exception. When someone comes to our attention with ability like the singular talent contained within this young man I'm about to bring to the stage, one has no choice but to surrender instantly in recognition of a true gift. It is an honor to include him on the program this evening, and I can promise you that you'll be hearing much more of him. Making his New York Philharmonic debut, won't you please welcome, *Everett Crisp.*"

A stagehand dressed all in black and wearing a headset pulled the stage right door open as light slivered itself into the wing. Everett, in his itchy rented tuxedo, swept onto the stage as though walking into the purist pool of warm water, his very own baptismal pool. There was polite, restrained applause but he couldn't hear it as he settled himself at the piano before utter silence replaced all sound, as though cleansing the palate prior to the next course of an elaborate meal.

Gazing from only the corner of his eye out into the expansive and world-renowned auditorium for merely a moment, the only faces he could see were those of Grant and Susan White, who sat silently with all of the pride that two utterly destroyed people are capable of. In some way, their child lived on in this young man, and they clung to that.

In the wing, Ruth Pickett stood in the darkness, watching from a closed circuit monitor, her current well dressed and wealthy gentleman escort at her side, whose hand she clutched tightly as more than a thousand people fixed their eyes upon the unknown young man from Iowa at the piano. Ruth trembled just a bit, not from nervousness, but rather an electric excitement that pulsated within her, strong enough to launch rockets. Her suitor, whom she had known for decades, looked at her with concern — this was not a woman to tremble on behalf of *anything*.

She was about to turn her boy over to the world at large, she was fully aware. Ruth, recalling her own first similar appearance on *The Ed Sullivan Show*, was filled with nostalgia. Tonight would be like witnessing a birth that, in light of all of the death that had just eviscerated her own New York City, was a pleasing thought. Yet, for her wonderful piano player, her dear friend, — pure joy, accented by flecks of sorrow, flowed through her blood. She felt very much as though she were giving him away with her blessing, casting him out onto a beautiful lake of success where resided such lovely things, yet also ample piranha. Her ears, laden with heavy brass jewelry, perked up as the whole of her attention fixated on the monitor that hung in the stage right wing and the sound that now emanated from just beyond those magic double doors.

It was just a single note at first. It echoed throughout the piano and then permeated the entirety of the hall. There was purity to it, like the first drop of rain. The smattering of droplets soon formed a pattern, a pleasing summer shower, and soon the orchestra slowly crept in, flipping through pages of orchestrations that had only been completed that very afternoon. It turned somber, to pitch darkness, the horrific warm stillness that descends prior to a hurricane, that strange green sky; and then — Everett Crisp took flight, catapulting himself and his audience right up into the center of the storm, hanging around the soaked rainclouds and drinking in the lightening. All of the notes and every bit of the power that had resided within him all of these years came pouring into Carnegie Hall through some of the most exquisite music ever to grace the space. It was raw and starkly honest, unadorned yet intensely beautiful and lonely. It captured the very mood of that particular month and that particular year, that *precise* moment in history. It was the first time that anyone within earshot could look upon the events that had so recently transpired with any level of eloquence.

"He's a star," Ruth's date whispered as they stood, side by side, in the dark of backstage. "He's the real thing." Ruth looked on with a distinct air of motherly pride. She had paid it forward, granted the same break she herself had once enjoyed when on the brink of surrender. But more so, she had done the world a great service, elevated a young man whom she knew would be more influential than even she. Well, perhaps not more than *she*, but still — very, *very* important. She put her Ruth Pickett face back on:

"You don't think I would have dragged Hollywood's most successful and best looking director off of a set in Norway just for nothing, do you? Especially one who has just so very publicly fired half of his creative team and whose movie is in limbo? Oh, — half of his team *including* his composer? Just listen."

The strings hit a climax only to be overtaken by the horns in what was less than a mere second as a single tear fell from the worn eyes of the Senator. Sweat poured from Everett's brow as he plunged forward through his own composition. In the stage left wing, Ruth's eyes widened with awe as Everett surpassed that which even she had thought him capable. How could a mere ten fingers accomplish so much glorious sound? It was a brand new day.

Light and color passed before him as he depressed the keys in configurations he could not even consciously fathom. Invisible nature performed the piece, something inbred, something buried deep within him guided him right through it, as painless as taking a pleasant stroll through the woods. He certainly hadn't had time to practice it. It was *effortless*. It was a bonafide masterpiece.

He could swear that Jamie White sat right next to him at the piano bench, just grinning that grin of his and messing with Everett's sweaty black hair before placing a single kiss upon the top of his head. Everett remained busy in pursuit of the notes as he railed against all of the outrage in this new world, channeling it into the eighty-eight keys that were his conduit. How could such a graceful man be plucked from the world so pointlessly? Who would ever have the patience to love him again? He would play for Jamie, seated right next to him. And he realized that, from that moment on, he would always be playing for Jamie. Every time he sat before an instrument, every time he wrote anything at all, it would be Jamie. There really was no other good reason to do it.

And then, with all of the gentility that had always come so naturally for him, the young man from Connecticut simply drifted through the hall, lingering around the ornate ceiling for a bit, gazing down at the brilliantly bright stage with profound pride and gratitude, before vanishing upward altogether, sailing high above the silent, wounded isle of Manhattan. The lights. He could see so clearly now.

Everett felt Jamie leave. A cold wind sat at his shoulder where only moments prior the familiar warmth and scent of the great love of his life had been. As he pounded his own notes out of the polished Steinway grand, he lifted his eyes to watch this most spectacular man, the one true thing he had ever known, make the most simplistic and graceful exit, high above the heads of both the music makers and listeners.

Surrounded by a sea of thousands of notes, each of which he had written himself, put forth by over one hundred musicians, Everett Crisp looked up from his piano, — and said goodbye.

Winter, 1978: Mason City, Iowa

All he knew at the time was that it felt right; it felt good, even. They were a unique pair who comforted each other, shielded in their lakeside retreat. But the day of the knock at the door from the uniformed officers, it was clear that Everett had done something horribly wrong. Again.

Everett's last look at Ken Moberly had been of a confused man dressed in sweat pants and a rumpled Mickey Mouse t-shirt, handcuffed outside of the little stone house by the lake, quietly questioning the officers as to his supposed misdeeds and gazing tearfully toward his friend, who faded away quickly, eyes blazing, in a police car. The word "kidnapping" was hurled in his direction. It would be one of the more mild words that would come to be associated with him throughout the coming months as he navigated the legal system from a jail cell, only really understanding that he had apparently done something wrong, and little else. Shelia and Jay Thompson had brought a major lawsuit, seeking significant financial renumeration.

But it was that last look that Everett would remember always, a man with pleading terror in his eyes, looking at his young friend who was already so many years his elder in most respects, bewildered, as the police vehicle pulled away.

There was not a single person he could ever recall, in his short life, who would not come to regret knowing him. Something from deep within him radiated evil. He was a bad kid; it was unmistakable. Perhaps all of those things that Jay Thompson had always insisted he was were true after all. His friend Ken Moberly, his momentary protector, would never again see the outside of prison, and this was entirely the fault and responsibility of one Mr. Everett Crisp.

Music would become more important to him than ever, but finding it would be increasingly difficult. He would wile away as much time as possible in the local library before returning home to whatever household would have him at the time. He had no record player or tape recorder of his own anymore, so his headphones were useless. Everett would drift in and out of people's lives, afraid always to get too close, for the next several months prior to his military school enrollment. The same shorts, the same jeans, the same few shirts he owned would have to do, no matter how ill-fitting they became as time passed.

A scholarship to a State University would be his only hope, the radiant light, the brass ring. School had always come easily enough for him, but now, he was determined not to get even a single answer incorrect. It was easy to trick the education system into believing that he was learning by the mere memorization and repeating of facts, there was even a certain musicality to it all. It was just such repetition that would lead to a full scholarship at age seventeen, thus setting him free at last.

The manicured lawns and lush surroundings of college life were in stark contrast to anything he had ever known. He stood in the center of a beautiful green park that first day, a late summer sky hanging low in the air and wafting through the trees. Closing his eyes, he breathed in an entirely new scent. He had grown to nearly six feet tall and acquired, though a search at the Salvation Army, a thin black leather jacket that would be his signature look, matching his dark hair that contrasted his pale face. Students scurried all about him on their way to various orientations and the bookstore. Everett stood still in the middle of all of the commotion. He would never again belong to anybody but himself. He was unleashed.

He was on work-study, of course, but it mattered little. He kept to himself, kept his head down, and embraced the library. One crisp October day, a package arrived at the tiny dorm room he shared with a young man named Russ whom he had actually only seen twice. The parcel was particularly heavy, wrapped in brown paper, and would be followed by four more similar shipments, spread out over various days. Records. All of Ken Moberly's beautiful records.

The bundles were a joy to receive, sent from the family lawyer who was also in charge of the trust that had been Ken Moberly's financial livelihood. Everett cherished each record, every cover, all of the liner notes and photographs, they even still smelled of the little stone house. He had by this time acquired his own record player and the hundreds of hours of fulfillment that would follow, throughout the rest of his life, were a gift beyond compare.

The final package was accompanied by a letter, set on official-looking letterhead, from the law firm:

Mr. Crisp:

As per the last will and testament of one Mr. Ken Moberly, whose last address, as you know, was Shankesville Prison in Shankesville, Pennsylvania, I am hereby forwarding to you his entire collection of recordings, which he expressly requested be remitted to you upon the occasion of his death.

Further, please contact my office immediately so that we might settle your financial bequest, as well.

Sincerely Yours,
Jonathan D. Johnson
Attorney at Law

Everett held the paper in his hand as it began to shake, somberly and then violently. He let the letter drop to the ground as the words tore though his mind like a saw separating the lobes of his brain. "The occasion of his death..." The records sat there at attention, ready to be called into service, but they no longer looked welcome, more like something from a threatening nightmare. Leaving his room, he began to walk then run for the library, sprinting through campus as fast as his legs would carry him, darting past students and faculty alike.

A search of *The Des Moines Register* on microfilm would provide the obituary, buried in the back amongst the used cars for sale and household services. He would finally find it, following hours of searching, printed a full four months prior:

MASON CITY CHILD MOLESTER
KILLED BEHIND BARS

There was a photograph of a young, beaming Ken Moberly, where they had found it was anyone's guess, which accompanied the three-sentence notice. The photograph was haunting. It had been shot, perhaps, during a family gathering, a happy day in June when he was surrounded by people who cared for him, before they had all left him one by one. Ken Moberly had perished from a life-ending blow to the back of his skull from a fellow inmate.

What had he done? What *had* he done? The room swirled as Everett tried to steady himself, but could not. He was falling down a drain that would wash him out to sea where he would surely drown. Had it not been for his own unfortunate existence, his own need to run away, Ken would never have stumbled upon him, lost and alone in the woods. He would be alive today, living out his life next to the reservoir and happily playing his records. Everett cursed everything that crossed his path, certainly anything that offered up kindness. It was simply his lot in life, like an extra-terrestrial power, that he would never, *not ever*, be able to smother: he was poison.

The sun faded as darkness fell upon the campus. Everett remained glued to his plastic library seat, staring at the headline, where he would remain until finally asked to leave by a shy and short librarian with mousy brown hair.

The cold metal doors of the library closed and locked behind him. A chill was in the air. The simple act of walking seemed the most impossible of tasks as the weight of the world crippled him, boring into him like a thousand tons of personal responsibility. In the pit of his stomach, he knew that it should have been him to die. On this day, he honestly wished it had been.

Spring, 2026: Malibu

His mother had always described him as fat. "Your father was fat, fat, fat just like you," she would say, going on to point out various overweight people whom they might pass on the street. "That's what *you're* going to look like," she would say. She could say such things, of course, because she had kept herself so perfectly trim and pretty, in line with her current husband's idea of the perfect compliment to himself. She would even dress herself in the ugly clothes he selected for her, crude and garish colors and patterns of jagged stripes and animal prints she had convinced herself were becoming because they were to his liking.

Her protestations regarding her son, naturally, were all in support of Jay Thompson's insistence that Everett, a cherubic boy of thirteen, occupied far more space than any boy should. Indeed, it was a protest against the abundant space he took up in the world and, more specifically, their lives. She even resented his last name. *Crisp*, indeed: something to be gobbled up and done away with. A thing of the past.

But the man who stood before him now, surrounded by the lush ocean and the sound of hunting gulls, was a shriveled stick of a man, far from robust. He had shoulder length white hair and a tired looking body, one that had given up on appearances and strived more so to exist, to remain on the Earth for a little while longer. It took mere eye contact to realize that the two of them shared that particular trait. In fact, it took only one glance at this man for all of it to come flooding back like snapshots, distant, dusty home movies which he saw in sepia tones. One had not seen the other since Everett was a mere child, but it mattered little, they were like opposing magnets to each other.

The old man gazed upon the younger version of himself, drawn, gaunt and exhausted. He thought not of all of the years he had missed and the things fathers are supposed to do and say, as that would be merely trite and stupid at this point. There was nothing he could offer other than a simple, "Hello, son."

Everett gazed at this man of whom he had spent so many years dreaming. His father, he once thought, would be his great savior, rescuing him from the treacherous life that he had endured, a man who would reach into the bonfire and pull him to safety. Only that never happened. His savior never came, and Everett came to realize that he was as disregarded as a leaf that falls into a fast moving stream. And yet here stood this man, all these trillions of years later; this man who had left him with a crazy man and a woman with such a low image of herself that she would simply surrender.

How Everett had strived to hold those thoughts, born so long ago, at bay, to let them be the reserve of emotion he need never again tap, safely locked away in the deep recesses of himself, like holding back lava. But one look at Charlie Crisp, one glance into that odd mirror, and Everett Crisp stood virtually naked and defenseless. He even turned to the boys for help, but they were drifting in the surf — far out to sea, having a grand time.

Everett had retired Sheila, seeing her in her own home and comfortable for the rest of her days, as was his duty. But he would not ever be in direct contact with her. Not ever again. Everett Crisp was not a man to be fooled twice. When a carnival ride throws you out of the funhouse due to malfunction, you don't get back in line to ride again. Jay Thompson had put a pistol in his mouth some fifteen years prior. It was Sheila who had found him. Whatever ghosts and demons haunted his life, whatever horrifying events that had turned him into the ignorant, arrogant, self-loathing monster he had become, had finally caught up with him. Oddly enough, Everett had felt himself closer to Jay Thompson on that day, the day he learned of his death, than he ever had, even though they hadn't seen each other in so many years, and even though he certainly felt no remorse. The two of them had always had at least one thing in common: one day, they would both die.

Joy wasn't the thing to feel upon learning of a person's death and that was not what he felt. Rather, it was a release, as though Everett had been untied. He would now take as long as he wished in the shower and no one would scream at him for it. He had heard the ridicule in his ear always, in the exact timbre of Jay Thompson's unrelenting voice, drilled into the side of his head via various bullet holes, regardless of all that had transpired since. Yet that day, the troops had simply deserted the city, and Everett was free on a cold, clear morning. And now, standing before him was the very man who might have prevented all of it, had it not been for his disappearing act. What his life would have been he would not ever know, and this was as it should be.

All of the things from those black days of his youth filled his brain now, things he had survived, things about which he had made efforts to atone. Throughout the years, he had checked in on the local paper from time to time. When McGregor's Sporting Goods was on the brink of financial collapse, Dan McGregor had received the anonymous check in the mail that more than kept the doors open. Adequate repayment for a stolen tent and so many hours of refuge spent browsing while awaiting the exact proper hour to return to Jay and Sheila's. How he had hunted down Mr. Walter Able and silently arranged for his granddaughter to attend

Juilliard after he had been informed, before even she had, that she had been rejected, and how he had picked up the bill in the form of a "scholarship." That black, cashmere coat of his, left in the coat check for whatever reason in mid August, could very easily have saved his life that night, and he was convinced that indeed it had.

Yes, Everett had always strived to clean up after himself, if nothing else. To, at the very least, leave the world as it was prior to his habitation. But lately, he had reminded himself that his goal had once actually been to leave it better. To carve "I was here" broadly in a tree, to honor the planet for allowing him shelter for these stretch of years. To be remembered. Just recently, the music, the symphonies, took up residence in his vast mind again, and it was of comfort, the very soundtrack of his life.

He never really felt as though he had lived up to his potential, which had always been his greatest fear. He had done many things, of course. Scored some movies. Loved. Been loved — briefly. That was a very finite period. But it was the top of the arc that he craved so badly: immortality. It's a ridiculous notion, pretentious, bombastic. But it's what keeps one in the game. Oh, in the beginning he had thought it was for the joy of creation or it fed his soul and then it was about money and for comfort and all sorts of things. But that's all a veil. Really, the whole time, it's one's self striving for *immortality*. To stay. To not be rushed off the stage. To defy the very anatomy of the universe. It's all a selfish quest, but we're all really quite selfish in the end, it turns out.

In the ten thousand lines that permeated the old man's face, a whole life story was itching to be told. Curious though he was, Everett thought it best that he just listen. The warm wind was laden with all sorts of new things blowing through these days, and Everett would simply absorb it all.

"So — beautiful day, hmm?" Why? Where had he been? Why had it all been as it was? Why had he been left to defend himself at the one and only time in his life when he himself was defenseless? Where were the *answers?* A slight chill filled the Malibu air as nighttime was upon them both.

"I know you're sick, son," he placed a firm grasp upon Everett's shoulder. "Those boys out there — they can't see it like I can — but I know you're sick." There was something so familiar about this man, even after all that had transpired, like two puzzle pieces coming together. "GOD, look at that sun... Now you just hold my hand for a minute... Good... Good." The old man grasped Everett's well-worn hands as though he were meditating, praying over them. "It's like flipping a light switch. Don't you be nervous about that. And I'm going to be there this time." He couldn't recall ever being touched by his own father. Despite it all, something felt altogether right about it, like a key that perfectly fit a lock. It seemed fitting that the man who had welcomed him into this world, would also usher him out.

Everett watched as the old man trudged on down the coast. It was appropriate that he was running on sand, for he struck Everett as the kind of man who strives to make everything more difficult than it need be: a family trait, perhaps. The whole day hardly surprised him. Ghosts had been coming to visit for a few weeks now. Charlie Crisp was running... and running... and finally he was no more, faded into the horizon.

Everett ventured inside and stared at his piano, the increasing ocean breeze at his back ruffling through his yellow linen shirt. But it was not at the keys nor at the polished wood that surrounded them that he gazed, but at the mahogany bench which stood before it, his office chair for these many years. He went to it with all the care that one approaches a newborn, and gingerly pulled open its lid.

There he sat, dutifully and patiently after all these years: Henry. Ah, to caress his great good companion who had seen him through so much but whom had sat loyally in the bench for these many decades was bliss.

To breathe in the familiar scent that came with burying his nose within his stuffed friend was an ultimate salve, a reminder that he had a team, too; he was both defender and defended. Henry, his worn exterior and the history he provided, had come back around to say hello once more, to share the kind of comfort that can only come from the familiar, the better sort of the kind. The monkey cared little about the aged face that stared back at him, only gratitude and pride filled his elated, stuffed body. Those glass eyes, as vibrant now as they had been back in those dark years, gazed into Everett's with a kind of wizened knowledge. Those wide red lips and that cunning little hat were exactly what Everett needed that afternoon. Oh, Henry was there, therefore nothing bad could happen, at least for a little while. Everett Crisp sat on his bench with his confidant tucked securely in his arms, and wept. In so doing, finally and not without struggle, he let go of the past once and for all.

Tide was comin' in.

12

Spring, 2027: Malibu

J EFF HADN'T SEEN Everett all day, having been all but ordered out of the house in the early morning hours while composer chained himself to piano. Jeff would occupy the day in his old neighborhood, West Hollywood and the surrounds — running errands, visiting some old friends, being nostalgic. It was good to be back, mostly because he knew that come the early evening, he'd be leaving it. It was a reminder of the person he used to be, a man he was quickly leaving behind. The bars, the random dates, the prowling and hoping, the perpetual hop from one ice flow to the next for survival, was a part of him that was dying.

He parked the car at that cliff, he had never known the name of it, the one that overlooks the Hollywood sign you see in all those old movies, and just stared for a while. Moments ticked by. Everett needed more time, and Jeff would give it to him. Looking at himself in the rear view mirror, he could see the faintest beginnings of lines around his eyes, just a vague trace of crow's feet. Bound to happen sooner or later he thought. Despite the tight blue jeans and muscle shirt he was wearing, his usual uniform, he had started to feel more grown up lately, and it was a welcome sensation.

The first time he had seen that famous white sign, those gigantic gleaming letters on the side of a hill, he was on a bus as it pulled into downtown LA. He had grinned from ear to ear. Jeff had accomplished what everyone he knew at the time said was impossible; he had made it out. Sunglasses and swimming pools would replace pick up trucks and marriage and boredom. But now, what he saw was the dirt that was gathered at the bottom of the "O," or the effect the weather had had on the whole thing, causing it to stand slightly lopsided. It had looked down upon him for seven years now, like a higher power, something to reach for; but it was just a sign, nothing more nothing less. He had learned enough now to know that he hadn't moved to Los Angeles to be an actor. He had migrated west to be famous. If he could only be famous than no one would ever question him again. If he could just achieve the great golden trophy of fame, the ultimate honor, akin to royalty. If trillions of people could laud him globally, than all would be forgiven and perhaps he could even forgive himself for his own past. But now, all of that seemed somewhat less important.

The famous people, he had come to realize, the truly famous, were only about fifty or so mostly troubled individuals. A handful, a mere smattering of folks plucked from obscurity for whatever reason to sit upon the bright golden dais. Jeff thought of the multitudes, the thousands, hundreds of thousands, his former self included, vying for those positions. It was stupefying.

He opened a bag of Veggie Chips he pulled from the glove box. Preoccupying his mind with various sundry tasks was the kind of mundane thing that would take his mind off of the obvious — Everett Crisp, whom he had grown to love, wasn't well.

Everett was a svelte man, but lately, there was even less of him. His face was drawn and his skin hung loosely around his skull. He hair, always full and even somewhat radiant, had begun to thin. Suddenly, in the span of just a few months, really, Everett Crisp had become an old man. Jeff knew there was something profoundly wrong with him, just as he knew that it wasn't to be discussed. There had only been one doctor's visit in all of the time he'd been helping out around Low Tide. It all seemed routine and even unnecessary, as though a dye had been cast and any preemptive action would be merely redundant. Everett, it seemed to him, was taking one last lap around the track now, a weary marathoner who could plainly see the finish line through abundant sweat and tears.

The wind would soon blow another direction, and Jeff contemplated what he really wanted as he grasped the steering wheel, looking out at all of that *world*. "You have to rescue yourself, no one's going to do it for you," he heard Everett say, a favorite phrase of his that was always rolling around Jeff's head somewhere, as of late. Indeed, he had been rescued; but perhaps, he liked to think, even though he knew Everett would not ever admit as such, but perhaps if just in the smallest of ways — they both had been. Jeff could see right through Everett just as he could most people after knowing them for only a finite period. It was a gift he had always possessed. He was capable, for better or for worse, of climbing right inside someone's skin and inhabiting their lives for a while. He could take on their joys and their pains for himself, swim around in them for a bit. He had always considered it, if not a calling, at the very least a gift. He knew far more about Everett Crisp than he would ever let on, and this was precisely as it should be.

Jeff couldn't wait to get back to Malibu, as he put the car in reverse and backed away from the overlook, leaving the looming sign in his rear view mirror, where it would gradually fade. Winter was blowing through LA, quite unexpectedly for early Spring. Strong gusts of wind ripped through the valley as he ventured down the Pacific Coast Highway in the convertible BMW, storm clouds already overhead and great dramatic swells smashing up against the California coast.

For the first time since moving to Los Angeles, he didn't feel dirty. He enjoyed Everett's company. He was asked for nothing in return. In many ways, it was the purest union he had ever encountered. He was needed for something real, this time. He had made a friend.

Everett had lit a fire. Something was different about him. He was clean — freshly showered and clad in ironed khakis and a crisp cotton shirt, a stark contrast to the unkempt mess he had let himself be over the past month. He sipped from a single glass of red wine. The expensive bottle from which it was poured stood breathing on the coffee table, the green glass reflecting the flames of the illuminated fireplace. A peace had descended over the house, a bucolic calm, as opposed to the frantic nature of the past many weeks. Everything was perfectly serene, nothing out of place. The rain began to fall and it was of protective comfort. They would spend the evening indoors, huddled in their own fort with wine, fire and good food. The sound of the weather outside beating on the skylights was soothing.

"I finished." It was a simple pronouncement that filled them both with pride. Jeff knew that this day was surely at hand. After all of the many hours of agonizing over treble clefs and key signatures, the rageful crumpling of whole discarded sections, 4 A.M. brain drains and agonizing hours of nothingness, Everett Crisp had written the final notes of his symphony, the pages of which sat at attention on the piano on perfectly arranged staff paper, not a note out of place. The instrument stood like a proud chariot, having delivered its occupant to his destination, only now to rest. Everett sank into the sofa; he had done it, it was complete.

Jeff went about making dinner, he had always been handy in the kitchen, as the rain turned to a full on storm, saturating all of Malibu, or the whole world over, for all they knew, as lightening reflected in the windows of the double french doors and thunder cracked over the Pacific Ocean. More wine was poured. Once dinner was through, Jeff cleared the table as the weary maestro retired to the adjacent living room to finish his wine in front of the blaze of the fire. Jeff looked at Everett, this man who had become much like a tough father to him, stretched out on his overstuffed sofa and glowing in the tranquility that comes with completion as the fire's light reflected from his pale skin in the otherwise darkened room. So much music in him. Standing over his teacher with a wry smile upon his face, Jeff made his simple request:

"Play it for me." And, although he had declared himself retired just two hours previous, Everett did.

Malibu: Spring, 2027

Everett did not emerge that day, remaining in bed from sun up till sun down, and sleeping on through another night. Every last bit of energy he owned had poured itself into the pages that remained at attention upon the lip of the carefully polished piano. Jeff kept the house orderly, kept Everett hydrated, but there was little else to be done.

Everett had entered his own world now; one created in his mind that began to fill the room and soon, it was everything, the only thing that existed to him. Shostakovich, Beethoven and ah, yes — Ravel — his old friend Ravel — all had returned to him, their melodies omnipresent. The notes churned around and around, providing a kind of underscoring to the events, the many events of the years that had preceded this one, the very things that had arrived him at this exact point. The music silenced him, kept him still. He had settled in to watch the perfectly scored movie of his own life. He recalled how, at one point in his youth, he had grown weary of merely hearing the notes, absorbing himself in their security. Rather, he wanted to *be* the notes for himself, bounce around forever, luxuriating in all of that *sound* that he himself might create. That was when he had first starting writing — way back then in that dark, scary Wonderland.

But today, the notes overtook him, as though a friendly fish had caught him, mid ocean, and invited him down, down, down to inhabit another world altogether.

He would sleep now.

Early Summer, 2027: Malibu

A doctor came, a doctor left. A feeding tube would take care of nourishment for the time being. Each day, Everett's few hours of consciousness were occupied by a phone call or two to various business acquaintances, ample complaints, and, on a good day, a grilled cheese sandwich with bacon and a card game with Jeff.

"How're you feeling today?" Jeff would ask when Everett was aware enough to hear him.

"Fine."

"Good."

"No." Everett would tug at Jeff's thumb and draw him close, as much as he was able. "Fine. It's a four letter word." It was all spelled out in the pupils of his weary eyes. "There is nothing desirable about fine... nothing at all. Every minute should be more than just *fine*." And he was asleep again. Jeff placed a hand upon Everett's forehead. He was getting smaller; the entirety of the man was shrinking, fading, right before him and he was the only one to witness it. Beneath his own trembling hand sat a mind he could never begin to understand, a strange and beautiful instrument that had brought both terror and comfort to the masses and to himself. And it was still in motion, still striving, still trying, turning — still punishing. But the body it inhabited was methodically shutting itself down.

Summer, 2027: Malibu

There are scores of people who are about to check out of this Earth. Most of them know it. Some of them make

THE LAST YEAR AT LOW TIDE

peace with it immediately but most of them stretch, they reach, they grab onto whatever they can to think that maybe — *maybe* — by some miracle, they can stay in this great mystery we've created here. That despite all of their complaining, their misery, their pain, they see the sunlight in a different shade and they *fight* to stay at the party, this divine and breathless beauty, the only home we've ever consciously known.

It was dusk, Everett's favorite time of day, when the beachgoers go home and leave a golden stretch of sand that glows in the sunset. That evening, the enormous sky had erupted in all sorts of color — shades of violet and deep reds and warm yellows which hung down all around them. Jeff helped Everett, so frail and wrapped in a blanket, down the patio step, onto the sand, right past the little wooden sign — "Low Tide," which caught Everett's glance as the two of them slowly made their way down to the ocean, Jefferson the dog circling about them both in anticipation of an early evening adventure.

It was the purest air either of them had ever inhaled, mixed with specks of salt water that were carried in on the crashing waves. When Everett could walk no further, he simply dropped to his knees, releasing himself to the sand, right at water's edge, while Jeff settled himself behind his friend, embracing his fragile body with his outstretched arms, Everett's head resting against the younger's welcome chest.

He would have made a good father, thought Everett. Although the thought had never before crossed his mind, sitting in the sand with Jeff Severin, it occurred to him. Had he ever taken the time to look up, he could have made a decent go of it. He would have made up for all of the mistakes and inadequacies that had befallen his own past, a past that he had finally, at long last, released to the ocean.

And all that would end with him: the hundreds of books read, the lessons learned, sunsets seen. The exams he fussed over, every note, rest, every drip of life, every flash of memory. His broken heart, his favorites, clothes worn and taxes paid, all gone now as though his eyes nor heart had ever set forth upon any of it. Ended. What had he been so worried about, as the hours turned to days and then years? Why had he always feared the tipping of the chair, anticipated the forthcoming storm rather than reveling in the calm that preceded it? It all ends in a blip of a moment, and all that builds up to it, to the event, the gaping unknown, the fear — is pointless. We are only the current cast.

He thought of all that lied undiscovered, that which he had never put to paper. Comfort, no, safety, so often trumps ambition. All of the compositions that lie right beneath the very sand that he clutched, waiting for him to unearth, would have to remain buried here. Only the few he was able to cultivate would survive him. Artists, architects are some of the few who have the privilege and the responsibility of leaving things behind that will outlast themselves. Others will leave memories embedded in the minds of their survivors, they will leave both the joy and the sorrow they inflicted upon the world. But artists and architects will leave something tangible to be heard, seen, felt, tasted, touched — properties pulled from the air and mingled with their own magic qualities until, like shaken cream that becomes butter or air that crystallizes — something *exists.*

But no time for pride, nor regret, now — the great undiscovered world lie just yards away. A warm breeze blew through Everett's alabaster hair as the water washed right over the two of them, huddled on the cool sand. Just then, Jeff's embrace felt familiar, like the treasured touch of a long ago suitor, a distant, remembered melody. Yes, he knew that touch, every singular curve of that particular caress. His eyes closed and he smiled in gratitude, in homecoming. The receding sun unmasked itself from early evening clouds and shone brilliant across the horizon, reflecting golden on the ripples of ocean below. Waves crashed right over his body, but Everett Crisp himself had already ridden one of them all the way out to sea.

Summer, 2028: Hollywood Bowl

Crickets supplied the music while the audience filed in and the Los Angeles Philharmonic tuned. Anticipation hung in the air that filled the amphitheatre, eloquently carved into the side of a hill, on this balmy summer evening. Jeff Severin, clad in his carefully pressed gray suit, watched from the stage left wing amongst bulky black instrument cases and scattered electrical equipment. Looking at the stage strewn with musicians, he remembered how Everett had always said that a symphony was like a big, luxurious king sized bed that you can stretch out in, while movie scores were like a restrictive twin you have to think twice about before you roll over and take all of the covers with you. He laughed a little to himself. Of the many things he had learned from Everett, gratitude was probably the most important, a lesson invisibly taught.

"Well, you did it. It's your night." Barry had come from behind to place a hand on Jeff's shoulder. Barry the bassoonist who would be playing Everett's work in just a few minutes; Barry the beautiful, of mind and spirit and certainly body. Still, Jeff couldn't help but wonder; what does he see in me?

"It's *his* night." A quick kiss and Barry took his place on stage behind the woodwinds and the strings. Half of Hollywood had turned out to pay tribute to a man who had always thought himself without friends. Now they would hear, thought Jeff — now they would hear the *real* Everett Crisp. In mere moments, his music, his brilliant final composition, would echo throughout this canyon and inspire the mountains, charm the trees. Jeff had been the first to hear this piece, but he certainly would not be the last. Perhaps years from now, centuries even, some miserable thirteen year old would stay up late listening to these very notes through headphones, dreaming of better days ahead.

As he himself had requested, there would no memorial, no services for the man who had scored many of Hollywood's most treasured films. He would have been wholly unimpressed with people gushing and lying and showing off their cleverness at some formal gathering at his expense. He would have got a kick, however, out of the handsome photograph, circa 2010 perhaps, they had shown of him during the "In Memoriam" montage on the Oscars that year, holding a baton and looking passionate if not half crazed. A pop star sang a sappy song about time as all those who joined him that year at Forest Lawn shot across the screen for one final bow. Yes, Everett Crisp would have thought all of that pretty damn funny.

The executor had offered Jeff anything from the house he wanted, but the only thing that he took was a curiosity he found far in the back of a closet: a framed poster board that bore a perfectly sketched keyboard, all eighty-eight keys, both white and black. It was kind of beat up, with stains and scratches and dents, but someone had taken great care to carefully mat and frame it. Why anyone would ever sketch a keyboard, and so exactingly at that, onto a piece of white poster board was beyond him, but it kind of summed him up, in a way. Everett was a deep mystery, and this odd piece of artwork, hanging on whatever wall in whatever dwelling Jeff might occupy, would always remind him of that. The ivory keys of a piano had always been Everett Crisp's greatest lover.

The lights dimmed. A hush fell over the crowd as the conductor took his place upon the tiny wooden box, the command center from which Everett had once made it all look so seamless. The stars had just begun to show themselves. Ghosts were everywhere.

The stars that shown over the concert also shown over a reservoir in that forgotten little town on the edge of nowhere, above Cambridge, above New York City, above Bel Air, above Malibu, and above a grave only a few miles from where they all sat, in which rested the grateful remains of a man and a stuffed monkey, both of them at rest, at long last.

The conductor raised his baton high in the night air as the opening chord was struck. Every eye widened, every soul stood at attention. An entire audience en masse took a sharp breath in.

Everett Crisp had become the music.

About the Author

PHIL GEOFFREY BOND is an award-winning author, best known for his debut novel, *The Last Year at Low Tide*, as well as his collection of short pieces, *All the Sad Young Men*, and the celebrated picture book, *My*

Friend, the Cat, based on the popular stage show. Often mixing dramatic prose with live theatre, his original pieces *My Queer Youth, The Disney Diaries, My Friend, the Cat, My Roaring Twenties* and *Small Town Confessions* have been embraced by a wide range of off-Broadway audiences. As a playwright, Phil has developed work at The Sundance Theatre Lab *(The Citadel),* and at many regional theatres throughout the states. A fixture on the NYC nightlife scene, he is a seven-time MAC (Manhattan Association of Cabarets), two-time Bistro and one-time Nightlife Award-winner. Currently, he is the writer/ producer/host of *Sondheim Unplugged,* now enjoying its ninth season at Manhattan nightspot Feinstein's/54 Below, where he also created the popular *54 Sings* series and served as the venue's first Director of Programming and later Director of Original Programming. In 1993, he was awarded the Presidential Medallion from President Clinton on behalf of his work as a young playwright.